PARASOL AGAINST THE AXE

Helen Oyeyemi is the author of *The Icarus Girl*; *The Opposite House*; *White Is for Witching* (which won a Somerset Maugham Award); *Mr Fox*; *Boy, Snow, Bird*; *Gingerbread*; *What Is Not Yours Is Not Yours*; and *Peaces*, which was shortlisted for the Goldsmiths Prize. In 2013, Helen was included in *Granta*'s Best of Young British Novelists.

Also by Helen Oyeyemi

Parasol against the Axe

Helen Oyeyemi

faber

First published in the UK in 2024
by Faber & Faber Ltd
The Bindery, 51 Hatton Garden
London EC1N 8HN

This export edition first published in 2024

First published in the USA in 2024 by Riverhead Books
An imprint of Penguin Random House LLC
penguinrandomhouse.com

Book design by Amanda Dewey
Printed and bound by CPI Group (UK) Ltd, Croydon CR0 4YY

Lines from 'The Secret Miracle' by Jorge Luis Borges, *Ficciones,* 1944,
trans. Anthony Bonner.

Grateful acknowledgment is made for permission to use the following:

The previously unpublished poem 'Gib acht' by Ivan Wernisch.
English translation by Petr Onufer and Mike Baugh.
Used with permission of Ivan Wernisch and the translators.

Vítězslav Nezval, 'Panorama of Prague' from *Prague with Fingers of Rain,*
trans. Ewald Oser (Bloodaxe Books, 2009). Reproduced with permission of
Bloodaxe Books, bloodaxebooks.com.

*This is a work of fiction. Names, characters, places, and incidents
either are the product of the author's imagination or are used fictitiously,
and any resemblance to actual persons, living or dead, businesses,
companies, events, or locales is entirely coincidental*

A CIP record for this book
is available from the British Library

ISBN 978–0–571–36663–7

2 4 6 8 10 ·9 7 5 3 1

Periphery is not a simple function of distance and accessibility vis-à-vis a center; rather, it is often the result of contradictory claims of two or more centers.

—Traditional Brno saying

༄

At home act
As if you were at home
But outside
Keep your tongue tied

And one more thing

Watch out

The steps going down
And the steps going up
Are one

—Ivan Wernisch, *Gib Acht*, 1986,
translated by Mike Baugh and Petr Onufer

1.

At some point—who knows how—I found myself a member of a WhatsApp group that seemed to have been set up as a safe space for sharing complaints about the capital city of Czechia. A couple of messages written by people who "just wanted to say I had a nice time there" were answered with polite but firm reminders that there was a different group for people who had had a nice time in Prague, and that group should be sought out independently. OK then . . .

. . . I thought I'd take a quick look at the complaints. I expected ten or twenty ill-founded grievances aired by the type of person who throws a tantrum when they come across locals who don't seem grateful that foreigners are "taking an interest" in their part of the world. (More like poking their noses in!) Ten or twenty stupid sob stories . . . but that wasn't what I found at all. Astonished, I scrolled for hours. So many harsh experiences, so much legitimate angst! Recounted in numerous languages. Some of the incidents referred to had taken place many years ago; apparently quite a few of them had happened to the narrator's grandparents (?).

The messages written in Czech were the longest, and pulsed with furious sarcasm. The messages written in Japanese were both the shortest and the most damning. The group members shared superficial information about themselves—nationality, ethnicity, age, height, in some instances weight and body measurements—it read as if they were victims trying to understand if their assailant had a "type." They were wasting their time; there is no "type." The city distributes its insults and outrages indiscriminately.

Once I'd read enough, I wrote and sent a riposte that was almost immediately lost in the horde of far more compelling messages that appeared at the exact same instant.

I wrote that I didn't remember any of these incidents; nor did I remember any of the people involved. Not if the characteristics they'd provided were supposed to serve as memory aids, at any rate. I was sorry for what had happened to them. However—however, I was no more to blame than they were. I was sorry for every bad thing that happened, every scam and every diminishment of their self-respect—but what is it worth, the sorrow of the onlooker? And that is what I was. The onlooker, not the cause. A little bit more than bystander, but still . . . what did all these people want, what had they really expected? COME ON, KIDS, I wrote. Don't go to the city and then get all scandalized by city life. I'm not even one of the grander metropolises! If I was I could have just eaten you and yours alive! I didn't, but no need to thank me! *My* self-esteem is in good health and doesn't require your gratitude!

That was the gist of the message. I slightly regret having used so many exclamation marks. I wrote the same thing in Czech and in German. As far as I'm concerned, if you don't know both languages, then whatever it is you think you know about Prague is fundamentally compromised. Which only really matters, of course, if compromise or being compromised in this context really bothers you. A quick test: I didn't write that WhatsApp message of mine in English, so all that you received just now is a series of paraphrases. How does that sit with you? Feels yucky, does it? Then farewell.

I gave that little message of mine five minutes to be seen by anybody who needed to see it—then I deleted WhatsApp. Quite a procedure given that I don't really understand phones and wasn't too clear on how I'd downloaded the app and acquired a user account. My competence ebbs and flows—the truth is I'm too . . . let's say "old" for telephones. I shouldn't use them. I should get a secretary. Hey, I'd like that: a secretary.

But back to my . . . what can I call this: An apologia? A defense? An excuse? Certainly not an explanation. The act of baring the soul has unpleasant connotations for me—mostly thanks to mallets wielded by bullies of the Catholic and Communist variety. And if only all the bullies were foreigners. Once they're gone you're still left with the homegrown zealots and chancers . . .

Well, all that's for me to handle, not you. I've thought about pleading special circumstances for the behavior I read about in that WhatsApp group. "Consider the exceptional latitude and longitude of this place" and "Give yourself a bit of time to really notice the way this city touches the stars, trust me, it's archetypal stuff . . ."—I could say things like that. Even if you were prepared to go along with such an idea, it entails comparative exercises I'm not equipped for. I mean, first of all I'd have to manufacture the impression that there's any such thing as an *ordinary* city, that there are any cities that don't incorporate some degree of optical illusion. (As for those mirages, be they repellent or alluring, don't they all reflect a refusal to be known "like the back of" some human hand?)

No—Paris wouldn't look askance at Prague. Istanbul would engage in a round of jocular and affectionate hair tousling; it would be like watching two bros completely secure in their insurmountable handsomeness. Shanghai would probably flirt a little bit . . . Athens would immediately agree to an impromptu fishing trip. And so on. In the eyes of its counterparts across the world, Prague has not broken any of the laws that the truly great cities abide by. What else do these places share? That's a tough one . . . we can quite clearly see that plenty is left to the discretion of geography, faith, history, economics. Perhaps when all's said and done the only non-negotiable feature is urban swagger. Audacity combined with a certain remoteness from reason. That's the temperament that qualifies cities to play the most extreme games of Truth or Dare with their rulers; games that end in catastrophe. Or revolution. Or both.

It's not that surprising, then, that a capital city so rarely channels the atmosphere of the rest of the country. When members of the populace outside the capital say, "But really that place is like another country," that's only to be expected. The tone of such remarks is envious, disgusted, mystified, forlorn, anxious . . . now that I'm thinking about it, someone once told me this: *The capital is the part of the country that most openly belongs to the world as well as to the nation. It's a way in for the stranger who can't or won't abandon their strangeness. And it's a last chance for the native who would otherwise rebel . . .*

I don't remember anything about the person who said this to me, except that I was very fond of that person, and I believed that they meant what they were saying, and I—well, adored the gaze that matched their words. Me and my rubbish memory, leaving me stranded with contusions that softly, so softly, glow.

I don't disparage towns or villages. You won't hear me claim that a city is a more stimulating or even more complex environment than a stable settlement that's faithful to its limits.

However.

The temperament of a town or a village is quite significantly linked to the expectation that between one year and the next, that town or the village will continue to exist. Cities—especially capital cities, have never been able to count on that. They test their footing from the moment they're founded to the moment they fall. So much has happened. So much that it can never be told. I feel stupid reminding you of that. You already know that about your own experience.

Also—also . . . speaking now without reference to other cities, or to your life, indeed, simply taking a statistical view, isn't it all right for a city to pull a leg or two when the mood is upon it? Prague already has a host of character references. For every single one of those WhatsApp complaints, millions of other observers have been permitted to come and go without anything too unusual by way of impediment. I'm talking about anything from holidays, conferences, concerts, and student residencies to entire lives lived out in this place, from birth to death. None of those people would recognize witness accounts of a city on the rampage. If you choose to, there isn't much to stop you from viewing the nature of this place as sedate, stoic, perhaps even shy. Home to souls that eat, sleep, and breathe reverie even as the bodies that accompany them gruffly get on with things.

Some—the deathless Dr. Ripellino among them—say that Prague will never not be. They say that Prague will glide along the banks of the Vltava for eternity, the heart of a nation that is itself the restless heart of a continent. Well yes, please. That would of course be my wish: unchanging change.

Even so . . . I say that if Prague never fails to be, then it was never a city in the first place.

And if it was never a city, then what is it?

Whatever (Whoever?) Prague is, its acts tend to be committed without warning.

You shall have examples. Not from WhatsApp—from my short-term memory. I'll tell you about Dorothea Gilmartin and Hero Tojosoa—a person who talked to herself, and a person who went quite enthusiastically out of her way not to do so. Hurry, while I still remember . . .

2.

W E'LL BEGIN WITH A BIT about Hero Tojosoa:

If you need to picture her, she stands six feet tall in socks, inhabiting this stature fully and with lightness. So she should; the first of her handful of growth spurts took place when she was ten . . . she's had thirty years to master this balletic balance. Her dreadlocks are both short and long, and a mix of black and gray— she claims she's "letting her youth go," but the overall effect is a silver-speckled, strategically parted mantle of twists that tickle the tip of her nose and slide to a downy stop at the base of her hairline. In minidresses her legs are positively dangerous, though mostly she's low-key gamine in jeans. It's possible to liken her most frequent facial expression to the "read" receipt that kills a conversational thread, or to a thumbs-up emoji sent in response to a confession of love. Her messaging protocols mirror her physical persona. Hostility? Callousness? Not really. Sometimes there just isn't anything left to say. Even when the other person seems to think there is.

Ms. Tojosoa was far from trigger-happy when it came to breaking out the *Got it, thanks* smile that caused her will to prevail. She didn't claim infallibility—she was the first to admit that career-wise she'd never really done well interviewing people in person. Jean-Pierre Randolph, the father of her son, outdid her several times over when it came to appearing entirely free of judgment or even opinion right up until the moment the encounter was fully converted into text. By contrast, Hero's tendency toward nonreaction (antireaction?) had an immediate effect. A luminous frost set in; one that gave even hardened egoists pause . . . it seemed so starkly unwise to reveal oneself to someone who wore this particular listening face. Friends and lovers, temporarily manhandled into compliance by Hero's subject-switching smile, would belatedly launch accusations from their seat in the vehicle that was taking them home, or via text message from the next room. Did she realize that she made it impossible to discuss matters of importance?? Was she happy now that she'd inhibited free speech?! Hero would protest that that wasn't her at all, that she'd heard you and didn't dismiss any of the thoughts you'd expressed. She proved willing and able to repeat what you'd said verbatim . . .

A great many books are firmly closed despite the general impression that they're wide open—they'll jovially present their back cover as page one and be baffled that you thought there'd be more. Some of these adamantly closed books are also people. There you go: you can picture Hero Tojosoa like that if you want to.

If you don't need any specific image of Hero Tojosoa, then forget everything except her age and the grace of her steps.

Tojosoa arrived in Prague in June 2018. At least, I think it was June. Could have been July.

The city had not seen rainfall for eight months. Or nine months. Thirst distorts dates. Out in the north of the Czech lands, along the knobbly coast of the Elbe, boulders rose as the river sank lower and lower. These weren't just any boulders—they were hunger stones. Just a few long and squelching steps across space that would have drowned you at the beginning of the year and you could kneel on these treacly slabs of doom and pick out the words chiseled onto them. Greetings from the seventeenth century. *Wenn du mich siehst, dann weine*, that one really set the mood. *If you see me, weep.* Yes, I saw that, and yes, I wept. Why not admit it? The hunger stones hadn't finished with me yet: I spotted another one in Těchlovice that upgraded my desperation to first class: *Wir haben geweint— Wir weinen—Und ihr werdet weinen. We cried—we're crying—and you will cry.* If you had a friend who sent you messages like that, you'd just block them, wouldn't you? But I didn't feel able to do that to 1617. It wasn't a bad year all the way through.

As for Hero and the drought—I'm not suggesting she was responsible for it. It's just that I don't think I would have begun talking to her if I hadn't been seeking pleasant ways to pass a little time during that dry, dry season. That's all I was doing . . . merely passing time, just having a little chat with an attractive, albeit semi-demolished woman. She'd been given a bag of frozen peas along with her beer, and she applied the icy pouch to different facial sectors as we talked about everything except her bruises.

"Would you believe me," she said, "if I told you I came here because there's a letter hounding me around my home city? I couldn't prevent the writing of that fucking letter—and I wouldn't have wanted to; let everyone write away! But that doesn't mean I have to read it. And I won't read it. Ever."

I raised my glass in honor of her resolve: "That's the spirit! Spend the rest of your life on the run from a letter. That'll show the letter writer what for."

Hero Tojosoa nodded, then hung her head. "Damn that man. Damn Gaspar Azzouz!"

She damned herself too: "I had to get away," she told me. "And Prague was the only place I'd been invited to. I only visit places with an explicit invitation in hand; that's how unoriginal I am. I'd have been better off almost everywhere else, but I must be one of those people who only learns the hard way."

Enjoying this case of mistaken identity (if she knew me she wouldn't have told me anything), I cast about for something to keep her talking. My question about what she loved was essentially an idle one. Her answer wasn't.

After a pause—the plummeting, frothing kind that precedes disclosure of religious faith, political conviction, or interclan enmity—she said: "Well—rainstorms."

And, oh no. Then I wanted her. After everything I'd said about really and truly changing my ways and not doing anything Agnes of Bohemia wouldn't do, and so on, I wanted Hero. But she must have been the one who started it this time, not me.

Consider my preliminary position: I'm someone who always longs to behave as they ought, and to let trouble pass by. Rabbis and Christian priests used to have quite a lot of time for me, but they've given up. I doubt they'd ever admit that, but it's true. I don't blame them. Even if hope is your default setting, you do eventually need some sort of promise that a more binding promise will be made at some point down the road, and I don't offer even that.

The Imam at the Central Mosque just off Národní třída is a

different story altogether. At equinox he plays Three Truths and Three Lies with me. The hour is one of my choosing: night flows through morning, and my opponent is not all the way awake. Sacred words shield the walls of the prayer hall as I tell the Imam of three acceptable deeds I've done since the last time we spoke. Examples: A service performed gratis for some friendless or near-penniless being. Or a Nice Surprise for the everyday Pája and/or Pepík who had been beginning to think that honesty is a handicap. The rehoming of a stray here, the engineering of a reunion there, all liberally sprinkled with hallmarks of the accidental so as to spare both parties their pride. Things like that. Then I tell the Imam three not-so-nice things I've been involved with: A spot of extramarital matchmaking here, some bureaucratic devilry there. Or a moment of rapt negligence when that which is beyond valuation slips out of reach and I watch it depart knowing full well that it can never return. Three acceptable things and three unacceptable things. Sometimes I've done all six, sometimes I'm making them up to scare the Imam, or to see what kind of thinker he is. Most of the time it's a mix.

I like the Imam, but he's not my friend. The limit isn't imposed by want of liking, but by my knowledge that once I feel I am someone's friend, I no longer test them.

All I have learned so far is that my opponent doesn't look for double meanings in what is said to him. Sometimes it seems that is the result of training. At other times he seems to understand that not only is the fear of being deceived a greater anguish than deception itself, but it's almost completely optional. And so he doesn't choose it. Shouldn't he recklessly embrace my fictions as facts, then, and lose the game? It's always the other way around; he always knows which is which. He's a winner who won't hear of prizes; he says the game was mine alone, but that if I'm moved to make a forfeit, I could propose a timetable for concluding my mockery of righteousness. Of course I answer in the words of Jirous (that beloved adopted son of mine who came over from Humpolec):

> *What you can put off till tomorrow,*
> *never do today.*
> *This also concerns redemption.*

The Imam looks at me and I look at him. After I moment I assay a cheeky wink, mostly to conceal the fact that I'm intimidated to kingdom come. The man is . . . supported by an influence that exceeds mine fivefold. Five times five times five times five times fivefold, actually. It's as if any boxing ring he enters is revealed to be a hexagon, and he is strong in every corner, his head and limbs clasped by the blazing digits of his creator. For my part I am quite conscious of not having made myself. I don't discount the possibility that the maker of my undividable rotundas is the same one who consolidates the Imam's strength along five vertices—that this maker has chosen different shapes to throw us off a trail that we'd otherwise take straight to their door so as to ask for even more favors than we already do . . .

. . . For all that, when I face hexagons, I have the diffidence of the middle child who has nobody's backing but their own. We can't know for certain whether zero is younger or older than five,* but if

---

* I'd assumed that zero was the starting point for everything until twentieth- to twenty-first-century minimalism got me scratching my head. Encounters with the void ought to feel like a return to the beginning; they oughtn't to feel like the next step. But if zero really was here first, would nothingness be able to present itself as a sumptuous bonus earned by pruning away all the baggage that's stalked us from the cradle . . . ?

zero is younger, then our mother's favorite is sure to be the elder. If zero is the elder, then Mum's bound to prefer the lastborn. That's how it feels when this zero comes up against the Imam's resolve to get it to do something about the state of its soul.

"We'll return to this topic tomorrow, then, just as you suggest," the Imam says.

I agree, and circumvent the agreement by treating six months as a single day.

As I told you, we are not friends, the Imam and I. But still. When I think about it, this may be the most committed relationship I have.

I strayed from Hero Tojosoa—or from concluding that either she is a predator at heart or I am. But we're returning to her. Tojosoa described her occupation as "ex-journalist." Her name is also attached to a handful of literary translations from French to English (and vice versa), as well as Malagasy to English and French (and vice versa). But these were all for online journals that could not pay enough to keep a person fed and housed. She seemed to be doing all right for herself quality of life–wise, though: she and her fifteen-year-old son, Jerome, lived in Dublin's Docklands. Nothing too showy: a small flat in a small housing complex. But I can't not mention that it was the kind of housing complex that has a live-in concierge who signs for packages and prepares a newsletter alerting you to one-off local events and altered arrangements at the nearby farmers market. Clearly there was income she acquired by some method she didn't feel like identifying herself with.

Tojosoa traveled on an Italian passport that stated her birthplace as Vatican City. She did not speak Italian.

She was a member of Sofie Cibulkova and Apolena Hrabíkova's

wedding party, Cibulkova and Hrabíkova being a Dublin-based couple who flew into Prague with a few close friends for their hen weekend. On the return flight, soon after the plane had entered Irish airspace, the couple were married by Conor Healey, a Humanist celebrant who'd come along with them to Prague for the sheer craic of it all. That's what was planned, and that's what happened.

Hero Tojosoa should have been on that return flight, but she wasn't. The previous afternoon, she'd incurred an injury in Sofie Cibulkova's presence and then staggered off on her own. The other members of the wedding party had looked for her for hours—there was concern that she'd lost consciousness somewhere, or was in some otherwise critical condition.

This concern was eventually dispelled by communications between Ms. Tojosoa and Ms. Cibulkova. More about those soon enough.

Touching the matter of the members of Polly and Sofie's wedding party being close friends: Polly consistently maintained that Hero Tojosoa was Sofie's guest, not hers. Sofie's friend, not hers. It was Sofie who went back and forth—and still does, for all we know. By the time the flight landed in Dublin, Sofie had confided in another member of the wedding party that she and Hero had in fact drifted apart a few years prior, that Hero had completely ignored the RSVP date on the wedding invitation she'd been sent months ago and had written to say she was coming just two days before everyone gathered in Prague. Sofie had (silently) questioned the suddenness of this development, and had felt she would have been well within her rights to tell Hero she couldn't come. But she and Hero had known each other for well over a decade. Hero had often exhibited "last-minute" tendencies . . . so Sofie had decided that for old times' sake, Hero would be welcome to join the party. She'd be paying for her own transport and accommodation anyway.

But we'll leave the accounts submitted by the newlyweds; it's Hero we're pursuing, not them.

Hero arrived on an afternoon flight a few hours behind the rest of the wedding party. Polly met her at the airport, briskly disregarding Hero's murmurings about having a mild headache and being keen to get to her hotel in favor of driving around a few different neighborhoods to make it clear that the real Prague exceeded the bounds of all the Baroque and Art Nouveau edifices that dominated Google Image search results. No, Hero was not permitted to exclude the bright-bannered hypermarkets from her sightseeing. Also on the outskirts: the angel-cake concrete of the prefabricated tower blocks and the taut and tidy facades of the commuter dormitories where beds and evening meals were paid for by the week. Only by reverting to teenagehood and unequivocally refusing to get out of the car was Hero able to shut down Polly's proposal that they stop for a coffee at the World of Pleasures next door to the petrol station that doubled as the most popular Prague stop for truck drivers.

"But it's good coffee! *Brazilian* coffee . . ."

Polly had the in-car atmosphere all thought out too. Hard rock playing at full blast. At the top of her voice, she obligingly translated some of the lyrics of Kabat's "Malá Dáma." "It's all about wanting the one person who's too wild to ever be yours . . . wanting them so badly you feel you could die. Or . . . turn into someone other than yourself . . . which is probably the same thing, don't you think, Hero? *Kdyby tam stála stovka žen / Vyzvu ji k tanci a to netančim . . . If she were among one hundred women, I'd ask her to dance though I never dance* . . . guess what, this was Czechia's entry for the Eurovision Song Contest one year!"

The lead singer's growl was getting under Hero's skin in a good way.

"Did this song . . . win?" she asked.

Polly laughed. "Win? We came last in the semifinal. Nul points. Standard treatment for those who don't have a feel-good song covered in sequins or some 'love conquers all' message. Not making it to the final that year was a real *You know what, fuck you, Europe* moment for me . . ."

Her tone held no rancor; it sounded like Apolena Hrabíkova had forgiven Europe. They were listening to the song just over eleven years after voters had rejected it. Also eleven years old: a virtually unclimbable strip of metal that had been added to Nusle Bridge's safety rail to prevent suicidal jumps. Yet drivers still exhibited gloomy caution as their vehicles passed through the pillars of that particular bridge. Or, at least Polly did. Loquaciously, at that.

Hero watched as Polly talked. Not directly; she watched Polly's reflection in the car window. Polly with her impeccably shaped, dramatically thick eyebrows and the wine-dark waves of hair cropped close to her head. Polly who was more passionate than Hero was (or was it that she was more opinionated and less dismissive?), Polly with her even, mid-olive tan, her Breton-striped crop top, her strong and slender arms, the brown onion tattoo that cuddled her left biceps like the love token that it was. It had to be, couldn't be anything other. If Polly had got a socialist-realist Glorious Fodder of the Proletariat–style tattoo before falling for

Sofie-whose-surname-meant-"onion," then—actually no, Hero decided. Sorry but no, that can't really be how things work.

As she drove, Polly ran through a sparkling series of neighborhood anecdotes that coursed through her great-grandparents' heydays and into the 2020s. These should have interested her passenger, yet didn't. Hero had already decided to skip that evening's cocktail gathering. The next day was Beauty Day: the group would get facials and massages and bond over their insecurities and all the rest of it; that was probably more meaningful in terms of post-wedding memories than the drinking bit. All Hero wanted was to go to her hotel room, lie down, and try to read the book she'd brought with her. *Paradoxical Undressing*, it was called. She'd never heard of it, and the handful of online reviews she'd found seemed to be talking about different books with the same title (and the same author . . . ?). But Jerome had bought the book for her. He'd got it secondhand and at great expense—he'd dipped into his *savings* for Hero's sake—so she was going to give it her full attention.

In the face of Polly's potted histories, Hero fell into a silence that she only broke once—to laugh out loud when, driving through the understated stateliness of a neighborhood called Bubeneč, Polly slowed down the car again, indicating her family villa without stopping. Yes, this must be the place, the pinnacle of the supremely real . . . an imitation shipping crate. That is, if imitation shipping crates came with a minimum of seven bedrooms and at least four balconies. The surrounding plant life had taken to the structure all the same, misting its corrugations with brambles and the airy flowering of linden trees.

It went without saying that Polly's family home had a far greater degree of actuality than 3-D picture postcards like the Astronomical Clock. (Or so Hero was supposed to think.) The Hrabíks' villa exhibited every half millimeter of the moderation that was necessary to be and let be. The Astronomical Clock was not like that at all; it seemed focused on botheration. As they stood in the crowd of hourly onlookers and watched that clock chime the hour, Hero could see why Polly denied it credibility. All eyes on these representations of wisdom and unwisdom, each one warped yet unwizened: a discursive astronomer, a reticent historian, twelve frosty-faced Apostles, an uncomfortably numb sybarite, a narcissist in thrall to his hand mirror, a miser holding his small and mighty bag of gold aloft, a skeleton handling an hourglass with the saucy verve of a professional nightclub dancer, and, bringing some bonus razzle-dazzle—a golden rooster. A few of these figures claimed attention haphazardly. The rest did so in an orderly fashion, moving in the time apportioned to them, each joint and lever mobilized with the jerky dignity of remnants clinging to the trajectory of an explosion.

Someone in the crowd began listing astronomical clocks in other towns and cities that were less hysterically hieroglyphic than this one, more evocative of the enigma of Time. Looking around, Hero managed to trace the commentary back to a brown-skinned, silver-haired someone in a long green dress. The clock critic's accent reminded her of Thea's and Sofie's—but then both friends had, at different times, expressed shock at Hero's inability to differentiate regional American accents. The lady in the blue dress jostled her way through the crowd as she spoke: "Excuse me, but who's calling this a clock? I don't see any clock here. Now, Brescia—Brescia's got a clock," she said, mostly walking backward, but with the occasional lateral move thrown in, seemingly just for kicks.

"What about the Arnemuiden clock? Do Protestant fisherman do it best?" Hero called out to her, inviting agreement, a rebuttal, or at the very least some eye contact. No such luck, but a stocky, ruddy-cheeked man standing between them thought Hero was talking to him and blurted out: "No ma'am—it's all about the Wrocław sun clock."

A teenage girl with a buzz cut quickly chomped down a chunk of sausage so as to be able to throw in the caustic remark that CLEARLY anybody who thought the Wrocław clock is as good as clocks get hadn't seen the clock at Ottery St. Mary.

Polly piped up that although the Ottery St. Mary clock was difficult to beat, it was the astronomical clock at Friedhöfe in Meran that really did it for her . . .

For all that it was being roundly ignored, the jingling timepiece under their very noses brought its spectacle to a dignified conclusion before it fell silent. The crowd dispersed as quickly as it had gathered, though a few people lingered to make clock recommendations in assorted languages.

The original dissenter raised her hands and pumped them: "Yes! I'm loving this brainstorming session. Embrace the Arnemuiden, Wrocław, Ottery St. Mary, and Friedhöfe in Meran clocks . . . and reject this one! Chartres, Olomouc, Padua too! Be strong, remember those names whenever you're tempted to lower your standards. And never! Settle! For a clock like this—"

Having put her foot down regarding horologies, the clock critic sped down her alleyway and reached her vanishing point, popping altogether out of earshot, too, though she was still shouting. The rallying cries she'd already made were sufficient; she'd established a distinction. Chiming on the hour really wasn't at all the same thing as declaring the hour. This music box setup inside a bomb (or bomb nestled in the cracked body of a music box) addressed quite another matter. So did the effigies who lounged with grainy insouciance on long pillows of stone above the double doors of buildings as they started and won street-corner staring matches with you. Also questionable: the buildings that splashed their way down the riverbanks like lava from a volcano that had erupted pastel hues . . . these weren't the kinds of things that ought to turn a twenty-first-century head. Better, less messy, to follow the raised firebrand and unsentimental outlines of Žižkov, or turn her face toward the ultra-bright functionalist lights of Bubeneč or Střešovice . . .

Well, maybe. But also: maybe not, you know? Hero certainly didn't feel like taking Polly's word for it.

Nicknamers tended to dub Apolena Hrabíkova "Polly" no matter how persistently she styled herself as a laid- back Lenka. There was just no shaking the impression that, on some prototypical level, Apolena Hrabíkova was THE Polly of the nursery rhyme; the one who put the kettle on. Putting the kettle on was what Polly H. was born to do, in life and in her art. Polly's style as a theater director was so unyieldingly linear it drew blood and tears; Hero couldn't deny its power. But power wasn't what moved Hero Tojosoa: in fact, she wanted out of that model. A life free of coercion, a life in which she sought no power over anybody and nobody sought any over her. That unthreatened and unthreatening position was the one that Hero, Sofie, and Dorothea had banded together to try to obtain for themselves, years ago, when if you came across one of them, the other two were never far behind.

Youth had been a factor in their failure. Of course they'd fucked up: Thea had, Hero had, Sofie had—sometimes all three at once. Repeatedly. But things might still have worked out for them if they'd continued to hold the plan down at three corners, i.e., if Sofie hadn't given up. Sofie Cibulkova had had so much more fear and trembling in her than either Hero or Thea could have guessed. She didn't dare to live under the name they'd chosen—the name they'd voted on, a single first name for all three of them. She'd kept calling it a pseudonym. The rules of the life they wanted scared her; too many tricks had to be played to secure it. More than were humane, Sofie said. And so, fleeing into the arms of honesty and humanity, fleeing from Hero, and from Thea, Sofie had run into . . . Polly. Who had presumably put the fucking kettle on before she'd proposed.

Polly and Sofie were staying in the posh shipping crate Hero had been treated to a safari-style viewing of earlier; the rest of the wedding party were already settled in air-conditioned comfort on the other side of the river. It was better like this . . . Hero had a feeling that the more she mingled with Sofie's new friends, the more headaches she'd find herself fabricating. They were good influences, these new friends—they had won. Sofie was one of theirs now. And they'd be impenetrably gracious about it because that's what good influences are like. Hero's accommodation was another mark of graciousness: in this, peak tourist season, a reasonably priced room had been found in a bed-and-breakfast owned by a friend of Polly's family. ("Obviously we would have had you stay with us, but it's cousins floor to ceiling at the moment, you understand . . .") This bed-and-breakfast didn't feel like a consolation prize. The building was centuries old, and so lovingly maintained that its bare rafters were assets. The staircases ran up at the pace of a trot. The rooms were minimally furnished—the eye laid them flat, and crossing their floorboards was like walking into an X-ray print. The glass in the windows was slightly foxed. Sunlight pawed at the panes. The host told her the house was fully occupied. Hero's room was on the fourth floor; most of the other guests seemed to be out.

She sat down on the single bed, kicked her shoes off, and allowed herself to feel that Sofie could have been the one to welcome her instead of Polly. When Polly had offered to pick Hero up, she'd succumbed to some feeble little need to be welcomed into a new place by a native, and, well, she'd got what she deserved for submitting to a form of authority she didn't even believe in. Sofie wouldn't have needled her with an insistence on the supremacy of the normal. She was a native Praguer too . . . the fact that Sofie's Prague was in Oklahoma was the kind of twist they'd have savored pre-estrangement.

Taking out her phone, Hero tried to think of something she could write and successfully send to Sofie. Half an hour prickled by as she revised and amended various abysmally insincere statements regarding how nice it had been to see "this beautiful city through Polly's eyes!"

Finally she came up with something similar to the direct tone they'd used to use with each other: I wasn't sure if you'd invite Thea. Would've understood if you didn't.

Sofie wrote back almost immediately: Hi! Of course I invited T! If only she'd said yes ☹

Forehead prickling, Hero wrote: She said she wasn't coming? Or she just didn't RSVP?

> She isn't coming, wished us all the best, etc.
> Can I call?
> Right now? You OK?

Hero was almost certain that she'd seen Dorothea Gilmartin at the airport, queueing with the holders of non-EU passports. "Thea?" she'd said, raising the volume as she repeated the name a couple more times. But the woman two barriered lanes away kept shuffling forward without looking up from her magazine. The off-brand bowler hat and the pitch-black lenses of the sunglasses the woman wore also made it all too possible that Hero was mistaken. However: Thea's hot-pink lipstick. Thea's fuzzy brown braid bouncing off the hem of that black leather jacket, Thea's slouch . . .

Hero typed and deleted until Sofie clarified the script for them both:

> I hear your head is aching.
> Anything you need?

Hero: Just some rest! I'll get that & see you in the morning.

Sofie: OK . . . if you're sure. The others are excited to meet you, though.

Hero: I'll call if I suddenly come alive again. HAVE FUN—

Sofie: We'll . . . try our best to? Here for you if there's anything you need before tomorrow, OK? Anything at all, just let me know!! Can't wait to see you.

Coincidence was allowed. Or Thea coming to Prague for personal reasons; that was allowed. Still, just to clarify the situation, she looked to see if she had any phone numbers for Thea that still worked. She didn't. And it was probably just as well. Many months ago—really it was years, but she counted the time in months to keep it closer—a short while after Sofie had moved out of the house, Hero had taken her own turn to depart. The house was Thea's, and Hero couldn't imagine being able to afford to live anywhere as nice as this again. As she'd handed the keys back to Thea, she'd spoken lightheartedly of the ease with which Thea would find other housemates—adding, half jokingly, that she might even try to move back in herself. The part that wasn't a joke was a genuine question about their relationship. Was it definitively dead?

"I hope you know, Thea, that I—that if you—I mean, if you ever—"

Thea took Hero's set of keys into her hand and squeezed; for a moment it seemed as if the metal would, must, bend. Or as if blood would, or must, run from fist to floor. Nothing of the kind happened, but it must have hurt. Looking into Hero's eyes, still squeezing, Thea said: "If you ever contact me again, you'll get what you deserve."

The clarity and calm of her gaze suggested complete withdrawal, and the tremor in her voice suggested blind rage. In order to verify which was topmost, Hero had said: "Don't be so childish, Dorothea." As she said this, she smiled and leaned forward slightly, inviting a slap or a key scratch. Thea's recoil—three quick backward steps—took her by surprise. She, Hero, had become repulsive. She'd better take Thea's warning seriously, then.

It had been all smiles and hugs when Sofie handed her keys back. What, then, was Hero to do with the frantic buzz of being more hateworthy than Sofie? It was too tempting to adorn her pride with it, like a living brooch that stung and stung again.

"Thea," she mumbled, unable to simply swallow the name in silence. Suppose you love someone and are petrified by the way that very same person does things—what is it you love in that person?

And what is it that you actually fear from them? And why did it feel possible to Hero that in thinking like this she was only handling film negatives, and the uninverted statement would be something like: *Thea scares me, and (or because?) I love the way she does what I don't have the nerve to do . . .*

Sidestepping this and other biohazardous recollections, Hero Tojosoa:

took two or three things out of her suitcase,

opened and closed *Paradoxical Undressing*, the "Prague book" that had eaten up her fourteen-year-old son's savings. Its cover image depicted a lace umbrella encased in slowly melting ice, and the book itself bore the hallmarks of a very, very limited edition. It was pamphlet slim, but some pages folded over on themselves and opened out to a size quadruple the length and width of the cover. The book's epigram was a few lines of translated verse originally authored by somebody named Nezval:

> . . . *My eyes drink in the lights of the great merry-go-round*
> *Whose ringing chimes call home*
> *All barges and stray horses*
> *Whose ringing chimes call home*
> *All sparks of light*

From this, Hero, who was most unequivocally *not* a spark of light, deduced that her home must lie elsewhere. She hadn't brought a backup book, and could only hope that this *Paradoxical Undressing* wasn't going to be a lot of operatic bawling that could have conveyed just as much substance in an indoor voice. She'd fallen asleep during *Rigoletto*. She didn't know how she'd managed to do it in the midst of all that earsplitting commotion, and yet she had.

Hero stared out of the window with her eyes out of focus,
checked her phone again. No new messages,
reopened *Paradoxical Undressing* and read the first chapter:

There's a secondhand bookshop near Lesser Town Square,
just a few steps away from that church with the tall, skinny clock
tower that scrapes upward alongside a shorter, much more
genial-looking plump, domed turret. The bookshop gathers itself in against the few cluttered square feet of pavement assigned
to its exterior: there are so many books that some have to live
outside in boxes, on a rickety shelf, and on two spinning carou-
sels that don't really turn anymore. The sign on the door says NO
MONEY. The bookshop's owner, Mr. Zapomník, is inflexible on
this matter. To customers who find it stressful to shop for books
this way (too many reminders of the complex negotiations
needed to acquire various goods when the Communists were in
charge), he says: "You really don't have to think of it that way;
mostly this is exercise for the books themselves."

Some customers have carte blanche: just take whatever you
want. Others have take-it-or-leave-it offers. For one Vančura
text you can take away two short story collections and one poetry
collection or play: no novels. For one Klíma text you can have
three novels, but *only* novels. Cortázar's *Hopscotch* gets you all the
Shakespeare, Marlowe, or Webster you can carry.

Certain books will get you nothing except an order to leave
immediately, though nobody is ever forbidden from coming
back and trying again another day, with a different book.
Though the decisions are made quickly, the rules are not made
up as they go along. The staff refer to centuries of precedent,
and they know their inventory. It's literature live.

Once a member of staff tried to explain that Mr. Z's aim is
to welcome all the *samizdat* and *tamizdat* home, keeping that destination as flexible as the editions themselves are. Mr. Z doesn't

know—no one knows—if it's too late, or whether there's such a thing as "too late" when it comes to books and remedying the punishments incurred by those who write them, read them, and circulate them. But this is the best he can do . . . *Lepší než drátem do voka, že jo?* Better than a poke in the eye.

Unfortunately for this eloquent staff member, Mr. Z overheard her. "What an interesting little speech," said he. And he formally accepted the chatty staff member's resignation in advance of her offering it.

A new staff member joined Mr. Z's team on the proviso that she speak only for herself unless possessed with explicit authorization to do otherwise.

The newbie spoke Czech, understood Slovak, and read Latin. You know, just like every Prague housewife whose kids have flown the nest and whose professor husband has recently eloped with a former student. The newbie tried to act like she'd seen it all coming, but privately, she was feeling really, really low. Mr. Z's comment that her Latin literacy would "come in handy with some things that have been occurring at the shop" was a little bit of a boost. She kept asking herself stupid "If I had done this or that instead of grappling with Latin would I still be in a loving relationship" questions, so she was keen to proceed with practical application of what she'd learned.

After a few weeks that didn't feature any Latin-related tasks, the newbie asked Mr. Z about the "occurrences around the shop" he'd mentioned when hiring her. Mr. Z's face lit up. "This house was built by one of King Rudolf's courtiers," he said, in an explaining voice. "I hear he had a gormless face and his family wasn't just posh, they were a bunch of pious scholars, so he always had an effective idea or two when it came to deescalating conflict between the astronomers and the clergy. Apparently over the years three different people gave him this house as a token of appreciation for his peacemaking—all three people thought they owned the house, but it was his all along, and he didn't make a big deal out of it, just let them think they'd been generous. *Thanks, thanks, so kind.* I'm thinking he didn't want so many people knowing this place belonged to him, anyway. People would ask what he used it for, since he didn't install any tenants or servants or anybody. But look at it this way . . . it's a convenient spot, this . . . close to the Castle and all its goings-on. You can dash back before you're missed . . ."

One morning the newbie was on the toilet in the upstairs bathroom. There was a little casement window to her left, and she reflexively checked the view from that window every couple of seconds, dreading the thought of catching a Peeping Tom in the act. The newbie would've preferred the window to be curtained, but she wasn't sure how to raise the issue without sounding like she thought everybody was interested in looking at her arse. It was difficult; everything was.

There was a bump in the plaster panel that centered the window frame. She flicked a fingernail against it, then pushed it, to see if it sank. It wasn't flat, but sharp—she almost got a paper cut. She ran a thumbnail around its circumference and it crackled. Paper, but not everyday paper. It seemed a folded banknote had infiltrated Mr. Z's money-free zone. She pulled. Oh. It was just paper after all . . . old paper . . . hang on, wasn't this parchment? She felt it should be handled with gloves, and not just because she happened to be on the toilet. Latin. In almost luridly rectangular hand, someone had written:

Only a matter that rests on three separate points can be settled for ever.

That sentence was crossed out, then written out all over again and underlined.

Over the days and weeks that followed, the newbie found further scraps all over the building. Her findings put her in a ticklish position. She couldn't in her heart of hearts approve of an entire, very old notebook (sixteenth century, according to a friend of Mr. Zapomník's) being torn into scraps that resurfaced at will. Within the current meanings of property-protective law, doing this to a centuries-old artifact was probably a criminal offense. Yet the newbie prized each scrap as if it were a medal . . . for what? Patience? Learning where to look? Taking over hoovering duties and closely examining the dust bag before emptying it out? Soon enough she realized what was going on: this was *gossip*. And gossip was just her favorite, irregardless of vintage. It made her feel like a wise person who knew how to avoid being talked about.

Knowing that it's absolutely none of your business probably makes you want to hear this too:

Fairly late in life, a nobleman at the court of Rudolf II fell in love with two physicians. Words like "smitten" and "besotted" barely approximate the nobleman's state of mind; his heart and brain were ransacked. What he felt for the female physician was something akin to a first love that both quakes and settles a person at their very core: there was no particle of him that didn't call to her, answer her. As for the male physician, the nobleman stood dumbfounded in his presence: that feeling, so sweetly distilled, was all the love that would go with him as he left this world.

. . . Talking about it later, the nobleman's wife said she thought he might have been all right if these two people had happened to him a good thirty years apart. An opinion to be regarded with caution: wifey didn't really seem to know what it's like to lose your mind over someone even once, let alone twice. The nobleman's wife, careful by nature, had been relieved that her parents had chosen someone who listened to her advice about what to do with their money and didn't bother her for conversation or fulfillment of conjugal duties once she showed him a doctor's note that stated that intimate activity was life threatening for her. She had another doctor's note confirming that the sound of her husband's voice *inflamed her brain and endangered her health.* She was no slacker, though—she had the dynastic side of things all settled. Before she'd seen fit to get the doctors' notes, the nobleman and his wife had had three children: one heir and two daughters to tactically marry off once their shrewd mother saw that the time was right. I say she'd earned the right to some rest.

The year was 1590. And in that royal court slathered with

the cream of the realm's crop of alchemists, astronomers, poets, painters, sculptors, philosophers, and diplomats, the two physicians kept a low profile. They did not aim to astound. And the nobleman who loved them employed many wily maneuvers to ensure that they didn't learn that he was wooing them both.

The female physician was interested in curative maltreatment. That was her term for it. Most people who saw her at work would say: "Oh, isn't she—isn't that—torture???"

An indisputably wicked business . . . unless you allowed Livia to assure you that her rationale was quite different. Livia was persuasive; her living situation had rubbed off on her. She was a member of the Florentine ambassador's retinue—an illegitimate daughter of the ambassador's, in fact, intermittently spoiled and neglected. In her teenage years she tired of that cycle and began to take notice of where she was and who was around her. She was mere centimeters from the throne of the Holy Roman Empire. And the throne was held by a King entirely composed of question marks.

If the world and its ideas are a jigsaw puzzle of boundless dimensions, then question-marked and question-remarkable Rudolf had raised a hurricane of puzzle pieces that flew elliptically, crashed to the ground, shattered in collision with each other, connected in mid air, fell upward . . . ? Instructors in various disciplines volunteered themselves: Livia represented a sliver of a chance to gain a precious moment of the King's attention. Say she mentioned some teaching of theirs to the head of her household, who went on to repeat the mention in the right company, even by way of amusement . . . well, the instructor's fortune could still be made. In return Livia was not unattracted, hesitating before turning away from Deep Mycology, incense making, and enfleurage.

She chose the one instructor who had neither the time nor the inclination to teach her anything: her father's physician. The Florentine ambassador's physician was one of the most respected in all Christendom, and he had some knowledge of Ottoman medical practice too—so he could not escape Livia. She assisted this senior physician tirelessly in any way that occurred to her until, for the sake of his patients, he was forced to intervene and tell her what would actually be helpful for her to do and why. You mustn't hold him responsible for Livia's eventual specialization, or her assertion that humans have knowledge of immortality, and that their lives only end (or appear to end) because they're estranged from that knowledge. Livia was very firmly convinced that only curative maltreatment could restore a person's sense of their true unkillability. And there was no use asking her who had taught her that, where she'd read it, or how she had come by the idea. She'd only name courtiers who agreed with her. Remember: those jigsaw pieces were boomeranging all around the Castle. Claiming the origin of an approach was futile even if you wanted to.

Considering Livia a challenge that he was up for, the lovelorn nobleman took care to woo her with sensitivity and eloquence. He made it clear that not only would Livia be able to hurt him in every way, but he'd tell her all about it in exhaustive detail. This was music to the ears of a researcher who wanted to hone the precision of her notes. Plus: certain of the nobleman's measurements excited Livia immensely: the circumference of his nostrils and the arched depth of his nail beds. These told her that not only was she going to be able to hurt him to a degree unprecedented for either of them; Livia had high hopes of being able to hurt the nobleman so much that he'd be in good health until the world itself came to an end, and probably even after that as well.

With Livia the nobleman played a double role. He was coguardian of her vision, which mostly meant buying all the equipment and materials she requested, instigating circulation of select findings from her experiments, and giving her pep talks amid the earth-, sea-, and sky-shattering squealing of every single one of his nerve endings. He did everything he could think of to magnify her sense of purpose, and it worked. Her focus cocooned the two of them in data—data concerning how much he was able to take and how far she was able to go. There would be no emergence until she'd cataloged it all. Despite all this, Livia never guessed that the body she subjected to curative maltreatment was that of her benefactor. He kept her very much in the dark about that.

This was a counterintuitive gambit on the nobleman's part: after all, he got off on the idea of unconditional love just as much as the next emotionally intelligent gentleman-about-town. But he'd got to the age of thirty-one without that ever happening for him or for anybody he knew. Also . . . life expectancy being what it was, he had about ten years left to enjoy any kind of ardent entanglement whatsoever. It was time to concentrate on "as ifs."

The nobleman had correctly understood this physician to be someone who liked a bit of intrigue. So, with the aid of a borrowed name and the wax seal of a third cousin of his who'd died in battle, the nobleman commissioned curative maltreatment research without meeting Livia: it was all done through letters she faithfully burned after reading . . . even the ones in which he praised her progress and asked helpful questions. His physical self he presented to Livia as a "servant," along with an introductory letter from his "master" that placed him entirely at her disposal. This worked well; he was pitied as a mere pawn of the man who commissioned the experiments. "You *must* outlast your master," Livia whispered to him. "Not by a few measly years: by millennia!" When she wasn't curatively mistreating the nobleman, she cared for him in other ways . . . well, it was exactly "as if" she loved him. Which made it worth all the hassle.

Livia wrote to the nobleman whenever she was ready to try a new method; he'd pay off her chaperones and meet her at a house close to the Castle. A house you may recognize. It wasn't quite aligned with the lane it was on; it was a bit too wide, faintly overstuffed somehow . . . no, it was evasive in its dimensions—that was it. Something about the way the outer angles stretched over the interior ones. It was the sort of house you could imagine eating the house next door, giving you a blank look with all openings very tightly fastened when you asked, *When did you last see your neighbor?* and then munching up another building as soon as you turned your back. Bones and all. A house like that gobbles up every other structure along the lane without ever admitting it. Still chewing, it'd tell you, *I wouldn't worry about it . . . just last week they were talking about going on holiday,* or *Aren't all these disappearances awful! Sometimes I almost worry that I might be next.* Just as you guessed, it's the building where Mr. Zapomník's bookshop stands now. If Prague Castle ever disappears overnight, I shall immediately release the address so that the bookshop can be thoroughly searched.

The nobleman's courtship of Livia included a month during which she mixed finely ground gold leaf into wine and had him drink that twice daily. He pissed gold and drooled gold and sweated gold, and in the third week it seemed to him that he was flayed by a *brightness*—a tingling spotlight, or two spotlights, one at his feet and one just above his head, shining into him and through him and melting him into a rancid puddle (later this was what he'd marvel at the most—that turning into a gold machine had made him stink, and that the stench itself was so excruciating). Livia was reluctant to halt that experiment—measure for measure, he was excreting a lot more gold than he had taken in, and she was interested in working out how that was even possible. But his cover story for the month had been a trip to Silesia that was supposed to be drawing to an end. And he needed a few days to retrieve the appearance of someone who'd spent the past few days talking and riding and banqueting as opposed to screaming and melting.

Another notable month was the one when she forced him to sleep all day, every day: she concocted a compound that she burned in the fireplace. After breathing in the fumes he couldn't stay awake, and could only be woken by blows so heavy that they broke a wrist or a rib. And each time he woke Livia asked him what he'd dreamed, she said he must have dreamed, but he hadn't dreamed of anything at all . . .

Had Livia been the nobleman's only love, he would've perished without leaving a trace of their quest to put an end to endings.

Luckily (?) the nobleman's second physician, Mikuláš,

patched him up. Occasionally the nobleman was on tenterhooks as Mikuláš arrived at the house; he'd rehearse stories about falling off his horse or being attacked by a bear. He never got to tell them. Mikuláš never asked; he just set about treating the wounds. Unlike Livia, he didn't equate medicine with healing. He was more inclined to argue that all doctors offered was long-term palliative care. Long term? Yes, from birth onward. Mikuláš didn't need to point out that the human organism is a frenzy of simultaneous processes; very often they could feel it. Blinking is a labor-intensive production, as is smiling, breathing, digestion, and everything else. Immortality?! How about being content with handling the wear and tear of a single day?

Mikuláš, the third son of a Moravian count, had spent his life cheerfully staying out of his eldest brother's way, the unspoken message being: *The title's all yours, psycho.* His medical training had been formally administered by monks. But the monks weren't responsible for his theory that we die when we can no longer hang on to the delusion that embodiment is a viable project. It isn't, and never was, and the longer we keep trying, the worse it gets. And if you asked Mikuláš how he'd come to think like this, he said he'd read it somewhere, and that it didn't matter where. He was no scholar; he was doing what he could to help his patients feel less humiliated by the patent truth that we are not able to be. An inability we demonstrate daily.

His nobleman was a model patient—rapturously exhausted and eager to fade away into pleasure. Mikuláš prescribed no bitter medicines, delivered doses mouth to mouth, and favored the most temperate alleviations: numbing ointments, cooling elixirs, dimly but warmly lit rooms, the gentle laying on of hands, physical exercise to shift melancholic humors.

Physical exercise: whenever the nobleman passed through the lofty columns of the Castle's míčovna and saw his dovelike physician playing so gravely there with shoe in hand, he recalled the bliss of release, of renunciation, even. With what looked like a mere touch, Mikuláš spun a leather ball across the tiled inner chamber and set off at a sprint to receive it on its return journey.

Sometimes—often—the ball flew from shoe heel to shoe heel with such whistling velocity that the nobleman missed the moment when it dropped out of circulation and saw nothing when he studied the ground: the aeronaut had already rolled into the shadows.

Livia, Livia's lovemaking, her curative maltreatments, and the sheer violence of her will: Livia was storm, stress, and carnage on every level. She had already begun training a more junior physician in her curative maltreatment methods: to take care of the nobleman after she was gone, she said (!). But in his own softly impersonal way Mikuláš was every bit as exacting: his was a love that wished you gone.

At times the nobleman felt himself becoming . . . slightly more and slightly less than a man. A channel of correspondence . . . ? His days and nights with Livia were answered by his days and nights with Mikuláš. Both physicians grew uncertain of their methods; their patient was not responding the way he should have if they were right. And yet it wasn't galling to be wrong, or to have their work undone. The contradictions felt sweet, the question you thought you'd answered returning to meet you as an equal.

"You're getting stronger and stronger," Mikuláš would say, running his hands along his patient's shoulders, arms, and chest, flinching slightly, as if the healthy musculature was tumorous growth. His fingers made alphabetical patterns as he spread ointment across the nobleman's wounds—well, one particular letter of the alphabet: a long sweep down, then a shorter sweep across. L, L, L, tessellations soaking into the skin.

Weekly suffocation practice with Livia began to take on the contours of a séance: gripping him by the hair and raising his feebly lolling head from the pillows, she'd stare into his eyes and tell him that she'd caught him again; he'd tried to resist breathing as the function returned to him. "Explain! What is this, who is this in you?"

The nobleman could feel his lovers coming to know each other through him. The closer they grew to each other, the further they drifted from their medical practice. Livia had three shaggy, golden-fleeced goats brought to her from Palermo and grazed them on some land bordering the King's vineyards. It was land that had been awarded to the Florentine Ambassador, so there were no legal problems, but the Ambassador had promised the land to his physician as a medicinal garden, and the physician had already begun planting. The goats' diet caused them to gambol in quite a reckless manner. Livia bought a lute and sang and played to them and it seemed to calm them down a bit; they'd settle down on the grass and nibble at her skirts while bleating their own lyrics. She milked them and made butter that even the garden-deprived physician had to agree was quite something.

Mikuláš bought a bakery in the Lesser Quarter and applied himself to the milling of flour and the application of caraway and sunflower seeds to his doughs. The crusts of his rolls and loaves crackled to the point of debauchery. One evening, the nobleman sat down with a slice of Mikuláš's sourdough. He topped it with some butter from Livia's goats; a layer that stood about an inch high. He added a bit of salt—let's presume that the salt represented him—and tucked in. Having patiently pandered to his ex-physicians' requirements, and having seen them both through to the other side of their ambitions, the nobleman now felt sure of his own. Livia and Mikuláš were ready to meet each other in the flesh. That is, in their own flesh, not his.

They had to get out of the King's orbit. The nobleman didn't want to blame the King outright for the fact that everyone who existed in his vicinity was completely losing their shit, problematizing the desire to live yet unable to forgive themselves for dying. This wasn't entirely Rudolf's fault, but pastoral care was lacking. You can't really have perpetual festivals of theory without that.

The nobleman lured his bread and his butter out to woods of Okoř, quite some way from Prague Castle. Livia's goats came, too, as she couldn't find anyone willing to watch them while she was gone.

The trees were meant to be a soothing factor, but they must have gone on the wrong day; it was like walking among the bristles of an exceedingly sulky green hog. (The boundaries of the city had not yet expanded as far as Okoř back then. They still haven't. But you mark my words: one day they will.) Regardless of the setting, Livia and Mikuláš had some enthrallment and some animosity to deal with before they could talk. "So! It's you . . ."

They hugged, compared hand sizes with their palms pressed together, Livia suddenly dealt Mikuláš a resounding slap, Mikuláš kissed Livia and then bit her cheek so hard that the blood washed down her neck—they both mocked and harangued the nobleman for thinking that he was so clever and so good at being in love, etc. Juvenile stuff. Around midnight, the nobleman almost got up and fled. Perhaps he'd got it wrong; the affinities were Livia's and Mikuláš's to pursue on their own. They could just name their first child after him and leave it at that.

But deep into the night Mikuláš got up and sorted out some food for all three. They hadn't had a meal all day, and even though they got on his nerves, he didn't think they should starve. Bread, butter, and salt: they began to talk. And it didn't take long for them to agree (Mikuláš perhaps more reluctantly than the other two) that finding out how to speak to the stars was not in their gift. Nor would they be the ones to learn what to do about the desolate beastliness of the body. So what actually *was* in their gift? It seemed to have something to do with the way they were together, and their way of perceiving and reaching each other that was one to one to one . . . possibly more; they'd never thought about expanding their resources this way until now. To reach out and touch she or he who opposes you. Without enmity, indeed with (or through) some emotion there still may not yet be a name for.

"It's funny that you're just some man," Livia said to Mikuláš. "Fine, a bit more than a man . . . a baker . . . all this time I couldn't talk about you or ask about you because I didn't know anything at all except that you *are*, and it seemed like finding out anything more would get me put into a madhouse."

"Just some man," Mikuláš said, contemplating the nobleman. "That's what I thought about this one. They grow on you, though, the ones you just keep seeing around."

Livia took the nobleman's hand. "They do."

The timing seemed right for the nobleman to propose that the three of them permanently forsake Rudolf's court and start all over again as bandits.

And that's what they did. For three utterly uninhibited years. Action suited them much better than thought had. At the end of the three years, the bandits bulletproofed their bonds by separating. Livia rode off to terrorize Bohemia's border with Germany, the nobleman picked the Silesian-Polish border, and Mikuláš went to raise hell at the Moravian-Austrian border. Each took with them four ways of dealing with those who crossed their path. If the weather wasn't too harsh and they were in a materialistic mood, they'd just take everything from you: money, jewelry, shoes, clothes, underwear. You and your party would be left to navigate the countryside stark naked. Then there was Livia's way: The Way of the Goat. She'd rob you and then keep you on as a surplus shepherd for her flock. For a few days—a week at most. If she liked you (that is, if you treated the goats as if they were your own children), you could make goat milk butter alongside her too. (For Mikuláš and the nobleman, however, the Way of the Goat meant they'd make you get down on all fours and bleat until they said you could stop.)

Mikuláš's way was fairly Dionysian; you'd be stuffed with bread and beer, told jokes you were too afraid to laugh at, and then suddenly released at dawn with all your goods intact.

The nobleman's way was to make you tell him the names and whereabouts of two people you loved. Then he'd go and kidnap them too! In that case the three of you were captives for months . . .

You really didn't know which way it was going to be with any one of these three. Travelers were scared witless; especially by the very thought of the nobleman, that mind changer, whose name none of them ever knew. So for a time, all nonessential travel to the Czech lands was curtailed.

The aversion lingered and made its way into lullabies that were sung about the bandits. Sleep, little one, or the shepherd milkmaid bandit will make you walk her Way of the Goat. Go to sleep RIGHT NOW or the mad baker bandit will make you eat bread until you pop . . . etc. Those lullabies are extant. When I sang them to my own children, it worked a treat every single time: the kiddies were absolutely bricking it. And so I tip my hat to those three lovers: immortal after all, impossible after all. Needless to say, the sharp drop in visitor footfall annoyed Rudolf II no end. It also served him right.

While we're on the subject of essential-nonessential travel . . . there's something I've been dying to ask.

Humor me. Tell me.

Where are you?

Hero went to turn the page, but didn't like the way her hand trembled. She had to admit that the question had thrown her; it combined reproach (a "Where are you" that doubled as "What's your reason for not being here?") with . . . what felt like actual inquiry. The narrator of the story didn't know where she was, and they wanted to know. Furthermore: it seemed to Hero that the story she'd been reading was narrated by a person distinct from whoever it was that had written the words—she checked the name on the cover—Merlin Mwenda. There was no refining the matter beyond that. Here Hero Tojosoa was with her right hand all unstable because, in the fissure between one printed sentence and another, someone had made a sudden attempt to find her.

She closed the book and drummed her fingers on the cover, saying, "What the fuck, what the fuck," until it turned into a half croon.

Then Hero:

walked in and out of the bathroom gargling with some Becherovka that had been thoughtfully placed where mouthwash would usually be,

opened *Paradoxical Undressing* again and took a look at the author photo. It showed a grizzled, bearded man about a decade and a half older than her. His physical frame was that of a wrestler, he shared her complexion, and wore a black eye patch. His outfit was the kind you've got to dive into with determination: waterproof dungarees that gleefully turn into boots. He'd tied some of his wildfire mane up into a topknot. He stood about ankle deep in river mulch and was brandishing his fishing rod in a good-humored imitation of wrath at being interrupted. The eye that wasn't covered with fabric held a steady look of astonishment; possibly a contradiction in terms, steady astonishment, but that's how it was. As if, upon seeing you, he exclaimed **THERE YOU ARE** at the same time as exclaiming *You're there?! I mean, **here**?!* And he had fans, or disciples, or something like that: a minicolony of nutria were fanned out around him, some of them watching the photographer, some of them with their backs turned and their paws a-paddle, seemingly checking the river for any funny business. Hero was reluctant to move on to the author biography; it looked rather long, and had very little chance of topping the thousand words the picture told. However . . .

In 1991, the author of this book, Sydney bartender Merlin Mwenda (born February 21, 1970) traveled to Prague on a one-way ticket, with a proposal for a chain of Aussie-style pubs and an oath that he wouldn't return until he'd secured investment partners.

Upon arrival Merlin scheduled a couple of meetings, and

engaged the services of an interpreter who knew business lingo and did all of that good stuff. Nevertheless, there was a misunderstanding that led to the loss of his eye. While he would, of course, prefer not to have suffered that, he doesn't have too many hard feelings about it anymore. For one thing, the lawyer he was romancing at the time assisted him in suing the City of Prague for damages. She framed the exercise as experimental, an exploration of blame culture, so he hadn't expected anything concrete to come of it. The outcome was a nice surprise: a note of unequivocal—though terse—apology from the Mayor of Prague (on genuine letterheaded paper), along with an ample out-of-court settlement. The money and the good manners helped Merlin come to terms with his injury, but so did his eventual understanding that it was part and parcel of the 1990s. That's the sort of decade it was: each year of freedom was a rocket ride. Unfathomable deals were struck in those days—deals he wouldn't have believed if he hadn't been there himself; only the reams and reams of postdated nondisclosure agreements reassure him that he didn't dream it all. And he wouldn't swap that (having actually been there, semi-sober and wide awake) for anything.

This being a first novel, the indignant reader will wish to know *why* it was written.

Hereby submitted for your consideration:

One spring day in 1993, Merlin Mwenda's only Prague friend took him for a walk along the pine-needled paths of Chuchelský háj. This friend was a man who appeared to be Merlin's junior by six or seven years: the lanky, fair-haired, and scrupulously clean-shaven Hynek Hejduk. Hynek Hejduk's friendship with Merlin was bolstered by nods, shrugs, hand motions, and eyebrow gymnastics. That was how they smuggled conviviality across an otherwise insuperable language barrier. Hynek was the perfect person for Merlin to talk to about Prague and how much he hated this city that had taken his eye. What Merlin felt was both hatred and painful love, the kind the writers of jazz standards know all about: *All of me / Why not take all of me?* He couldn't risk talking to somebody who could understand what he was saying or offer advice. He was afraid of being advised to commit some deed so brutal that his beloved enemy would take notice of him once and for all; he could resist such thoughts as long as he never heard them from anybody else. So Merlin felt perfectly safe as he told Hynek that there were no two ways about it: Prague was a joke city. "Prague's for ginks; I'm getting out," he said (he was always saying that). "Brno's so much better." The mention of Brno didn't seem to sit right with Hynek.

Merlin tried again. He only wanted to say that Brno had much more intellect—there no playing the fool in the capital of Moravia, no behaving like one who has no idea what time it is. Hynek stared off in the other direction; he seemed to have decided to give Merlin a moment to collect himself. But Merlin didn't feel like collecting himself just yet: first he wanted to show some appreciation for a thinking city. A city that steadily breathed life into theory. "Brno," Merlin bellowed, attempting to startle Hynek into warming to this theme, "Brno is—" But Hynek Hejduk grimaced and made the universal sign for *Shhhh*. They walked on through the woods in silence; there was fresh breeze and Hejduk pointed at a few clusters of bluebells, making sure Mwenda saw that they were coming up nicely. Eventually Merlin settled down on a bench in a scenic spot. His drinking buddy remained standing, happily surveying their surroundings. They had a pale-gold-colored church behind them and the Vltava River crackling along below. The only thing missing was beer. Merlin Mwenda thought he'd have a go at communicating that thought to his drinking buddy, but only made it halfway through the process of turning his head before Hynek Hejduk knotted both arms around his neck and pulled as if he meant to pop Merlin's skull right off his neck there and then. Merlin roared and, being highly incensed as well a lot bigger than this fellow, would have surged up from his sitting position with relative ease if not for Hynek's speedy introduction of a switchblade that prodded a couple of arterial pressure points and made it clear that cutting a throat would not be a complicated problem here. He suggested that Merlin calm down and keep still. Merlin complied as best he could. He also attempted to reflect on his mistakes. Had he . . . overpraised the city of Brno?

Adjusting distances and proximities with disturbing ease, Hynek had words with Merlin. Hynek's muttering went in at Merlin's left ear while Hynek's knife tapped out a triangular pattern on the right side of his neck. An upside-down triangle— a heart emptying itself. Hynek Hejduk spoke an English so centrally European (with differently influenced pronunciation for every other word; at times there was a Magyar melt to his consonants, in the next moment rich Dutch vowels rolled out, next his intonation flickered around the edges in a manner that felt fairly Italian &c) that, fascinated by the cumulative neutrality of this accent as well as by the proximity of death, essentially mesmerized by form, Merlin almost forgot to attend to content. In due course he overcame that obstacle.

Hynek told Merlin that there wasn't going to be any more moping from the depths of a beer barrel. Not for a while, anyway. No, Merlin Mwenda was going to take a break from all that and write a Prague book. As for what a Prague book was, they'd find out once Merlin had written it. Hynek Hejduk was leaving town for a bit, he said, and when he came back he was going to want something to read. He told Merlin he was going to visit him a year from now . . . and if, in a year's time, Hynek found that Merlin hadn't written the book that he was after, he'd slit his throat from ear to ear. No matter where Merlin Mwenda went, no matter who or what he tried to hide behind, only the novel that he owed could save him from Hejduk's Abbatoir Special. That's about the long and short of what Hynek said.

All this was a lot for Merlin to take in, of course. Not just the ideas, but the expression of the ideas.

Brain ticking over, Merlin asked if this was some sort of windup.

Hynek only tightened his grip and answered that if there was any doubt in Merlin's mind, he had only to wait and see what happened a year from now. In the very instant that he released his hold, the younger, sprier man was off at a sprint, leaving Merlin with the church propping him upright and the river to swear at. He combed every bleary pub memory he could access, both dreading and longing to find Hynek Hejduk's first appearance in them. That first meeting kept slipping past him, as did the first overture. Looking at the situation sensibly, friendship was always going to be Hynek Hejduk's least likely motive for establishing a rapport with a maudlin skirt chaser. As for the most likely motive . . . that would be taking the aforementioned maudlin skirt chaser to a secluded spot in order to jump him for cash he didn't even have. Merlin knew that he had to get back to his bedsit, but for some reason he had a hard time getting off that bench. Ultimately it was the thought of Hynek circling back to finish him off that did it.

As mentioned before, this took place in 1990s Prague; the local economy was hulking out and no commission was truly off-limits, including (especially?) that of having to write for your very life. Rather than take any unnecessary risks, Mwenda knuckled down and bashed out *Paradoxical Undressing*, the novel you hold in your hands today. Meanwhile, Hynek Hejduk took his gap year, or whatever it was. His absence actually lasted about eighteen months, and his reappearance was quiet, emotionally refined—one afternoon Mwenda arrived at their usual pub to find Hynek Hejduk just sitting there, at their usual table. Hejduk looked a bit better: his hair was thicker, or he'd raised his hemoglobin levels, or something—it was hard to pinpoint what department the improvement had occurred in. There was a handshake, and an apology from Hejduk. He was sorry for having stayed away so long. Not for anything else. He addressed Merlin in Czech, and did not seem to know any English anymore. Despite ignoring all efforts to address his alarming conduct that afternoon at Chuchelský háj, Hejduk has remained Merlin Mwenda's best drinking buddy ever since.

3.

HERO TUCKED *Paradoxical Undressing* into her bed, placing the book on the pillow and then drawing the covers up around it. She'd go for a walk first, and read more when she got home. On her way downstairs, she recorded a voice message for Jerome. Exactly who was it that recommended this book to you??? Sending that by SMS wouldn't have conveyed the chuckle that gave rise to the question.

Jerome's reply, even more slowly and carefully enunciated than usual, came as she walked out into the soufflé of sunlight and shadow that was late afternoon in Malá Strana. Her son's voice had broken about a month before, and its new huskiness sometimes agitated his stammer. He'd hear himself, reject the sound, then run all over the place gathering up the juddering syllables. It was Dad . . . I asked him what book you should take with you. He said that one, but he wouldn't lend me his copy. Do you like it?

Not "Is it good" but "Do you like it?" There was the young man she, Jean-Pierre, and Claudine were raising between them. *Three*

Journos and a Baby. Jerome had had notions of pure objectivity debunked at around the same age other kids' parents sit down with them for the talk about the actual providers of the presents underneath the Christmas tree.

Hero FaceTimed her son, and he answered—there he was, with his square jaw, languid, bespectacled desert-dweller eyes, curly quiff of hair, and ears that stuck out so sweetly they undermined any attempt he made at projecting bad-boy energy. The bad-boy energy was very much there, though—she knew that; sometimes she thought she knew it better than anyone, though she hadn't yet cracked a way to address it. An anxiously loving mother imagined things, that was what J.-P. and Claudine said. And yet this is what Hero knew: until fairly recently Jerome had shown no physical partialities in terms of new company he'd seek out. Now Hero's son liked women. Shape and pigmentation weren't a factor, but age was. Saying that Jerome had started liking girls or liking "older girls" would downplay the significance of the shift. These days Jerome Randolph made quietly and irresistibly intense advances on females who had so many years on him (ten? fifteen?) that they were guaranteed to see him as analogous to a nephew or younger cousin and laughingly pet him in ways he seemed to find increasingly unsatisfactory. Hero was not imagining that. The desire was as guiltless as any appetite: your body seeking out what it likes with no thought of what it means to like that and no plan as to what will happen afterward. Hero had already ridden the roller coaster of feathers and scales that was Agnès Varda's *Kung Fu Master!* a couple of times, and she kept thinking, oh please, please please—Jerome, can you really not slow down, can you really not wait until . . . ?? Hero wasn't pinning her "until" to Jerome's reaching the age of consent in a year and a half. It wasn't as if certain faculties showed up bang on time for your birthday: *Your ability to give yourself to somebody without being used has now been authorized! Ditto your ability to take a lover without depleting them! Hip hip hurray!* It was just—wasn't there some way for an appetite to . . . defer fulfillment just long enough for the subsequent giving and taking to be *fair*?

On to the part that Hero surmised, but didn't know: she thought Jerome might have been meeting women. A woman? Which was worse? She thought that might have been happening on a couple of occasions when he'd lied that he was with certain friends and had set up such an intricate tangle of interdependent alibis that it took hours to establish that none of the friends he'd mentioned were with him or actually knew what he was up to. Another proficiency more speedily acquired by the son of three journalists, she supposed. He'd pulled that trick once with Jean-Pierre and Claudine, who'd had heart-to-hearts with him and then decided to wipe the slate clean without telling Hero what had happened. Which meant that Jerome was free to repeat exactly the same exercise the following week, when he was staying with her.

According to Jean-Pierre and Claudine, this personal time wasn't troubling in and of itself. They didn't believe Jerome was doing anything that broke their trust. The way he went about securing those three or four unscrutinized hours: those were the lengths they'd inadvertently made him feel he had to go to. They'd banned solitude and that made him curious about it.

The thing was, they could be right. Except for the slightly charged interactions with older women that Hero was not imagining. He was like her, so he would keep pushing to see what else he could get away with. The pushing was never fully intentional. In short: something was going on with Jerome and he was possibly not 100 percent aware of what it was. But even asking about it felt like a way of twisting the entire thing into a label that *told* him what he was doing, how his behavior should make him feel, and what anybody who wasn't some sort of degenerate would think of it.

Confrontation is probably overrated; they went off on a mobile-data-blasting walk together instead, roaming the aggressively coded streets of Prague while the daylight lasted.

Walls spoke in etched and welded symbols. So did doors and many of the window frames. And they were most emphatically not talking to Hero and Jerome. Their route took them past The House of the White Peacock, The House of the Two Suns, The House of the Three Degrees, hat shops that looked like patisseries, and patisseries that looked like clinics. Occasionally Hero heard a squeaking sound . . . rusty and rubbery. Wheels on cobblestones. Sometimes the sound was behind her (she didn't turn to look), sometimes up ahead (she made a point of not scanning the horizon), or around a corner. Sometimes the sound of this selectively sticky wheel was drowned in surging traffic, human chatter, or the screams and sighs the pavements and buildings made as construction workers battered and restored them. But as soon as she forgot about the wheel, she heard it again. Jerome didn't comment on the sound—it probably didn't carry, and the sound equipment on her phone could only do so much. But the lumbering wheel soundtrack seemed like a counterpart to something else that couldn't really be reproduced over FaceTime . . . a trailing ripple of . . . not really attention; more *intention?* Not a perception of pursuit—it was more as if she were being processed by pneumatic post. Whether it was an address, a terraced courtyard, a landmark square that turned like a circle, an impromptu deviation to look at a poster or a sculpture, each stop seemed to send her sailing onward to the next. No wonder she kept hearing people exchanging nautical greetings in a landlocked country; cries of "Ahoj" and "Ahojka!" rang out all over the place.

All this was basically the opposite of what Hero liked in a city . . .

Jerome was reading her a list of key events. Uprisings, defenestrations, and self-immolations weren't anywhere near the half of it. Hero Tojosoa would have liked to see a tiny bit more decorum in evidence, a little bit more homage paid to the bravery shown here, as well as the magnitude of spirit—or of despair.

There was a moment that somewhat reversed this impression. Taken unawares, she stepped onto a bridge lined with statues that curved her sense of the sky above her and the water beneath her in such delicate increments that upon reaching its midpoint she seemed to be either approaching a position behind herself or coming from somewhere she'd never been. Jerome said, "Hmmm," tapped away at his laptop keyboard for a few seconds before announcing: "Yeah, we're at the Charles Bridge, Mum."

He took his leave as she walked back to the bed-and-breakfast; it was dinnertime, and Jean-Pierre and Claudine were sticklers for sit-down family meals during which everybody exhibited interest in the kind of day everybody else had had. Hero was more than glad for this help with Jerome's socialization: it fell into the category of good stuff that her disposition prevented her from giving her son. All the same, she had to bite back a pathetic request for Jerome to stay with her a little bit longer. She was following a lane that had already zigzagged across the dimmest stretches of a number of other lanes and led to dead ends in every direction she'd picked so far. "Dead ends"—well, that was the point of view of someone who had stumbled into a beer labyrinth and didn't want any beer. She was greeted by a pub or a dive bar at almost every turn; the buildings on either side of her swelled with multilingual warbling. The pavements were encrusted with tables, chairs, foam-topped glasses, and perspiring organisms. She was getting closer and closer to nowhere; that is, to finding out what nowhere is. Wheels squeaked directly behind her—*those* wheels that had seemingly run errands in her vicinity for much of the afternoon—and she whirled around to face them down.

Firstly, it was a single squeaky wheel. The force behind it was twentysomething and bronzed Mediterraneanish in aspect. Or Middle Eastern? She wore floral dungarees and brown strappy sandals that did very little to close the height gap between her and Hero. She was pushing an outsize (and empty) wheelbarrow that had the symbol of the City of Prague—two crossed golden keys—very neatly spray-painted on either side of it. "It's OK! I'm Jitka!" she said, undaunted by Hero's best deity-peering-from-the-empyrean stare. She took out a wallet, held up a license that confirmed her name and her official designation to . . . ?

"Take you home," the woman said, indicating that Hero should sit down in the wheelbarrow. Hero inspected the steel tray, and Jitka supervised her inspection, whacking the cushions to show how plump and comfortable they were, showing her the umbrella that would protect her from rain and sun as she was carted to her destination. "Just three hundred koruny for delivery to your door. Lost lady discount . . ."

"Oh, no. No thank you, er—Jitka," Hero said at last. Close up she could see that the pink and white peonies on Jitka's dungarees were hand embroidered. Boosting people's confidence with nonin-trusive notifications that they're looking good being a matter of city-dweller courtesy, she took a moment to compliment Jitka's out-fit before walking away. Jitka beamed but didn't say anything, and Hero set off along the side street once more, eyes on her GPS map. According to that lying little blue dot, she was at Prague Castle.

Squeak, squeak, squeak, and the clacking of heels. Hero felt authorized to ignore this; she'd been clear with Jitka; they were probably just heading in the same direction for a while. She kept her eyes above street level, comparing the names on the red-and-white plaques to the street names her phone was showing her. She couldn't remember the address of the bed-and-breakfast. Fuck.

Screeeeech. Jitka drew level with her, tossed her ponytail, thrust her chin out: *J'accuse!* "You don't know where you're going."

"I do," Hero lied, waggling her phone without conviction.

"No," Jitka said, her gaze compass true.

"I can find it. It's probably just on the next street or something. Enjoy your evening, Jitka. Thanks for . . . caring? Bye . . ."

Hero tried the opposite direction this time, walking as fast as she could. The alternate rasp and swish of the wheelbarrow still rode her eardrum, though Jitka didn't rush to overtake her this time, merely followed at a leisurely pace. Table legs rattled, and al fresco boozers whisked their feet out of the wheelbarrow's path, complaining as they did so.

"Racist?" Jitka called out to her eventually, sounding as if she were inquiring about a food allergy or dietary preference. "As soon as you see me, you say here's a liar and a stealer? Already you're so sure that as soon as you sit down in this bad Romani's wheelbarrow she'll run away with you and dump you at the skip . . ."

Hero turned around again. "Jitka. Jitka! Don't piss me off, my dear. It's really simple: put yourself in my place. Would you want to be wheeled around like a sack of grain?"

A withering stare from Jitka: "What's your name?"

"Hero."

"*Fakt?* Well it doesn't suit you."

"Er . . . and how would you know that?"

"Oh, I'm a know-nothing; don't mind me. I'm a know-nothing, and you're a Hero who's more worried about not looking strange than finding her way . . . sorry for bothering you."

"Apology accepted," said Hero. "Just don't do it again."

"I won't! Best of luck to you!"

"Thanks so much! You too!" Hero couldn't seem to find the right moment to pivot into wordless scorn. So now she had to out-nice her opponent, who folded her arms and said: "Two hundred and seventy-five koruny." Then she nodded slowly as she evaluated her own offer: "Absolute best deal. You left the place where you're going to sleep without making even a tiny bit of a plan for returning—personally I would never do such a thing, but OK, that's how you do things! We'll find the place . . . I will not give up until we do. I could just walk beside you and help, but why not take a seat, since this isn't for free."

"Two hundred and fifty," Hero tried. She wouldn't have to phone Polly to ask where the bed-and-breakfast was; it was worth it . . .

"Two hundred and eighty! Didn't you hear my guarantee that we will find the place? I'll wheel you around until you recognize the house. Anyway, racists pay more."

Jitka turned the contraption around so that she could lead the way, and Hero sank down among the cushions, limbs jolting as Jitka heaved her along the paved lanes. She'd never felt or looked more ridiculous. This would inevitably be the moment they collided with Polly, Sofie, and their bridesmaids. Or with Thea. If Thea was here. Darkness was falling; Hero fumbled in her handbag, found her sunglasses, and put them on anyway.

"Know what this neighborhood is called, Hero?"

"Castle District?"

"That's the part of town we're in, yeah, but the neighborhood is Nový Svět. New World . . ."

Jitka was incredibly strong armed. Strong all over, actually— she went at a clip and made no effort to conserve energy by speaking less; only looking over her shoulder every now and again to make sure Hero hadn't fallen out onto the road. She explained that she made good money in these corners of the city that were too much hassle for car drivers. She usually turned up to transport those who drank until their legs turned to water and then found that their friends were too weak to carry them home. She pointed out notable houses; here was an address where you could place an order for an ultra-light chain-mail vest; they were made by a history professor who specialized in the Přemyslid era and boasted that his work could have saved King Wenceslas. They were pricey vests, but Jitka had no complaints, since they were sexy as well as stabproof: she wore hers over a strapless bra when she went out man-catching. On an adjoining street there was a digital whiz who specialized in wholly convincing manipulation of photo and video images; photoshopping dead (and slightly bored-looking) family members into family gatherings, providing clips of the deceased telling one last off-color joke from beyond the grave. The effect was mundane and pathos-free—it was as if death were just another stamp in their passport. Jitka had heard that this girl was the daughter of a TV newsreader. The project that had led to the discovery of her talent was a video clip in which she tried to make her father say: *I'm proud of you, girl.* She watched it over and over, and it was never quite right. The digital whiz tinkered and tinkered and it got a bit better, but she was still perfecting it and might never manage, because it was the reverse of what she achieved in her projects for other people: the emotional note it struck was too high, plus she was trying to replicate an utterance that had no original version.

Hero wondered at Jitka; she had all the information that nosy people managed to extract from their neighbors, but she wasn't exhibiting the behavior of a nosy person, i.e., trying to glean information about Hero that she could tell others. For Hero, this increased the possibility that the information Jitka was sharing was . . . made up . . . ? Yet she listened more avidly than she had to Polly.

"That house over there"—Jitka swung a foot in the direction of a house with mullioned windows the shade of smoky topaz. Her attempt to kick the house from a distance was overambitious; she stumbled and swore—"is that where you're staying?"

"No, the one I'm staying in looks back to front somehow. And there's a lamppost nearby that's more like a fountain of bulbs . . . ?"

"Oh, that house! It's right next door to Jiří who makes the snow globes . . ."

"Jiří who makes the snow globes?"

"Yes. He calls them banishing globes. But I don't think he knows what they actually are, or if they really do what he says they do. It's all a bit—"

"All a bit what? Did you buy one to go with your chain-mail vest?"

"There's nothing wrong with supporting each other, Hero. Jiří needs all sorts of help. He went to art school . . . I don't know if he went there because he isn't normal and needed some arty camouflage, or if they did something to him there so that he can't do honest work. Anyway, I feel bad for him. And I was talking about it with somebody else who thinks what poor Jiří is doing with the snow globes is some kind of Action or whatever the art kids call it. Something that's meant to make you take a second look at the basics. Like those vending machines where you put a coin in and a little bottle labeled AIR comes out? I myself would be raging, but at least with the snow globe you get something that looks nice."

"Are they expensive?"

Jitka ignored the question: "It's like a classic city landmark snow globe—you'll have your St. Vitus Cathedral or your Žižkov TV Tower in there—but Jiří also puts in another figurine of your choice. It's not made out of the same material as the landmark. The figurine he adds in for you is made out of something that gradually gets lost in the snow every time you shake the globe. Do you see what I mean? You shake the snow globe and the Cathedral or the TV Tower don't go anywhere, but the thing you asked Jiří to add, it crumbles away bit by bit, but not evenly . . . kind of crazily . . . like there's a tiny killer in there who only comes out under the cover of snowfall and goes mad with a saw."

"Huh, so that's the 'banishing.' If you want to give up smoking, you can get this, er, Jiří, to put a little carton of cigarettes in the snow globe and shake the snow globe until it's gone. And then you don't want to smoke anymore. Something like that?"

Jitka thought that over—seemed to worry about it, actually—then gave up on articulating the worry and nodded.

"So what was in your snow globe, Jitka?"

"Er . . . nothing," Jitka said, looking straight ahead.

"Nothing?"

"The night I went to see Snow Globe Jiří, I . . . wasn't in the best condition. Wasn't holding my drink too well. And I was starting fights . . ."

"With who?"

"Oh . . . my sister, my man, anyone who wouldn't sing sea shanties with me . . . everyone."

They reached the lamppost that Hero had noted when she'd first set out: its lit lanterns drew the dusk into themselves and blazed like lions' eyes. Jitka took a couple of turns around this apparition. Hero tried to get out of the wheelbarrow—her head and heart were jive dancing, no longer able to endure the dragging of the wheel on the heavy cobblestones. And all the nearest houses seemed to rock back onto their haunches . . . this was Nový Svět, the New World, and she thought she'd really better get up and run, run far and fast, back toward the old one.

"When I got to Jiří's place he was still up," Jitka said, pushing Hero back down into the wheelbarrow's pan. "And he wasn't all that sober himself. He made me a snow globe within two hours—maybe three hours? He was pouring more beers for us both as he went along . . ."

"Jitka, could we please stop circling this lamppost? I'm going to throw up. Ah—thanks. So. Snow globe. You don't know what you asked Jiří to banish . . . is that what you're telling me?"

"I don't. And he says he doesn't either! Once he gave me my

snow globe I just sat there on his sofa, making it snow and making it snow because I wanted the thing out of my life fast, whatever it was."

"And in the morning . . . ?"

"Nothing in there but a mini Astronomical Clock."

"Maybe he was so drunk he didn't actually add anything at all," Hero said optimistically.

"God, I hope so . . ." Jitka drew to a halt outside Hero's bed-and-breakfast. "Sometimes I think I might have asked him to put in a little Jitka figurine. I was just really fed up with everything!"

"He could never have made a Jitka figurine that quickly, though," Hero said, after a long moment.

"No. No he couldn't . . ."

Unless he had one ready-made, Hero thought.

"Unless he'd already made one . . ." Jitka mumbled.

She looked back at Hero, who smiled instead of answering. Then, helping Hero out of the wheelbarrow, she held out her hand for her fee and halfheartedly went through the motions of making change for a one-thousand-koruna note. When Hero told her she could keep it all, she made the peace sign and departed without looking back.

Hero stared hard at the house to the left and the house to the right of the one that was hosting her.

"Jiří . . . Snow Globe Jiří . . . are you there?" she whispered. There wasn't anything Hero wanted disappeared—not really—so it was a relief that nobody answered.

Both the neighboring houses had windows lit at every level. Quite a contrast to the building Hero was staying in, which was only lit up on the ground floor and the fourth floor. The fourth

floor: her floor. Hero hoped this was another guest's doing, but—
ugh—something told her she'd left a light on. She'd left the room
during daylight hours, but switching on a light just to make sure
that it was working and then . . . forgetting about it—yes, that had
been the cause of Thea's one and only threat to evict her. Hero
had left a light on and a tap running at the same time, and Thea
had told her that this amounted to an ultimatum: me or precious
resources. *And I choose resources, Hero. I'm always going to choose
resources over those who squander them!* Hero hadn't meant to issue
an ultimatum of any kind, and couldn't have been more remorseful.
But Thea wasn't one to heed intention; she only addressed what had
happened. Intuiting that Ms. Dorothea Gilmartin had converted
her existence into an equivalent number of water and electricity
units and strongly preferring not to be told what that number was,
Hero had opted for continued groveling, and had spent the rest of
her time under Thea's roof checking and double-checking taps and
light switches. Forgetfulness had returned as soon as she was left to
her own domestic devices.

She took the stairs two at a time, pleasantly surprised by the
minimal creaking but wondering about the stillness and the darkness. So much for being fully booked. She swept the staircase with
her phone flashlight until she reached the second floor, where she
found the hallway light had been switched on. The bedroom door
to the immediate left of the staircase was wide open, though the
light in the room itself was off. She glanced in as she passed—it was
an unfurnished room with no one in it. Hero sped up, taking three
steps at a time now. When she reached the third floor, the hallway
light was already on, and she heard the light on the floor below
being switched off. This didn't exactly gladden her heart; she looked

back down the staircase and very nearly missed the furtive opening and closing of a door at the end of the third-floor hallway. It had been flick-book-animation fast, but she'd caught it.

"You—oh—stop right there!" she said, striding forward to knock on the door that had just shut. It stayed closed; she knocked harder, and grew sheepish . . . there was too great a disparity between the row she was making and the hush that enfolded her. She'd encountered an introverted guest who didn't like running into strangers on staircases and wanted to wait until she was out of the way, that was all. Why was she acting like this?

She stopped knocking, and someone sniggered. They were immediately—and quite angrily—*shhhhhhhh*ed by somebody else. Now she turned in the direction of these sounds. Another bedroom door had opened, and the room was emitting the tremulous light of candle flames. Two people began talking; the female-sounding voice spoke in Czech, and the male-sounding one responded in Malagasy. It was three doors down, but she hesitated. Firstly, what she heard was very clearly a recording, and secondly, the female voice was too familiar. She'd transcribed so many of the interviews she'd conducted that she'd know her own voice anywhere. That was her, those inflections were hers. Furthermore, the tone . . . no, more precisely, the tenderness she was hearing in her recorded voice—Hero never talked like that. Not even when she actually felt that way. In fact, she made an especial effort not to sound soppy when she felt soppy. For all that she longed to seize that recorded self by the shoulders, give her a good shake, and shout, *Don't you know who we are? We never, ever whisper sweet nothings*, the actual endearments Hero heard herself uttering were a matter of conjecture. This other Hero was, after all, speaking in a language she did not speak. The male-sounding voice, though—the Malagasy that voice spoke was heavily accented (he put a Germanic spin on most of his words), but Hero comprehended what he was saying all too perfectly, and it was enough to give her hyperglycemia. All right, she'd take a look. She had to know what this was and how it had been done.

"Let's get the timing right for once," the male-sounding voice said. "We have to make it look like—"

The door slammed shut as Hero reached it.

"Don't knock," the Malagasy speaker from the recording entreated her from across the hallway. "Please, no more knocking . . ."

A third door had opened; a rectangle of lamplight framed a markedly autumnal man. He was the one who'd just spoken. The coloring of his hair, eyes, and skin were different blends of ochre, russet, and cinnamon, though his features were Slavonic. He raised one of his one hands and eyed it attentively before asking: "Is there writing on my forehead?"

"No . . . ?"

"I just thought I might be the Golem tonight. Never mind."

His gaze was fairly explicit; it appeared to perceive every inch that was ripe for heady revelry, it was touch and taste at once. Was she wearing clothes at all? Her hands and arms . . . they were gloved all the way up to the elbow. Violet silk. Her shoulders were bare. As was her chest, her midriff . . . ah, bare all the way down to the soles of her feet. Nonplussed, she looked at the man across the hall; there was no way he didn't have anything to do with this. But—this delight she basked in—they were in the same condition. No, his was more acute, as he was gloveless.

"Not now, Hero," he said, smiling and walking backward into the room he'd emerged from. "And not here. Be patient . . . this happens later. As you were . . ."

He closed the door, opened it for just one more jubilant glimpse, closed it again, and then the hallway light clicked off. Or, quite possibly, Hero had been traversing the third-floor hallway knocking on doors in the dark all along. Because she was wearing the same vest, flannel shirt, jeans, and trainers she'd been in all day. The very flatness of this restoration (recovery?) brought to mind vicissitudes that members of her circle had had to accommodate . . . the onset of seasonal migraines in Sofie's thirties, the crustacean allergy that had hit lobster-loving Jean-Pierre out of the blue right at the beginning of his forties. *Alors*, her own time had come. Now that Hero was in her forties, rising to her feet after half an hour or so of being joggled around in a wheelbarrow would not fail to propel her into a trance. Good to know.

I think there was more to Hero's light-headedness than the red herring that she'd just thrown herself. She had something like second-date nerves; tension that slithered down a double helix of decisions—hers and that of the book she'd begun reading. People who only ever feel like this about other people may raise their eyebrows as high as they like: the fact is that reentering these premises had reminded Hero that there was a book in her bedroom that was thinking about her. Where are you, that book asked, and there was no way of finding out what it would do with her reply. Would her answer be instrumental to the book's approach to her (in some form even truer than bound pages . . . ?), bringing her to its location, fleeing her, sending her something . . . ? Hero half feared it was the latter—there was already a registered letter she'd been on the run from for weeks—her real reason for being here instead of at home. But *Paradoxical Undressing* played no part in that. Or did it!

This wasn't a standard settling-down-for-the-night scenario for Hero, or even a typical just-going-to-bed-with-a-book scenario. Something sought to enter her life—or already had.

As for the fourth-floor light she'd seen from the street . . . it had indeed been coming from her room. Not just the main overhead light but the bedside lamp, and—following the sound of dripping water—she'd left the bathroom light on too. She must also (this was hard for her to picture, but there was no other hypothesis to hand), she must also have absentmindedly run a bath and decided not to get into it. The water was frigid. The bathroom window was open just a notch. She closed it, and saw that *Paradoxical Undressing*, the book she'd left on her pillow, was now propped up at the edge of the bathtub, at the top corner where the tub met the wall. This—this she rebelled against. Whatever else she might or might not have done, she'd definitely tucked the book up in bed, reveling in the treatment of a book as if it were a person. Also . . . come to think of it, this wasn't the book that she'd put to bed. The cover was the same, the author photo was the same, the publication year and printing press were identical, and so was the biography (as far as she could ascertain by skim-reading). The book was significantly heavier; there were more pages than there had been before. And when she opened it up at Chapter One, there was nothing about a shop where books could only be bought with other books, or a building that regurgitated scraps of a Rudolfine love triangle. She hunted that other chapter, feeling her way along the seams of later chapters, delving into the pages that had pockets and opening out their supplementary pages, to no avail. She wandered back into the bedroom and sank down onto the mattress as she read the pages that were now calling themselves Chapter One:

Matouš Brzobohatý lived in fear. He was a (rightly) reviled High Court judge, but that wasn't what troubled his sleep. He didn't think well of anybody, so why should any of them think well of him?

The Judge wasn't an unfeeling man: this was perhaps the worst thing about him. Having ensured an absence of admiration among his subordinates by insulting each and every one of them (nonverbally . . . it was all deeds), he fully registered their humiliation. Abhorred by those complicit in the harm he did, the Judge challenged them all to act against him—to make any move against him at all—and nobody moved a muscle. Instead, the desire for violence either struck those in his vicinity or it flowed over the Judge in heady, ambrosial waves, warming him in chilly weather and cooling him down when the sunlight sweltered. No bribes or favors for Judge B.: this simultaneous consciousness of both hatred and its impotence before its true target was the only occupational perk he prized.

Over at the court in Nusle he sat in judgment between arches and columns and bars, tight semicircles of marble and tile, and everybody was cheating and nobody felt sheepish about it anymore. Brzobohatý was on the side that tried to steal everything from people who, in turn, tried to steal some puny scrap back, or to conceal it, while protesting that they had done nothing, didn't have anything, didn't want anything. Or, most galling: *I'm not the criminal in this situation*. How wonderful to be such a serene and august judge of one's actions; it almost made his job unnecessary. Except that you can't absolve yourself of deeds that destroy others. It's all very well to be creatively absentminded, "losing track of" records and "mistakenly" authorizing documents that ultimately allow some bourgeois crybaby to slip out of the country. Well done you! We're better off without the boys and girls who hate sharing anyway. But now that you've committed an act that insults both the intelligence and the authority of the State, what becomes of everybody even tangentially connected with you, eh? Can you confirm the forgiveness of each and every person whose already tricky living conditions you've now volunteered for additional scrutiny and higher barriers? Questions like those ran through the Judge's mind when the desk jockeys and filing-cabinet rodents appeared before him to learn their fates. Most of them were silent, but every now and again he got somebody who'd tell him their clerical mistake had been misinterpreted or ask him to consider the possibility that ordinary life had become a nightmare in which obedience to the law actively eroded the common good. At times like that he'd very much wish he could jump up, clap a hand to his head, and cry, "Ah yes, now I see it all! You're free to go"—and then lengthen the term of their custodial sentence if they actually dared try to walk out. Helenka, the court stenographer, didn't really have an ear for sarcasm, though, so he held back. One woman, weeping with rage and sputtering words out anyway (*You—you—how—what—*) managed to tell the Judge that because of him—yes, little old him—she, who had never wanted to hurt anyone, now had no hope of ever escaping evil. Because of Judge Brzobohatý there was no Right Thing left for her or anybody else to do, there were only wrong things, greater wrongs and wrongs that were greater still. As soon as the defendant was sufficiently crushed by the silence all around her, the Judge shrugged and directed her attention to pale, inert Helenka, allowing a single fact to impress itself upon all present: not a word of the defendant's outpouring had been written down.

Helenka's indifference may have been absolute, but the Judge's wasn't. He listened to the defendant's every word without taking his eyes off her. There was an appealing disconnect between her seamlessly color-coded appearance and her slightly coarse figures of speech: it struck him as decidedly odd that somebody as newly glamorous as this young lady was causing such problems for herself. She'd finally become chic beyond her wildest dreams, then somebody asked her for help and she'd pressed self-destruct—was that it? She might as well have just pleaded psychological instability. (Even if she had, Brzobohatý was well aware that he represented an entity that invented crimes, demanded you grovel, promised to forgive you, and then threw the book at you anyway. As hard as it could . . .)

The next defendant was a professorial type who only pleaded guilty after an extended discussion of the grammatical errors in the written charges she'd been presented with. *"Oh, so THAT'S what you were trying to say I did? Yes, I admit to that."* Anyone could see that she was frightened, dreadfully frightened, that clever woman who seemed to have understood from the beginning that no matter how interested she was in mincing words and no matter how good she was at doing that, there was no way for her to be spared the ordeals prescribed for everybody else. Still, the thing Judge B. found most galling about intellectuals was the way they always had their noses held up in the air, no matter how blatantly those damned noses trembled. It was the combination of those two scoldings from defendants—attacks from differing directions that were both somehow located above him, above his way of thinking—that left the Judge in shock. The Judge had been judged and found inadequate.

Brzobohatý was dapper. With his side-parted salt-and-pepper-shaded hair, and loosely cut yet perfectly pressed suit and tie, this 1957 sword of justice looked like a lesser-known member of the Rat Pack. The one who wrote and delivered verdicts that knocked all the wind out of first-time offenders. If the sentence struck the offender as disproportionate—if the offender had taken their one chance at confirmed illegality and made it a puny act instead of doing the very worst that they could possibly do, then that was their own affair. Authors of articles in the underground literary journals poked fun at his apparent absence of mercy. He was a bogeyman; one of hundreds that the deviants had to mock in order to shrink the paralyzing shadows they cast.

Someone doused Judge Brzobohatý in vinegar once, before his minders could emerge from their concealed positions to intervene. Or perhaps the Judge's minders saw what was about to happen and just thought, *He's a big boy, he'll survive.* They didn't like him either.

Brzobohatý's attacker was a wispy young waiter who said that Joan of Arc had told him to do it. Anybody could see that the boy really wasn't all there; Joan of Arc had had an earthly messenger who had supplied the waiter with vinegar and told him who to throw it at, where the target would be, and when. But all the boy would talk about was La Pucelle, who, realizing that some evil must have found its way into her mind (how else could the cruelty of her trial be explained?), had humbly apologized for her misrepresentation of the beautiful things her voices had told her. The vinegar thrower kept telling the Judge that Joan had thought that "the voices were good, but the fault was hers," when actually both Joan and the voices were blameless. As for this time: "The voice was good, and the fault was yours, sir . . ." All right then!

Wisely or unwisely, Brzobohatý didn't believe real harm could come to him from members of the general public. What distressed him was the absence of an exception to his animosity. That's what his son should have been. His son was the spitting image of him in his midtwenties, and at one point seven or eight years before, the boy had been the entirety of Brzobohatý's reason for taking this so-called path of least resistance.

Knowing that self-determination wasn't in the cards, that it never had been, that nation after nation was queuing up for their turn to rule his country, there'd been a strong temptation to break his own head against a few others' and go out knowing that he'd at least caused some inconvenience. And that's how things might have gone with Judge Brzobohatý. No compliance whatsoever, just like so many of the boys he'd grown up with—some of them Communists, some of them not, some of them suicides, most of them not—the ones who went from vehement man to unceremoniously crumpled corpse in a flash and could only silently be remembered by the little things you tried to do anonymously for their widows or their children. Brzobohatý didn't dare leave Aleš to a life as the recipient of queasy favors. And of course, imagining the kid's attempts to survive as the son of official, on-the-record scum was even worse.

The Judge's background and social circle had contained so many subversive elements that it wasn't possible for him to do the bare minimum and be left alone. Had he not set about dominating his immediate environment he'd have been eliminated. Luckily for him, his father had been a die-hard anti-Nazi long before the German occupation; that was a point in his favor. But Brzobohatý had to build on that himself, with words and deeds of incontrovertibly Communist intent. He did this without hesitation, because he was the father of a young man who garbled proverbs with a poet's knowing grin.

Their next-door neighbor, an almost-elderly man who often seemed sad and confused, rarely remembered Aleš's name, but knew that the two of them were friends: "Oh, there's my friend," he'd say when he saw Aleš, and called him over to the fence to talk for a few minutes. For a couple of months one autumn, Aleš and the neighbor passed their time together pondering the skies. According to the neighbor, one of the clouds was a floating cameo image of Antonín Zápotocký's head (side profile). Looking cheerful for a change, the neighbor brought magazine photos of Zápotocký out into the garden. "Look," he said, holding the photos up in the air. "The nose—the chin . . . it's him. Don't you see that it can't be anyone else?" Brzobohatý's young son held out until their neighbor pointed out that this cloud had appeared exactly two weeks after Zápotocký's death.

"Oh," Aleš said, "that changes things. That cloud is an obvious sign that the President's soul isn't at rest." To all appearances he was completely in earnest—as was all the vigorous nodding from the man who lived next door: "A terrible thing to see, really . . ."

All three men put their hands behind their backs and reviewed the patchwork of impending rain. The Judge wasn't sure which tuft of this sullen fleece was supposed to be the spitting image of the late President—they all just looked like clouds to him—but after a few more moments of pretending to look where the other two were looking, he considered the timing appropriate to ask: "Why isn't Antonín Zápotocký at rest? I mean—why wouldn't he be?"

Aleš and the neighbor "haha"-ed until, gradually realizing that Judge Brzobohatý was waiting for an answer, they stared at each other, then at him. Though these two were on different sides of a garden fence, in their unblinking perplexity they were one.

"Well?" the Judge said. "You're looking up at this cloud and you're saying it's President Zápotocký. Wait a moment, I apologize—I put a few words into your mouths there. You didn't say that the cloud is Zápotocký himself—you're suggesting that the cloud is like a message from his soul, yes? A demonstration of his unrest?"

"The profile is an unquestionable match for his, if that's what's bothering you," their neighbor said, starting again with the magazine photos.

"All right, all right, let's not go through all that again; I'm not calling you a liar. But come on, this isn't difficult—I'm only asking you what you're getting at with this claim that the President isn't at rest. I heard he finished writing his final novel before he went. It sounds like he left with his affairs more or less in order. I just . . . why wouldn't Zápotocký be at rest? Why wouldn't he, eh?"

Aleš asked: "Are you OK, Dad?" and their neighbor said: "Respectfully, Your Honor—how would we know? We can see he's got something on his mind, but surely only he could tell us what that is?"

Brzobohatý's son had had an unaccountable taste for stewed chicken neck, which he prepared himself according to a recipe he'd got from God knows where and sat up eating late at night while he wrote essays that did not meet his teacher's requirements: a nonchalant rebuttal of Loos's *Ornament and Crime* in place of a glowing appraisal of the Monument to Stalin at Letná, for instance. He put away a substantial amount of his parents' precious whisky, too, but they couldn't be angry with him for having good taste. And what had Aleš done immediately after his grandfather had had a talk with him about not being such a smart Aleš and taking care not to stand out for the wrong reasons? He'd got himself a gigantic cardboard box, drawn a smiley face on the front, and pinned a paper cutout of the uniform of the National Ice Hockey team onto the back. It was the 1949 team he was honoring: the team that had won the Ice Hockey World Championships despite the death of six players in a plane crash on the way there. When Aleš went out "disguised" in his cardboard box, on certain errands or for his weekly Relaxation Appointment, he pinned a different paper shirt to the back of the box, alternating between the names of all six of the ice hockey greats who'd been lost in '49: Troják, Stibor, Jarkovský, Šťovík, Pokorný, Švarc. An onlooker might not know who was shuffling around inside that cardboard box (it wasn't always Aleš; he lent it to friends, and sometimes to pairs of friends, since there was room for two inside), but they should know that the box remembered losses. Aleš's Weekly Relaxation took place between the bushes just out of the river's straggling reach as it ran under his favorite bridge, the one that was coral and gray. That's where Brzobohatý's boy liked to perch in his memorial container, having a quiet drink or a smoke.

Aleš had had something that must be protected; exactly what that was, was not for a father to say, it was his job to safeguard that spark, not wax lyrical about it. Maybe in a few years, after all of this was over, Aleš would still . . .

. . . what was Brzobohatý thinking, that Aleš could still be whatever it had looked as if he were going to be? A stand-up fellow with a sunny disposition—sunny, yet not naïvely so?

Almost a decade passed. Years of relative safety, the best that could be procured. *Lepší než drátem do voka, že jo?* Better than a poke in the eye. Aleš qualified as a lawyer . . . and became a kind of sentient Party placard. He took to speaking in slogans, as a joke, his father thought, a derisive nod toward the fact that their home was bugged to its back teeth. Within weeks the hectic syntax of the slogans dug into Aleš's levity and chipped away at it until— well. Joan of Arc's vinegar-tossing henchman sounded more sound of mind than Aleš Brzobohatý did. It was around then that some preparatory instinct led Brzobohatý to remove his son's name from the forefront of his consciousness: he took to calling the boy "Junior" instead. Yes, he was afraid of his son. No, not of his son, but of certain moments. When Káča Brzobo-hatý commented that their son was going to be "one of the Par-ty's brightest stars," for instance. Matouš kissed her hand, giving her her dues as the mother of a heavenly body (Káča gave him the look he'd first fallen for; wryer than wry). And though Ma-touš's smile exhibited pride, in his head he said: **I'll see him sent to a labor camp first.** It was the scheming cogency of such thoughts that frightened him. If only there was some sign that Junior still had character enough to reject his old man; if only there was some aspect of the young man's speech and acts that betrayed unseemly haste to climb the ranks. Haste might have indicated anxiety, trepidation, anticipation of the system giving way. But Junior was in no hurry. The youngster had no doubt that the invincible obliterators of Western depravity were here forever, and the order of things would infinitely perfect itself. So the son would continue to venerate his father's role in all this until the fulness of time itself relieved the elder man of his duties and it was the son's turn to take them on. Couldn't the boy be lazy, a shirker of responsibility, capable of a little bit of independent thought, something or someone *natural*? Wishful thinking . . . Aleš was on so many committees, all you heard from him was "we" this, "we" that, it was only their incompetence that stopped those committees from implementing the majority of their foul plans; the truly regrettable thing was that incompetence wasn't enough to prevent all accomplishment.

The last straw: Brzobohatý Jr. brought his intended bride home for dinner. She was a chirpy blond prison guard who'd been transferred from Olomouc after quashing a hunger strike. The transfer was a promotion, not a punishment. And she LOVED children, she was so good with children, she told them, making sure her prospective in-laws knew she was an all-rounder: tough yet nurturing.

Káča spent the rest of the evening with her gaze fixed on her son, mesmerized; the boy was always saying he could never bring another woman into their family unless she was "at least as good as his mother," so who on earth was this girl, what was she?

At dead of night, the Judge took a seat at the desk where he composed the majority of his official correspondence and took out a typewriter that he'd pulled a preposterous number of strings to acquire anonymously. Brzobohatý cracked his knuckles and began writing in Brzobohatý Jr.'s name, copying the slightly allegorical language he'd seen the dissidents use in those journals of theirs.

The Judge began with the intention of framing his son. There were a number of ways he could incriminate "Junior" without seeming to have anything to do with it. Somewhere around the middle, though, the Judge began to develop arguments the way he thought Aleš might have before he'd become so invested in his social position.

Brzobohatý fumbled through several exhortations to free thought, knowing that he didn't know what that was. He kept at it because he was sure the concept would have meant more than just words to his boy. When he read his writing back to himself, its mechanical gusto pained him about as much as the sound of Aleš replacing his own naturally occurring thoughts with Party slogans had. But it was only a first draft, and he was not permitted to stop there; it turned out that the silencing of his son had not been an unanswerable act. Suppression fucks up any dialectic; there's no going forward or back, only a sideways pull. That which is made silent in the son speaks in the father. That which can no longer speak in one can no longer keep its silence in the other.

Before we continue—look up from this page. Have a stretch, have a look around, preferably through glass. Yes, it can be a drinking glass.

Where are you? (Do you know?)

"And you?" Hero asked the book. "Do *you* know where you are? Also, what have you done to yourself while I was out?"

She found her jewelry pouch in her hand luggage, took out the longest earring she had, and marked her place in the book with it. Her first thought, even after all these years, was that Thea and Sofie should be told about this. Then she wondered if Merlin Mwenda was still around, and whether she could contact him, though she wasn't sure how to ask about the completely different editions. She left her phone on the bedside table, sat by the window, and eyed the city instead. A seemingly fractal array of towers, turrets, and spires. She tried not to frown—glassy indifference would have been a more comprehensive put-down—but she couldn't help it. What right did these paired steeples have to hold the full moon between them like that? Before her very eyes, the moon escaped its stone guards, then fell into and struggled out of a series of verdigris-coated oubliettes. The poor thing did this until dawn, when it was the sun's turn to rise into its own peril. She couldn't have witnessed the entire saga, must have dreamed some of it. Or most of it . . .

Either way, in the morning Hero Tojosoa was still draped across the window seat. *Paradoxical Undressing* was still hugged to her chest. And as soon as she opened her eyes the statues started showing off. A cloud-skimming troop of stone figures, some gesturing toward each other, others signaling the heavens. Not really being in the mood for all that, Hero drew the curtains. She thought about the way that even in the parts of town that were ostensibly edgier or more modern, grit and grime flitted evenly across surfaces as if applied with a fine brush. If the bruises were painted on, then what about everything else? The more breathtaking the visions, the more melodious the duet between grandeur and humility, the more suspicious Hero Tojosoa became. She'd had a lot of misgivings about coming to Prague. Some of them were to do with her having taken the city's name in vain so many times. For a good while, at least as long as Jerome had been alive, whenever Hero had needed a fictional place to stay, she'd picked Prague. "Oh, I'm really sorry, but I can't—I'm in/on my way to Prague . . . I thought I told you last week . . ."

The recipients of such messages didn't even ask "Where's that?!" or try to find out any more. They seemed to accept that it was all out of their hands, that Hero was on some trip of unutterable necessity, and communications were concluded.

But now Hero was well and truly in it, in honest-to-goodness Prague, with a book that kept . . . looking for her?

She checked the book: Chapter One, *Matouš Brzobohatý lived in fear*, good . . . the text hadn't changed again. Be that as it may, she still had to get out of this place. With any luck, Beauty Day would go past quickly and they'd all be back on the plane before things got out of hand.

4.

Now, if Hero Tojosoa was an axe, then Dorothea Gilmartin was a parasol. Really both were both, of course, but you try telling them that.

Hero wanted out as soon as she arrived. Out was what Hero always wanted. It was her reasoning behind befriending Sofie in Paris and Dorothea in Dublin: they were so unmistakably nonlocal.

Dorothea, on the other hand, longed to stay. Which was very awkward and unexpected, because she thought she'd successfully hardened her heart against this place during her years as an Oklahoman.

Picturing Thea: Neither tall nor petite, she fits in wherever there's room for the average. She appears resigned to the vulnerability of holding this middle ground, frequently baring the back of her neck to the elements and not standing up anywhere near as straight as she should. Yet if you took some sort of poll, the general first impression of Thea would be that of a Bearer of Glad Tidings. Factors contributing to this: the roundness of her face, the bright solemnity of her green eyes (she tends to close those while laughing, and her laughter is like a low-key fit of hiccups), the long-winding chestnut plait that's most often looped up into a bun, or subdivided and twisted around her head like a crown. Lastly, there's the soft specificity with which her mouth shapes itself around the words she speaks. Have a care; Ms. Gilmartin's deportment is treacherously receptive . . . in the middle of a shouting match she can pause for a moment of mirth before returning to wrath—or, at some point during a jokey conversation, she'll take grievous offense, not necessarily at what you said, but at the *way* you said it and what that way revealed to her, and then—*Oh, ha ha, actually, never mind, got to go now, but as always, it was a pleasure talking with you*—you're left in doubt as to whether she considers you toxic waste and you'll never hear from her again or whether she sees you as the Roger Federer of repartee and will very soon be back for more. Dorothea Gilmartin's gaze seems to say "So . . . ," "So?" or "So!"

Thea and her father attended two Sarah Vaughan concerts in 1978: neither of which she remembers, though she's told her deportment was excellent; she was a model jazz baby. She tells this as a cautionary tale. Considering spending time and money taking your toddler to a high-culture event? Well, the choice is yours, of course, but Thea feels duty bound to mention that when she was very little, she heard Sarah Vaughan, *the* Sarah Vaughan, live in concert twice in the same year, and it didn't make her a better person.

The first concert took place in the bone-simmering intimacy of Prague's Reduta Club, and the second was at New York's Carnegie Hall, postdefection. What had happened in between? Well. When Thea's father, Štěpán Dlouhý, heard Sarah Vaughan singing—directly to him, with no machinery in the way—the *blue* of her voice (he sounds a bit unhinged trying to describe it and keeps try-ing anyway), the neither daytime nor nighttime blue of her voice almost made him . . . throw up. It took Štěpán a few beats to under-stand what this sound was doing to him, what was wrong with it—what was right about it, really. It was melting the gray gelatin that kept him immobile. And afterward there was nothing for it but to follow the sound of Sarah to its source. Thea takes this and several other of her father's rationalizations after the fact with a few kilos of salt; particularly his oft-repeated claims that he's "never been an ideology guy." Štěpán tells her that he signed no Charters and no Anti-Charters—those documents were so dangerous in so many different ways that reading them left paper cuts on the mind. He condemned no one and collaborated with no one, just lived with his head down, "staying out of it," "not getting involved," not even in his thoughts. And the man continues to exhibit profound caution about entering into any contracts, actually reading all the terms and conditions three to four times before signing his name or pressing "accept"—that's the reason why there are so few apps on his phone. That kind of convenience is in itself an ideology too risky to buy into; Štěpán Dlouhý tells his daughter things like this and seems to consider his activities and his inactivities explained, but when he's finished, Thea lets him know she doesn't really buy any of it. "Tati, I hear you. I do. But can we talk about the fact that you could've looked for a brand-new base anywhere in the States but moved us from Prague to . . . Prague? Do you get how the real-life decisions you make have me struggling not to see you as 'an ideology guy'?" As if there could be any other basis for such sentimental bridge building.

It wouldn't have been like that if Thea's mother had come with them. So Thea likes to think. But getting two out of three members of a nuclear family out of the country was enough of a feat . . . Dagmar Dlouhá stayed behind. Not being the type to languish in idleness, she sent letters and photographs in the post and obliterated the time spent waiting for replies by writing and illustrating some children's books that Thea really, really hated. The more Thea hated the picture books, the more widely they got translated. Then there was an animated TV series that was dubbed into even more languages. Classmates sang catchphrases at her. *Don't thank me—thank Progress! It's UNSTOPPABLE.* The main character was a girl Thea's age, who had the same name as Thea, and very similar physical features. The girl in the stories was excruciatingly empathetic, clever, and brave. The kind of girl who never had anything to be ashamed of. This was the type nonstorybook Thea would have gone all out to intimidate, but would more likely been beaten up by, since she was nowhere near as fast and strong as the mountain-climbing, roller-skating, deep-sea-diving, Alpine-cyclist version of her. The entire Eastern bloc was storybook Thea's paradise, and she roamed its landscapes at will, joining forces and sharing regional delicacies with other manifestations of Socialism's future.

Book 1: Thea goes rafting on the Tang River with Li Jie. Crazy fun: he saves her life and she saves his. But at dinnertime they have a falling out: Li Jie has suddenly got some stuff he wants to say about dumplings. He tells Thea that Czech knedlíky are tastier than Chinese jiaozi, and he wants to know their secret so that jiaozi can improve. Thea is distressed to hear this, as she believes that jiaozi are superior to knedlíky and was hoping to discover something that could bring Czech dumplings up a level. Emotions run so high that the pair turn to empirical assessment, assuming operation of a highly efficient dumpling factory for the day. Thea and Li Jie provide knedlíky AND jiaozi to thousands of Dragon Boat Festival attendees, and when the eating experience questionnaires are returned, the children arrive at the happy realization that when it comes to dumplings, there is no competition: there is only deliciousness.

Thea hasn't actually read this adventure all the way through—she's tried, and just couldn't do it—but she's had the storyline narrated to her in detail by two out of the three long-term partners she's been with so far. When they did that, Thea fought and overcame the urge to curl up into a spiky wrecking ball by reminding herself that these weren't deliberate attempts to get her down. Unlike Thea, Inzhu and Mina had grown up with tongue-in-cheek fondness for this cartoon character, and had never even imagined that when they grew up they'd meet and fall in love with, ha ha ha, the real-life inspiration for her.

I'm helpless before Thea. Much more so than with coolly closed-off Hero. When I told Thea she couldn't stay, all she said was: "Hmmmmm." Which made me uneasy. I almost wished she'd ask me why she couldn't stay. Until I saw and heard that "Hmmmmm," I'd been thinking of giving her a reason before she thought one up. But that would most likely have backfired. There are times when reasoning aloud is like dangling scraps of compassion in front of someone's nose just to show that there's more where that came from; just not for them. No, when sending someone away, best to spare them the carousel ride of reasons that make no difference to what's permitted and what's restricted.

Still, I waver in Thea's presence because her mother died here. In the spring of 1989, just a few months before everyone who'd been calling for democracy finally got it. Actually, Thea wouldn't say, "My mother died," she'd say, "My mother killed herself." Addressing the fact of it in this way provides shelter from her father's belief that there's more to the matter than has yet come to light. Of course there is . . . but that figure in the dark is one and the same as the person who was killed. That's more than enough for Thea and her father to try to get their heads around without inventing additional malice. Thea does agree with her father that the word "suicide" doesn't feel correct; to Thea that word suggests a predominance of sorrow or numbness. In Dagmar's case, "self-murder," the literal translation from Czech, has more accuracy. Sadness had to have been part of it, though; this is what Thea's father knows about his ex-wife, that she was well attuned to every manifestation of hilarity, and just like a collector of pocket monsters, really wanted to keep going and catch them all. He doesn't see that as the disposition of someone who dies at their own hand. It does make sense that Dagmar would have been sad to have been halted like that. But there was probably also a lashing out, a howling, split-second conviction that she should, must be removed—and that couldn't be withstood.

Dagmar did this when Thea was twelve. The super-duper Thea in those picture books is still twelve, will always be twelve, and she earns Thea's keep several times over, partly due to contemporary nostalgia for the kitsch accessories to tyranny and partly due to two grievously garbled stories that seemed to hold equal weight. The first—the story Thea's father publicizes—is that of a satirist with the ingenuity to work in plain sight while permeating the borders of the very milieu she derided. That sounds good to Thea: that's the Dagmar Dlouhá Thea would actually love to be the daughter of—except that she doesn't trust her father's memory. To be clear: it isn't Štěpán who Thea mistrusts, but memory itself, the parts of the past we latch on to and stretch further to cover up other parts we ignored or were otherwise unable to take in. Thea Gilmartin is *that* jury member. Enraptured by paper trails and camera footage, unmoved by eyewitness testimony. (All those honest spectators who don't realize that they aren't telling the truth . . .)

The other Dagmar Dlouhá is the one Thea gets dutifully litigious about whenever sees it hinted at in print: the story of the passionately anticapitalist author who missed her defector daughter so much she made up another, better daughter who stayed loyal to Socialist ideals but still couldn't make a dent in her mother's loneliness. If that one's true, it's too harrowing a truth for Thea's father to be expected to live with. She knows him: Štěpán's Dagmar has to be an unbeliever who never could be converted. Vulnerable, yes, but with more nerve than all those who menaced her put together. If the woman Štěpán married and left was anyone other than the woman he remembers, following that blue brick road of his was a betrayal he involved his own daughter in.

Thea's cordial relationship with her stepmother is partly facilitated by their worry (one of many worries associated with deeply loving a man through all the rods and bolts of the current framework) that on any given day Štěpán Dlouhý could vanish because he doesn't know what he needs to say. Or because he does know, but is so accustomed to being responded to rather than listened to that accurate expression seems pointless.

Thea's uncle Vavřa, Dagmar's older brother, reckons there's a third Story of Dagmar in which Dagmar Dlouhá is a true believer.

Her ideals match the stated ideals of the Party, and at first she regards the majority of the Party's actions as necessary. That changes, but she can't let go. OK, she says, the functioning of this Party is far from perfect, but it's still the world's best bet for achieving the equality of all peoples. Not being someone who ignores contradictions, Dagmar Dlouhá has more and more difficulty maintaining this position, and yet greater difficulty abandoning it. The reasons for pulling the plug on her belief proliferate: the biggest being the gulf growing between her and her daughter, who is swiftly absorbing notions that freedom is mainly the freedom to consume. Meanwhile, little goody-goodies send Dagmar fan letters from all over the place; she begins to wish them dead. She almost has to do that, since these Progress Girl enthusiasts write things Dagmar's own daughter would never write. Dagmar cannot ever wish her daughter dead. Nor herself . . . or can she? It turns out that not only can Dagmar wish that for herself, but fulfillment is within her power too. He's describing a heart-splattered woman. The unacceptability of Dagmar's beliefs—both to her daughter and to herself: *I can't believe that I believe what I believe*—picked up speed as they circled her. It was like a cyclone in her head that ripped solid from liquid.

To Dagmar's husband this is just as appalling as the story of the bereft Socialist discovering that fiction can't salve the wounds of fact. But Štěpán doesn't argue with Vavřa; he only shrugs. There's no way a marital partner's understanding and a sibling's understanding can be the same—or at least, Štěpán reckons that in this context, differing views are more desirable than not. Besides, everyone who knew Dagmar thinks they know why her life ended the way it did. Most of them won't comment, and the ones who are able to talk about it disagree on most points.

Hero Tojosoa is probably the only person who's said anything pertaining to this that makes complete sense to Thea—and she wasn't even talking about Dagmar. She and Thea had their feet up one night and were watching a hospital TV drama with the chin-in-hand attention they also gave to Fellini films. And at one point, while one of the doctors was shown making a breakfast that would very soon have to be abandoned, Hero suddenly said that this kind of story always gripped her with its will-they-or-won't-they. Will they or won't they admit that the cause of death can't ever really be known, that the reason why someone couldn't manage to keep living for one more minute is an impenetrable secret?

"I feel like the chances of that happening are higher if it's a non-English language show," Thea had said, trying to downplay her reaction to that comment.

Eyes glued to the screen, mind entirely elsewhere, Hero had replied to her in Malagasy.

That was one of the things that made Thea happiest of all; the times that Hero forgot that she couldn't understand everything she said. It happened a lot . . . and only with Thea, as far as she could tell.

But oh God—the note that Thea's mother left. The note convinces Štěpán that it wasn't suicide. Someone got Dagmar to write some of it, but when they tried to make her complete it, she saw this was her last chance to expose them, and refused. Thea doesn't buy this for various reasons, but whenever she stirs herself for a proper discussion of plausible letter dictation methodologies, she finds herself hurtling overhead and landing in the void of extreme self-censorship . . . a jurisdiction in which you're not able to say a single thing that you think, feel. or know. Not even your name.

> My beloved [blank]
> I'm [blank] [blank], please [blank] [blank]
> [blank]—we [blank].
> This was never [blank] [blank] [blank],
> your [blank]

The missing words are cut out of the paper, and according to those at the scene, they were never found. Thea knows how she would have made sure of this if she were Dagmar: she'd have cut those rectangles out without writing anything in them.

As you've probably gathered from the names of her family members, Dorothea Gilmartin isn't the name in our axe-parasol's (American) passport. It's the name she started going by in her late twenties. Thea hasn't answered to the name in her passport for a very long time, but feels she can't change it because it's the name that Dagmar wanted to give her. Should I have got that out of the way first? Maybe it isn't a crucial point. They just sort of shrug at each other, Dorothea and the picture-book adventurer who's made her birth name notorious. If naming was once a fraught issue for them, they're over it now. *Because of me, you get to exist*, Thea tells the girl in the cartoons. And if the girl in the cartoons ever responds, she'll doubtless say *Yeah, well, because of me you get to fund a Dagmar Dlouhá scholarship on every continent.* The scholarship is for postgraduate studies in psychology, and for Thea, keeping up with the scholars' work brought on the dopamine fluctuations typically associated with social media. She was employed: she led her father and stepmother to believe that she ran a pistachio nut company that had a cult following on Instagram and a lot of high-end customers, from luxury pâtissiers to Michelin-starred chefs. She had founded the company and still owned it, but someone else ran it in her name. Thea's true work was pursued for her own fulfillment. It was the (vengeful) change she wanted to see in the world.

Hero doesn't want her book talked about, but I'm afraid it's not going to be possible to leave it out, since Thea took her name from that book. Hero Tojosoa's only one: nonfiction. She'd published it five years before she and Thea met. And Thea's name is taken from its cover. That's right . . . Dorothea Gilmartin is (was) *Hero's* pen name.

This omen was extensively analyzed when Hero and Thea first met; Jean-Pierre (Hero's boyfriend at the time) was consulted, and so was Sofie. Did Thea know that Hero had written a book under the name she'd introduced herself with? If so, how? Did her name just happen to be the same as Hero's pen name, or had she assumed it after somehow becoming familiar with . . . that book, which had only sold about three copies in English despite the exceptional translation? Should Hero be flattered or frightened? Who was this person really?? etc.

One evening Thea proposed that she and Hero play a warm-up game of darts before the pub quiz proper; it very quickly transpired that they were both rubbish at darts, so Hero could only assume that this exercise was Thea's way of telling her that she'd love to talk about what they were pretending to ignore. She broached the pseudonym topic directly, and the truth of the matter appeared to be a disconcerting mix of coincidence and design. Dorothea had read Hero's book the very same year it came out in translation. She'd also employed investigators to ascertain Hero's identity, mainly to satisfy her own curiosity as to whether the book had a single author. (Thea had had a hunch that it was a collaborative effort on the part of at least three people.) But becoming a pub quiz teammate of Hero's had been an effort to make new friends in her neighborhood. Friends with general knowledge, as she didn't really get on with specialists, Thea said. She hadn't recognized Hero until she'd heard her say her full name. She was so markedly withholding her opinion of the book that Hero ended up asking about that too: "So, what did you think of it?"

Thea said: "Think? I couldn't. It walked all over me and wiped its feet on my hair." Her tone didn't reveal any particular attitude toward being handled in that way either. Dorothea Gilmartin was maddening in just the way that Hero Tojosoa loved best.

Sofie prided herself on her patience, but after a few weeks of topical phone calls, even she had reached her limit. She gifted Hero the Adventures of Progress Girl; all eight books. Once the reading had sunk in, she drop-kicked Hero's stalkee narrative: "Do you need the name Dorothea Gilmartin right now? No. Were you planning to use it ever again? No. So, what's up? You're not gonna let your new friend—your new friend who would otherwise have to be identified as the tragic real-life version of Progress Girl—borrow your spare name? Which she'd chosen before she even met you anyway?"

That tugged at Hero Tojosoa's conscience. She was conversant with the procedures that made a name unusable. She'd lived some of them. She was the daughter of a man who refused to acknowledge her as his, yet paid all her school fees and expenses promptly. This blank check might have been underwritten by a sense of duty, but it was more likely issued on account of the rumors about him. Rumors that Hero's mother personally kept just a rumble beneath common knowledge, altering enough details to prevent full plausibility. For the first half of her life, Hero had found that wherever she was, her name was pursued by murmurs regarding her parentage. She was an old hand at dispensing the "So what?" shrug that let the archivally inclined know that not only was she not interested in being told whatever it was that they thought they'd found out about her, but the telling didn't place her under their control. By and by she learned how to rid herself of those absurd intelligence briefings; they abated as soon as she moved beyond the reach of Yolande Tojosoa's public relations network.

Hero hadn't bothered with a university degree—one less sordidly extorted decoration. Instead, she cast herself squarely in the mold of the reporter who spends more time at her chosen district's courthouses and local government meetings than she does at her desk. Her reporting was done in her own name, but her book was quite a different matter. As the book dripped down both her arms like cold, clear fluid, she became convinced that its strongest seal of protection would be a name other than her own. That which she had found remarkable would be addressed as "everyday life from the perspective of the daughter of a Roman Catholic priest and . . . his sister!" or some other such garish fabrication of persona. It only took a handful of facts to transmute "Hero Tojosoa" into mere overspill from another tale. And how does that tale go? It's about a teenage boy who turned to religion in the hope of being saved from his sibling; this boy's sister so unmoored him from his own sense of what was right and what was wrong that at times he refuted her physical existence.

In her midteens, obeying a chant of unknown provenance ("Now or never, now or never, now or never"), Hero sought, found, and read unsigned love letters among her mother's belongings. As she read the words of the man who'd fathered her, she made her peace with the strong probability that they wouldn't exchange a single word as long as they lived. *Oh*, she thought. *I've got your number.* This priest had a mind that threatened and was at threat. She pictured him as a figure perpetually aflame in a deep sea, his thoughts and feelings dealing harshly with him and anyone else he thought about or felt something for. That which remained inviolate after such treatment was the only thing in the world the writer of these love letters could find beautiful. Hero's understanding of her mother's nature correlates with this model: Yolande must have been hundreds of people's last beloved by now. Hero's mother is an end-of-life guide who commits to a sidekick role as her patients search for the reasons their farewells are proving so bitter, angry, or fearful. Once the reasons are identified, she's there to accompany you past them. At walking pace, lest the shadows take issue with your haste to part ways with them and give chase. After that there's only surprise. Yolande says some of her patients look very pleasantly surprised—excited, even. Other patients look up at nothing with expressions that seem to say: *Oh, for fuck's sake, does it really have to be you—you of all people?* Yolande doesn't seem to have a plan to retire; she'll probably be her own final patient. She wonders if she'll be startled herself, after all that she's seen.

Hero wondered if the love letters Yolande received were a

foretaste of the . . . what to call it, monumental alteration, or amend-
ment, that so confused the dying. Yolande Tojosoa would've been
thirteen when she first read her sixteen-year-old brother's attempts
to imprison what he felt for her in writing. The boy was so pain-
fully in thrall to Yolande (or to her wholeness?) that the tendons of
his paragraphs kept tearing. He wrote that she was more than flesh,
more than air, more than light, more than blood, and more than
water . . . so it is with the saintly, and with the diabolical. The writer
of the letters went from altar boy to lector to seminarian to deacon,
leaving Antananarivo with a jacaranda sprig inside his jacket, faithfully serving parishioners in various corners of Europe. And his
sister, Yolande, followed wherever he went. He'd send her away,
then fall wretchedly ill and beg her to return. Yolande's brother was
the only person who disturbed her equilibrium; even if she wanted
to, she couldn't think of anyone but him.

Finally the priest sought—and achieved—a placement at a sem-
inary in Vatican City, leading scholarly interpretation of Old Testa-
ment texts. He and Yolande both thought that would pull a full
stop to their torment; they couldn't carry on right in the heart of
Christendom, even they wouldn't dare. But they did. When it became clear that Yolande had fallen pregnant, there was no discussion of paternity; he knew there hadn't been anyone else for either
of them, ever.

Enter Hero . . . and the identification of this love-hate fresco as
the keystone of her psyche. Except that it wasn't. Mystery was the
priest's obsession and notoriety was his sister's; their daughter's psyche had its own activities and concerns, very few of which turned
out to be congruent with theirs.

Yolande Tojosoa seemed fond of recalling the morning that

nine-year-old Hero had woken her up to ask if they could get a second bathroom because "it's uncomfortable sharing a bathroom"—the subtext being *with a stranger . . . it's uncomfortable sharing a bathroom with a stranger.* And the stranger was Yolande!

If Hero really had made such a request, she would've remembered it. She looks upon the "let's separate our hygiene arrangements" story as an oblique expression of something Yolande wasn't temperamentally equipped to communicate: that she often felt as if Hero had chosen her as an incubator and then drawn indelible boundaries as soon as possible after birth. Not that Yolande had any complaints about their relationship; she was somewhat touched by Hero's unfailing politeness to her. Over the years that came to count for more than the spontaneity and high spirits that Yolande tended to prize in girls and women. Her standards for boys and men were more nebulous, but apparently Jean-Pierre and Jerome met them fully; in Yolande's eyes they could do no wrong. Perhaps it was simply being handsome and laid-back that did the trick. Especially the laid-back part. No more exorcism rites that positioned Yolande as the unclean spirit to be cast out, please, no more . . .

All of this made Hero Tojosoa an unsuitable name to put on the book she wrote—the book Thea claimed had walked all over her and wiped its feet on her hair. "Hero Tojosoa"; the sheer destructiveness of the act would have been tamed by biographical attribution. Hero staved this off by combining the names of characters in two of her favorite books, *Middlemarch* and *Confessions of a Justified Sinner.* Thus the author Dorothea Gilmartin came to be. Until she was supplanted by Dorothea Gilmartin the reader, anyhow. The reader who had accurately perceived that Dorothea Gilmartin's book had been assembled by a committee of hangmen who happened to live inside the mind of one person.

Sofie had her own issues concerning Thea. Issues she felt were more portentous than Hero's, but much less . . . lucid. So it took longer for her to bring them up. Sofie's issues revolved around the disparity between teenage Thea and adult Thea. Adult Thea's memories corresponded with what it's feasible to remember about anything fifteen years or so after it happened. The correspondence was perhaps too feasible, or adult Thea's manner when she talked about the past was too studied: you (well, Sofie) felt she was referring to . . . notes? It almost seemed to Sofie that this wasn't the grown-up version of the girl who'd attended the same high school as her. This Thea struck her as another person who, for some cryptic reason, preferred that Sofie believe she was "her" Thea. But half a heartbeat before opening the topic with Hero, Sofie was forced to admit that this misgiving came down to physical disparity and not much more, her impression of teenage Thea as an imposingly free spirit (heated gaze and strident tone of voice, comfortably overweight, strong preference for Lagenlook outfits) and her impression of adult Thea as a mute siren.

The Thea that Hero (re)introduced Sofie to was eerily slender— though no skinnier than Sofie was herself, so this shrinking was only eerie when recalling Thea's schoolgirl stature. The new Thea's elocution struck Sofie as vaguely Scandinavian somehow. And this Thea's affect was cold—though that might have been because she had been somewhere, something had happened . . . she was coming back from it, but she was still underwater. She seemed ready to remedy the aloofness, beckoning to you to come and warm her up.

To make things plainer: at school Thea had been someone Sofie said hello to and complained about homework with—no personal chats, no physical contact, nothing that Thea could construe as Sofie's being interested in her in any way. As an adult, Thea was someone Sofie stroked and snuggled with, linking arms with frequently, just as she did with Hero—except that Sofie never thought about going further than that with Hero. For the first time since she'd left school, Sofie lacked the audacity to proposition someone she wanted. Wasn't Thea looking at her and thinking: *Is that it? This is all that became of Sofie Cibulkova? I thought she'd be more . . .*

There was, of course, no need to worry about all that if this Thea was not actually Thea from school. Her forehead was lower, her hairline higher, her eyes more deep-set, what had this person done with the real Thea! Or had this Thea impersonator made some sort of revenge pact with the Thea Sofie had known? But then . . . Sofie had never mistreated Thea . . . had she?

Keeping company with Dorothea Gilmartin altered the very gait of Sofie's mind. Her thoughts tottered and dipped; it was like trying to walk with a stiletto-heeled pump on one foot and a flip-flop on the other. Over the course of a single day Sofie accosted her newfound friend and fled from her—doubts clanked against counterdoubts and coincidence French-kissed design. Blurting out: "What happened to you? Did something happen to you?" only made Thea laugh and tell her, "Yeah, twenty years happened, Sofie. Same as with you."

Sofie accepted and disbelieved this at exactly the same time. She was reading much too much into body-weight variation ("I mean, hello? Are these not the basics of existence as a hormonal organism? Levels rising and dropping, size ranges as opposed to fixed sizes?" Hero's words, when Sofie finally began to say what was bothering her), and yet every instinct told her that this particular sea change was some feature of an aftershock. Sofie oscillated. To her own detriment. For Sofie Cibulkova, kaleidoscopic vision was an impairment, not an enhancement; she'd never flourished in protean conditions. Hero had and still did; Thea too. Just not with each other. Though, again, Thea was willing. And Hero wasn't. Either way, Sofie's leaving them was always a matter of "when" and not "if"; theirs was one of those incompatibilities that no amount of fascination can lessen.

That arid summer, the summer that Hero was here, and Sofie was here too, I wasn't able to pass Thea by without speaking to her. I asked her what she hated. It wasn't a casual question. Yet she smiled as if it were, and she said: "Tears."

5.

THEA'S TAXI TOOK HER straight from the airport to a five-star hotel in New Town that shimmered all over with sepia-toned glass, the entire building an upbeat accessory to the smog-blackened undulations of a nearby monument to some olden-day monarch or other. She'd booked a room there because her escort for the night had recommended it. It was a good base of operations, smilingly discreet, not winkingly discreet—the distinction was vital. And Bára, the escort, was good with her. In her photos she'd borne a resemblance to Sofie Cibulkova . . . or was pretty in the same long-nosed, soft-focus watercolor way in which Sofie was pretty, right down to the ever-so-slight tilt of the head that made it seem all she ever listened to was birdsong. That plus gray eyes and ash-blond hair: *Job done, your Sofie C. substitute is ready for collection . . .*

Thea had only fleetingly been attracted to Sofie in a nonplatonic way—for seven angsty days or so, decades back. Substitution was still welcome: she missed her friend. In person, the nature of the resemblance was clarified by the way Bára sat, stood, walked, talked, and wrinkled that nose. She wasn't a giggler; she guffawed; she was more like a distant and disarmingly gallant cousin of Sofie's. Thea had been a bit worried about the age difference. Such parameters weren't inhibiting when you assessed a partner by eye alone; any appealing adult could easily be "about your age" as long as you set your guesses on autopilot, allowing them to add or subtract enough years to keep you comfortable. But in this instance, Thea and Bára had built trust by swapping passport information and the results of STI tests. It was a drill they both knew: sacrificing some anonymity and mystery to minimize unwelcome surprises. Thea had stopped short at running a background check on Bára (she didn't care if Bára had been arrested, and not having been arrested isn't that significant in terms of indicating an absence of malevolent impulses—Thea herself was a living example of that), but she'd offered up the squeaky-clean results of criminal-record checks run on the name in her own passport. For Bára's peace of mind. The escort was twenty-seven, though she'd appeared younger than that in unfiltered photographs. There'd been a defensive flurry of messages when Thea had asked how recent the photos were: *They were taken yesterday, why do you ask / We can FaceTime right now if you want / Somehow I haven't had that much stress in my life. That could mean that I could come across as immature / If you have any concerns about my suitability it's better to cancel.* Suitability went two ways, though: What if this twenty-seven-year-old shrank from Thea's withered attentions? Forty-year-olds had been Thea's own hard limit when she was Bára's age. More on their side than on hers, actually. Ms. Gilmartin tended to butt heads with older women, making a split-second choice to become a brand-new

ordeal for her presumably much more experienced adversary to sur-
pass. The partners under forty had taken a mostly lenient attitude
toward this gratuitous antagonism, whereas both the over-forties
she'd had romantic dealings with back then had told her to fuck off
without further ado. Now that Thea was where those women had
been, she could understand that. She was no longer invested in the
effort of displaying uniqueness, or forcing somebody else to exhibit
theirs. It was beginning to look as if she and the loves she pursued
really were just like everybody else, even in the ways they tried to
prove that they weren't.

Bára didn't think like Thea—she didn't seem to be facing a
panic-inducing projection of a future self. They were just two
strangers meeting to mutual benefit. She knocked on Thea's hotel
room door with her motorcycle helmet still on and relaxed into the
awkwardness like a champ, gently teasing Thea about the textbook
formality of her Czech: "You're sure you left in the 1970s? Not . . .
the 1870s?" Then she asked if she could show Thea something.

"Yeah, why not," Thea said warily. Phone in hand, Bára connected to the hotel wi-fi and displayed livestreaming footage of a
pear tree she'd adopted in Jablonec nad Nisou. The tree had been
double-grafted, with bated breath . . . if all went well it would bear
red, yellow, and green pears simultaneously. It was still about a year
to a year and a half away from bearing any fruit; when it did, the
owner of the orchard would send Bára all the pears, or invite her to
come and pick them. For now the pear tree was relishing photosyn-
thesis and the late afternoon breeze soughing among its thickly
massed leaves.

"They really get into your head, don't they—trees," Thea said,
after a couple of minutes.

"Yeah, you've got to watch yourself with trees," Bára agreed. "Lately I haven't been able to get to sleep until I've said goodnight to mine."

"You haven't named it, have you?"

"I have. I'm screwed, aren't I . . ."

"'Fraid so, Bára. Look—don't tell me the tree's name . . . tell me why you chose it."

Bára swept a hand through her own hair, drawing thoughts out along dirty gold filament. Her eyes narrowed when Thea reached out to tuck a few strands behind her ears: *Made you touch me.*

"Well. I've named her after the patron saint of childless people, difficult marriages, glove makers, hernia sufferers, and . . . woodcutters . . ."

They continued to watch the tree growing as they undressed. Then Bára tapped her phone to close the browser window, and they lay side by side in the four-poster bed listening to an Iva Bittová album. No alcohol, nothing to smoke, just warm, bare, Bittová-bitten skin and some very frank eye-fucking. The sex started off very quietly and grew overwhelmingly meditative. One delectable indulgence at a time, like pulling a gossamer glove on finger by finger. As they tore through the throbbing mist they broke sound barriers too. Knees tucked around Bára's heaving hips, Thea lifted her head and howled at the chandeliers.

Bára left a little after eleven p.m., lining the waistband of her jeans with banknotes. She'd requested payment in two-thousand-koruna notes, because they had Ema Destinnová's face on them, a hallowed face: "That's my woman . . . my wife . . . have you listened to her singing "Song to the Moon"? I can't get enough of it, it's like sonic Sachertorte . . ." Bára smiled down at the notes, folding them so that they frilled out around her. Then she patted them flat, and Thea very briefly enjoyed the thought of Bára interspersing cross-country rides at breakneck speeds with stops at petrol stations where she'd peel off a damp, salt-soaked Ema Destinnová portrait to pay for fuel. She walked Bára to the lift, and then paced her hotel room, reviewing her client's instructions for the next day. After about half an hour, sensing that the risk of running into Bára on the street had dissipated, she went out herself. Just looking for something to eat, she thought, walking past the online foodie-hyped hotel restaurant without a second glance. She was here for work, not for a trip down false-memory lane. This was what frolics with Bára was supposed to distract her from; it was bad enough that she'd connected to wi-fi on the plane just to look at the block of flats in Kbely on Google Street View, zooming in on the main door of the building. Having darted out at the age of three, what could happen if she walked back in at the age of forty-two? And the people who lived there now . . . in their old flat, and in the neighboring ones (it was Mrs. Novotná next door who'd found the body), how many of them knew that this was where Dagmar Dlouhá had lived and died? If they knew, how many of them ever thought about that? Štěpán Dlouhý was still lobbying for installment of a plaque announcing that fact, and would probably get his way; he had the unflagging stamina for admin that's only feasible for those who've had segments of their brains occupied by authoritarian regimes. Thea zoomed in on a few of the building's second-floor windows; all she knew was that they'd lived on the second floor. Her dad had sold the flat long ago, without telling her which one it was. Now that she was here she kept thinking about going over to the Kbely flat to knock and knock and knock, asking that box of walls and doors and windows to tell her what Dagmar's parting note couldn't. This thought was going to be like Bára's tree for her now . . . from now until she left the city. Luckily she was only here for one good-night; tomorrow she'd fulfill her client's request and then go somewhere else. She wasn't sure where yet. Already Thea was thinking: *Would it be so bad if I just . . . don't leave?*

Thea's client kept asking if she was really going to be able to do what she'd been hired to do, saying that the conflict of interest was bound to override her actions, even asking Thea to supervise while somebody else took on her requested task. Thea never changed the wording of her response. "Emma, I'll get this done for you." What she didn't say was that anything she did to another person she was equally prepared to do to herself. Some mindsets may be verifiable through speech, but not this one.

One blessing: outside the air-conditioned hotel, it was too hot for much more rumination. A bit alarming, though, that heat. The sun had set hours ago. She walked down to the riverbank; there were bars on the boats moored along it. She was going to have a drink, and she was going to have to find another woman. Risky, partly because it wasn't possible to be as strict about not letting someone stay over if they weren't being paid for their time. Dorothea Gilmartin may not have earned her own living, but she budgeted as if she did. Not only does this child of Marx and Coca-Cola know which enhancements of her property or state of mind she wants, she knows precisely how much she's willing to pay for them. Her estimation of a fair asking price sifts down to the penny. Unkindness is an expense too: anything that isn't income is an expense. And "I don't want to pay for more time together" costs marginally less than "I don't want to spend any more time together." The good ship Bára having already sailed, Thea would have to take a chance on picking up someone who didn't like sleepovers either. Or she could just grit her teeth and cuddle. As long as they fucked first. When it came to distraction from potentially devastating acts, sex was yet to fail Thea. And she was a woman immeasurably favored by fortune in that almost everywhere she went women checked her out.

When they'd still been friends, Thea's pheromone halo (or whatever it was) had pissed Sofie Cibulkova off a little bit; being someone who was far more often looked at by men, as well as someone who struggled to persuade women that she wasn't toying with them, Sofie badly wanted to learn how to flip the switch. Thea would've liked to help, but couldn't. "Just go out into the street, walk past a woman, and she'll look" was shit advice, but that was how it went for Thea. She had no idea what it was about her the women were looking at, or how they knew that they could get lucky if she looked back. She did know that she varied enough from scenario to scenario and environment to environment for the looking to be unrelated to any boyishness or unboyishness she projected. There didn't seem to be a link between the looking and aspects of her shape that she accentuated or downplayed either. Nothing to do with hair length or style, or whether she was wearing makeup or not—other women in her vicinity just went *OK, who's this?* It had been like that since late puberty. Seventeen, eighteen. Girls who couldn't stand silence would inform her that they'd been looking at her because they thought she'd been looking at the boy they liked. Then they'd look at the boyfriend to see if he was looking at Thea, never catching him in the act, which mean this guy must either not actually fancy girls or, wow, he must be more devious than she'd thought, because he had to have been staring, that girl was so . . . (meanwhile this girl who was so . . . was looking at the girl who was trying to catch her boyfriend out, and some essays on feminine sexuality basically write themselves . . .). But diffidence was the official name of the game, and Thea was supposed to take the other girl's self-doubt as a compliment. Other girls took a quick sidelong look at Thea and then did a surprised and somewhat nervous double take, possibly wondering how to keep this from being an exercise in just the kind of objectification that depressed them. Yet other girls just . . . outright . . . looked. That's who Thea would take home from the boat bar; someone forthright.

She couldn't pick a boat to step onto. Peeping through the windows, everyone onboard seemed to be coupled up or uproariously grouped. She kept walking; there were still a couple more boat bars further down. She strode through the dully echoing arches of a bridge, the night sky melted into the water; the very mud seemed to sweat, and someone advanced upon her. Someone eight or nine feet tall and twice her shoulder width. All around them the darkness trembled and the sound of the water was like gums being sucked and lips being smacked. She would gladly have written off this furry black colossus as a side effect of dehydration, but it was making straight for her with its equivalent of a hand—a floppy beige paw the size of a spade—held out. Not a warding-off gesture; something must be placed in that supplicant paw, or there'd be trouble. Black fur—well, black with a shaggy gray bib over the torso—eyes with gigantic whites, a round red nose, and a three-tuft antenna atop the head . . .

Backed up against the slippery stones of an embankment wall, Thea saw it now, she saw it all . . .

What a world, this world in which muggers exploit the face of Krtek, the friendliest and heretofore least money-minded little mole ever imagined. All Thea had was the nuclear bomb–proof Nokia 3310 she carried around at night—Krtek waved that away—plus some bar money. Not even a credit or debit card: she'd decided that if she ran out of cash trying to pick someone up, she'd accept this as friendly advice that she was better off masturbating. Swearing and shuddering, she scrabbled around in the pocket of her jeans, found a two-thousand-koruna note, and crumpled Ema Destin-nová, the soprano of First Republic sopranos, into Krtek's out-stretched paw.

Krtek backed away a bit—she seemed to have managed to disconcert him. And no wonder: suddenly, between scratchy breaths, Thea heard the sound she was making . . . a buzzing and a clicking, as if her teeth were wasps. She swore louder, more deeply, cursing with all the hellfire in her chest, thrust her shoulders forward, and rushed him. Krtek stepped smartly aside and, swearing back at her just as loudly, plucked her wrist up toward him with the genteel flick of an illusionist conjuring a scarf out of thin air. He turned her palm over and placed something very small and bendy brittle in it, then closed her fingers over his deposit. Still rushing—rushing away from him to the lamplight on the other side of the arch now—Thea opened her hand and found something only slightly larger than the nail on her little finger. A teardrop of flaked enamel, mostly the color of sunlit sand, though it darkened to gray-brown at its misshapen tip. She knew this thing: it was the scale of a carp. Uncle Vavřa gave her one of these each Christmas, and by New Year's Eve she was always disappointed in herself for having lost it already. The scale was meant to stay in her wallet, multiplying whatever was in there, but that wasn't the reason she regretted her negligence. Her peasant inclinations wouldn't let her off; that was all . . . she wanted to keep every pretty gift that was given her, whether that be a carp scale or a birth name.

Carp scale in hand, she turned and followed Krtek, who was now galloping south, in the direction of Podskalí. She wasn't sure why she turned back—she supposed she wanted to thank him, or to apologize for the verbal abuse. But as she closed the distance, the man in the giant mole costume started yelling in a distinctly reedy voice that the deal was done, what else was she looking for, one thousand koruny was a miraculous price for a carp scale like that, she couldn't find a more perfect specimen anywhere, and if she didn't stop this harassment, he was going to call the police. She stretched an arm out as a sort of placeholder while she thought of some mollifying remark—and Krtek took the carp scale from her hand and replaced it with a coin.

"What—" Thea held the coin up, examining it front to back as Krtek stood there with his hands on his hips. A one-złoty coin, rather worse for the wear. She tried to bend it, to see if it was made of chocolate or something.

"Well?" said Krtek. "Is the lady satisfied?"

"I don't—I want the carp scale back!"

"You realize that this is not what comes of not being happy with what you already have? Now it's too late."

"Just let me have that scale. Please."

"No, it's gone."

"Then give me back my money. That was *two* thousand koruny, by the way—not one."

"Haha! Whether it was one thousand or two thousand, that's gone as well," Krtek said. As Thea grew more accustomed to his voice, it occurred to her that this probably wasn't a he.

"Now listen here!" she told the giant mole, who struck such an attentive pose that her setting-things-straight declaration abruptly ran out of steam. She looked for slots in Krtek's fabric—the barely perceptible slots the costume's wearer would be observing her through. She couldn't decide . . . there were at least seven or eight glassy little gaps. Eyes and false eyes.

"Americans speak Czech so well these days," Krtek (semi-insultingly) complimented, then swiftly elided Thea's chance to blurt out something about actually being "from here" by adding: "I'm not messing you around—I'm telling you how my business works. Exchange yes, refund no."

"Then—take this back and just . . . have a good evening." She handed the coin back—its vendor took it and turned away. And she was unable to resist addressing the businessmole's back: "But can I just say . . . I'm no stranger to this stuff; you could even say I'm something of a pistachio baron. Entrepreneur to entrepreneur: two thousand koruny, or a carp scale, for a one-złoty coin . . . that's difficult to justify by any standard."

"It wasn't just any one-złoty coin, but that's your loss. Thanks for the feedback—I'll take it on board . . ." Krtek pocketed the supposedly remarkable złoty, waved a hand, and jogged away—this time in the direction of the Castle. Thea's subsequent pursuit was more reasoned than it had been before. If Krtek was female, she wanted to know more. Maybe Krtek was her type.

"Would you mind keeping me company for a little while?" Thea asked.

Krtek's only reply was a rather nasty chuckle.

"Are you meeting someone?"

Another chuckle.

Undaunted by the cold shoulder she was being given (and ready to give up the moment Krtek told her to go away), Thea followed her ... what could she call this being, her mugger, her trader? Thea followed her mole down a few side streets and stopped where the mole stopped: at the glinting grille of a gate set in a wall that rewarded her attempt to gauge its height with a crick in the neck.

"Wait here," Krtek said, twisting a finger in the keyhole—this appeared to unlock the gate ...

... Thea tried to go in, too, but the gate was slammed shut. She curled her fingers around the bars and peered through them: long, neat boxes of bulging earth, vines snaking out of terra-cotta urns; some flowers here and there. Most surfaces were labeled with a surname or a naïvely drawn representation of a salad vegetable, and the air was thick with rivalrous gardening methodologies. So far, so allotment. And apparently there was some business Krtek conducted here at around one in the morning ... or there was some rendezvous to attend? Plus, just now with the finger used as a key ... Thea no longer quite trusted what she was seeing. The very pavement beneath her feet seemed to elevate into a sweltering ramp, and she was dehydrated besides. This Krtek didn't seem to be the type who'd try to catch her if she swooned. Perhaps she was already in a swoon. All in all, it was high time she disengaged and made her way back to her hotel, buying a cold bottle of Kofola on her way there. Had Thea obeyed common sense, she would have missed the sight of Krtek through the iron bars—Krtek pulling off the Krtek costume, leaving the head on and touring these plant patches in otherwise perfect nakedness, making a leisurely barefoot trail around and between the tomatoes, cress, and baby aubergines, her pearly buttocks lingering a little way above the soil as she squatted, soaked it root-deep with piss, and then trampled the mulch. Such profuse streams, unstopped with so few pauses between each patch—was there any way for these plants not to overdose on ammonia? Also: one almost began to wonder how that frame accommodated such an outsize bladder . . . but no, Thea would not allow her attention to be degraded by guesswork, worry, and supposition. She was here for this sight and nothing more.

Having completed her plant-watering parade, Krtek looked around, saw that Thea was still there, and remarked: "There's a drought on, you know."

Thea nodded, thinking, *Don't speak, Thea, if you don't interject this can run its full course and the Krtek head will come off too.* Krtek gathered a handful of fallen leaves and gave herself a quick rub, *Don't speak, Thea, wait, just wait*, yet Thea found herself saying: "What now?"

Krtek's answer was delayed—she was busy getting back into the rest of her costume—but eventually she said: "Well—you can't stay here."

"'Here' as in . . . ?"

"Prague. You can't stay here."

"Hmmmm." *We'll see about that.*

"I suppose you'll still be wanting something before you go." Krtek was beginning to sound anxious. "Something for your koruny and your carp scale and your złoty?"

"Exactly that. So . . . aren't you coming out of there?"

"Not until you're gone," Krtek said. "Sorry. You might be a good person—anybody might be, I suppose—but I can tell that you've got some intentions toward me. You know, not so long ago I used to be up for anything. I've moved on from all that, though."

"What if I told you my intentions might not just be for tonight?"

"That's what they all say! Pull yourself together and stop this, please."

"OK. I'm stopping. I've stopped. You're only into serious relationships now; I get it, and I respect your change of lifestyle." But now it was Thea's turn to put out her hand. "Just give me something for my koruny and my carp scale and my złoty, and I'll be off."

Krtek approached the allotment gate from her own side, remaining one careful step out of arm's reach.

"You promise you won't stay?"

Thea hissed "Yes."

"Hands up," Krtek said.

"What?"

"I need to see that no fingers are being crossed!"

Thea raised her hands above her head and kept them there as, facing her at all times, Krtek walked over to a plant pot near the back of allotment. Thea couldn't tell what was growing from it, but whatever it was, the growth was accompanied by profusions of tiger-striped greenery. Krtek dug around in the earth with her droopy beige paws, pulled up a thin paperback or thick pamphlet, brushed it off, and brought it over to the gate.

"Here you go." Krtek passed the pamphlet through the bars. It had a photograph on the front: a block of ice sloshing back into liquid form. An umbrella was still held aloft close to the core of the ice; its canopy looked like interlocked snowflakes. There were words too. *Paradoxical Undressing, Merlin Mwenda.*

"Thanks . . ."

"You're welcome."

"Have you read it?"

"Ha ha—no. No time."

"You're really not going to show me your face?"

"Huh? I already am. This is it."

Thea walked away down the street thinking about that. She'd been considering wearing a mask for tomorrow's job; so fiddly, though, since she'd be getting her hair dyed just moments before crunch time.

Hearing the allotment gate creak open, she looked over her shoulder. But she'd misheard; the gate was still closed, and Krtek was still standing there making sure that she was really leaving.

"By the way," she called out, "I'm Dorothea. And you?"

"As you can see, I'm Krtek," the mole said smoothly, her mood seeming to improve with distance. "But Dorothea—"

Thea stopped walking and turned to face Krtek, the heavy gate, and the gloss of all that was thriving behind it. "Yeah?"

"I was just wondering . . . about . . . I mean—what do you hate?" Ms. Mole was afraid to hear the answer; Thea could hear that in her voice.

Don't worry, I'm not going to tell you, she thought, and smiled. But just like every other time she'd instructed herself not to speak tonight, she went against herself and spoke. "Tears," she said.

It was the most honest answer she was able to give. She was thinking about the way an incorrigible wrongdoer cries when you make them give reasons why they shouldn't have to atone for what they'd done. If you ask Thea, tears should be abolished because whatever meaning or function they have is—well, liquidated by those who otherwise do what they do (or try to) either quite merrily or without much affect at all. It's only when such people are challenged by someone or something that's stronger than them that they try to change the rules, expelling water from their eyes. Water that wails: *I'm not that bad, I don't deserve this*, when you are, and you damn well do. Thea went a long way down in her own estimation when she cried, and she was only slightly less disgusted by the lamentations of others. On several of the occasions when Hero made phone calls to her and wavered over their actions, Thea would only ask, "Is he crying?"

If Hero said "Yeah," she asked Hero to take screenshots of the weeper watching the numbers tumble as she drained every last penny from his account. For she, Hero and Sofie were Florizel, the habitually incognito Prince of Bohemia from three crime stories Robert Louis Stevenson wrote in 1878. Stevenson's Florizel dearly loved to out-pretend a pretender.

A few hours later, Hero or Sofie would sour the celebrations by parroting what they'd just been told: Their mark had blubbed that most of the money in that account wasn't even his; it belonged to people who'd have him killed when they found out it was gone. Or it turned out the target had a one-month-old son; he'd held the kid up to the camera, pleading for a squalling innocent who still had his whole life ahead of him. What the fuck was going to happen to that kid now? Wasn't there some other way to collect this debt that would've been better for everybody in the long run? And so on.

Thea would listen to them without interrupting, and made no

reply other than to scowl into her champagne. All this wobbling had been induced by tears. It was tears that redirected Hero and Sofie's loyalty from the dazed unfortunates who'd managed to gather their bearings just enough to come to Florizel to reclaim what had been taken from them. It was especially strange to hear such talk from Hero, after that book she'd written, and what that book had brought about. A dry-eyed tale always loses out to a tearful one, so oh, yes, Dorothea Gilmartin hates tears.

6.

A T AROUND TWO A.M. Thea took a seat on the balcony of her hotel room, positioning the pages of her expensive new book so that they were legible against the lights switched on behind her. This was her compromise between what she ought to do (go directly to bed with her eye mask on to ensure at least a few seamless hours of rest) and what she had wanted to do (seduce Krtek, or make her pilgrimage south of the river to the flat that would neither welcome her nor break its pact of silence with her mother).

The epigraph was from Austen's *Northanger Abbey*:

> *Alas! if the heroine of one novel be not patronized by the heroine of another, from whom can she expect protection and regard?*

All right then, Mwenda—another glance at the cover confirmed that that was the author's name; Merlin Mwenda. OK then, Mwenda, off we go, Thea thought. But the view laid out before her was more than momentarily distracting. Only in the small hours, when Kampa Island's life-size queue of plastic penguins lit up, did Thea fully perceive what a desperate yellow those birds are. Live penguins waddle around sneezing salt and not seeming to expect anything in particular: the Kampa penguins are counting down to doomsday. Which just might be today . . .

She held her book up; a silent request that the penguins hold on while she had a look at this thing. The author photo was monochrome, and what she saw took a full second to sink in, then brought her to her feet with a yelp. There were no people in the photograph: only objects. A two-thousand-koruna note, a carp scale, and a one-złoty coin, side by side on what appeared to be the sleekly padded surface of a surgical table. This stunt put her on alert—she glanced over her shoulder, then across the river, and had to talk herself out of double-checking that the door to her room was locked—but by and large the . . . personalization aspect pleased her more than it troubled her. No refunds because the items had already gone into the book, eh? She flipped through to the author biography:

Merlin Mwenda (1970—, motto: *Molto dolce far niente*) carries pebbles in his pockets so he can add just one more tier to any cairn he comes across.

A large gulp of Kofola, and then Thea waded into Chapter One:

Nineteen forty-three was the year that Leah Loew went to a party every single night. At least one, but normally two or three.

It was unavoidable: her hotel was in the party parallelogram, a twinkling convergence of ley lines you had to drink a lot of champagne to see. It had to be champagne, though. Not hard spirits. Livelihoods depended on it! That's what Leah's boss told her. Mr. Deutsch gloried in the struggle of keeping his hotel open. He'd given it a name that was memorable in its incongruity—*The Silver Złoty* ("Wait a minute, wait a minute, what city is this? What's the currency here? Did we . . . overshoot somehow and end up in Poland?" first-time guests quizzed the receptionists)—and he'd been the first to employ full-time taxi dancers, two men and two women, and house them in the eaves of his Jugendstil palace.

He'd hit upon the idea after overhearing a conversation between two officers who'd just arrived at the main train station. One officer was telling the other that Prague was all right for a day-trip; it was a nice little set of reasonably well-preserved ornaments that were still up to the job of relaxing the eyesight— but it was best to leave by nightfall. "Why do you say so, sir?" Mr. Deutsch broke in, ready to reassure both officers that the city streets were safe enough at night, though they should already have known that; they were in themselves the greatest danger wherever they were. The officer giving the advice had turned to Mr. Deutsch and said: "Don't you know how deathly boring Prague is at night?! It's as if the city has an early dinner and then goes straight to bed. There's absolutely nothing to do . . . so as I was saying, Voss, make sure you're well on your way to Budapest or Vienna by the time it starts to get dark . . . Krakow would be quite all right as well . . ."

Mr. Deutsch asked around; he surveyed hotel guests, and most travelers concurred—an overnight stay in Prague was something you did when you were defeated by logistics or just didn't feel sociable. Past a certain hour the city was alive only for locals who already knew each other and invited each other to the kinds of pubs that might as well be Masonic lodges for all the welcome an out-of-towner received there. One notoriously unfriendly pub landlord would throw handfuls of peanuts down onto coasters as a snack—sweaty peanuts out of his bare hand! No, no, such hospitality couldn't be borne.

And so Mr. Deutsch had issued an appeal to his rival hoteliers' self-preservation instincts. Profit lay down a capricious path. "What do you feel like doing right now?" Mr. Deutsch asked all the owners and managers who attended the meeting he'd called. Nobody answered, so he guessed: "You're feeling pretty useless and wouldn't mind just turning out all the lights and skulking, right?" Lethargic nods all around. He continued to address them, sympathetically but with the utmost obstinacy. Mr. Deutsch gradually wore his audience down, got them to agree that doing the opposite of what they felt like doing was the only way that they could all benefit. Starting a chain of parties that ran from late afternoon until breakfast time would make this city *the* place to be for panicked insomniacs and covert surveillance operatives who need their targets' tongues to be loosened with drink. Over and above all that, staff could supplement their earnings and raise their standing with the authorities by selling juicy stories to the highest bidder. All they had to do was create the right environment . . .

The Silver Złoty led the way, showing all the others how it was done. Any of the Złoty's paying customers only had to snap their fingers and appealing dance partners would appear. Leah had earned her role in this by hurtling through an audition that had lasted all day; she'd found the physical demands far less strenuous than the hamster wheel her mind ran on. The girls who wheezed that Mr. Deutsch was asking for too much should have read his advertisement properly. DRASTIC DANCERS ONLY—WELL-BROUGHT-UP KIDS GONE ROGUE: as such they had to know how to tango, waltz, Viennese waltz, quickstep, fox-trot, and rhumba, and they had to know the moves well enough to imperceptibly downgrade their difficulty when paired with a less capable dancer. Leah, Irma, Vojtěch, and Dušan danced for hours, seemingly growing more energized the longer they danced. When the atmospheric buzz dwindled they didn't wait for more patrons to come in, but went and brought nicely dressed pedestrians in from the streets, reprimanding them for trying to go home without telling the Złoty gang all about the evening they'd just had, or issuing assurances that the later this new dance partner arrived at that other party they were on their way to, the more eagerly they'd be awaited; besides, it was essential to have a practice party first. Leah and company kept this befuddling conviviality flowing even as the action moved from the ballroom or bar to the underground bomb shelter (and back again), they ate standing up, and when they saw that further cultivation of a patron's bar tab was no longer viable, the patron was released with good grace. Just another night in the life of a fearless and fun-loving Praguer: *Come back and cheat death with us again sometime very soon!*

The taxi dancers slept in seashell-shaped beds and felt safer in fancy dress. Safer? More themselves, or something. Leah and Dušan were sexed-up versions of the eagle you found on the back of a one-złoty coin: silvery caps instead of crowns, feathered tailcoats, long, tight breeches, short boots. Irma and Vojtěch were a pair of two-tailed lions who'd climbed down from Bohemia's coat of arms and were ready for anything.

Whenever Leah saw Vojtěch go for a cigarette break, she went, too, even though he usually made a point of ignoring her. She was curious about that. It couldn't be that Vojtěch was the type who tried to go incognito by avoiding other Jews; Irma was Jewish, too, and he couldn't seem to get enough of Irma. Vojtěch liked to smoke in the mosaic courtyard, where squares of amber and garnet streamed beneath their feet, climbed the pillars in arrow formation, and shot for the moon. Leah lit Vojtěch's cigarette, then her own. They smoked, and Leah hummed "*Škoda lásky.*" After a while, Vojtěch blew out his longest stream of smoke yet and, looking straight ahead, told her that from her first day on taxi-dance duty the doormen had been taking bets on how soon she, Leah Loew, would become a German officer's mistress.

"Oh yes? Which officer?" Leah said. Perkily, since Vojtěch was not ignoring her tonight. There was no bursting her bubble now.

She regularly danced—only danced, nothing more—with a few officers. And had not been wooed by any of them. She recited "Erlkönig" for her dance partners, advised them on their woman troubles, or in the case of her favorite lieutenant, discussed the merits and drawbacks of different water cures. He was from a placid Bavarian spa town and found the Moldau spiteful—a characterization that enthralled her partly because she knew what he meant as soon as he said it.

"*Genau!* Any day now that river will tear this city open and pull all its stuffing out," she told him, dipping far, far back into his arms.

"It's like a baptism of whips," Leah's spa lieutenant said, letting her rest near the floorboards for a moment—long enough for the glacial drip of the chandeliers to wane one by one, as if they were being unscrewed from above—before raising her with a smile. Leah's spa lieutenant liked her because he'd never met her. The woman he danced with was the one described in the false identification papers Leah had purchased. The documentation stated that Leah's genetic heritage was an adequate mix of Nordic and Slavic, and her cranial measurements were in the superior range, along with various other bits of numerical nonsense that confirmed that the country was being run by catalog-clutching, tape-measure-wielding perverts who had no understanding of what mattered and what didn't matter about a person. Elke, a former girlfriend of her brother's, had helped her out. Elke Glauber, racially pure by SS standards, and psychologically anarchic by almost all standards, was what Leah thought of as a "machine person"—someone who seemed to speak the language of filing systems and understood how to feed them data in such a way that whatever she told them was accepted as fact. There was very little personal rapport between Fritz's girlfriend and little sister; the little sister found the girlfriend immature and the girlfriend had no thoughts whatsoever regarding the little sister. Leah didn't have a persuasive amount of money either. Nor did she have anything else that would have been of any use to Elke. But Elke draped an administrative cloak over her ex-boyfriend's little sister all the same.

Leah's request for the cooked-up paperwork had been brief, composed, almost impassive. She'd sensed that if Elke was going to have a go at this, it wouldn't be due to a desire to keep Leah safe, or even because of anything Elke felt she might owe Leah's brother. Assisting Leah in the deception of would-be supermen was a(nother) chance for Elke to express her serious problem with authority, as well as her love of turning clockwork against itself. For this reason Leah wasn't really grateful to Elke herself—it was the anarchy in Elke that she thanked. It had given Leah the camouflage necessary to remain a Praguer . . . at least until some official sent word that Leah Loew was required to board a train to a work camp. Her no-show would trigger a search, the false papers wouldn't stand up to triple or quadruple scrutiny, and. Beyond that her imaginings suffocated her. It was all a problem for another day; it just had to be. These days and nights Leah donned a countless number of good-natured grimaces when her dance partners told her that in certain lights and at certain angles she looked almost Jewish. Did she mind it, they asked . . . was she teased or harassed because of this unfortunate impression? Her spa lieutenant brought her a little case of imported cosmetics once; he'd discussed Leah's problem with his second favorite girl, who'd guaranteed that these tinted powders and liquids would eliminate troubling illusions and showcase her true beauty. Leah was keeping count—the spa officer was the sixth of her regular dance partners to perform such gallantries for her, and each time she took increasing care to tone down the truthfulness of her "Oooh, *zlato*, you shouldn't have . . ."

Then again, perhaps she needn't bother. When she thought about who she was dealing with here—Vojtěch, the doormen, her spa lieutenant, and other officers—she felt a calm assurance that their feminine gall–detection equipment was busted, if they'd ever had any to begin with. She'd have liked to place a bet of her own on that, but settled for asking who the doormen thought was in the lead. "You can't make up your mind whose mistress you'd rather be, and you want us to pick the fellow out for you, is that it?" Vojtěch asked her. "You really don't give a damn, do you?" A look of condemnation crossed the heavenly planes of his face; El Greco's heaven . . . stainless glass. Captivated by that look, and pleased to have inspired it, Leah just had to stroke the man's cheek. "Jealous, Vojta?"

Vojtěch Tlustý, bane of husbands, fiancés, and hopeful suitors far and wide, drew himself up to his full height, stubbed out his cigarette, and set about disillusioning Leah. He didn't dislike her, he said, but being nice to her was probably more trouble than it was worth, since she was bound to "take it the wrong way." She ought to try taking a leaf from Irma's book, he told her. Now, *Irma* was a girl who knew what was what. Irma understood that flirting was mere entertainment. Vojtěch had never had to have this kind of talk with Irma . . .

Somehow Leah didn't laugh, though she felt a violent need to. Poor Vojtěch, having to parcel himself out equally among all the women trying to claim sole rights to his affection. Except Irma. Thank goodness for one-in-a-trillion Irma . . . Now he was going to have to let this dim-witted acquaintance of his get strung along by some soldier who'd make her a target for the resentments that nobody dared show her man. Leah had heard what people said about Milena, that taxi dancer at Hotel Isosceles who had taken up with an Austrian of ambiguous military standing and was having his baby; Leah had seen Milena treated with a deference that dripped venom. She was still a girl, Milena . . . not yet eighteen, tossing her ringlets and steering her walk with her stomach. Milena was not in love, not exactly . . . the father of her child was too erratic in too many areas—kindness, truthfulness, financial support—but she was proud of bringing forth life while everybody else was busy killing. Milena wasn't the only military mistress Leah was acquainted with, but she was the only one who neither became reclusive nor surrounded herself with lifestyle-compatible companions. And Vojtěch and the oh-so-worldly doormen of the

Silver Złoty thought that Leah was keen to throw herself off the same cliff—

Not just Vojtěch and company . . . Irma too. The first thing Irma had accused Leah of was loving men. "You're not even picky," Leah's suitemate said, casting dark glances between her calves. She liked to talk as she huffed and puffed her way through her pre-bed calisthenic routines. "You look at them with such enjoyment. And you speak with them so gladly—as if it never once crossed your mind that they might not be a good thing . . ."

Leah shrugged. "Irma, if you're waiting for me to apologize for having a father, brothers, cousins, and friends who behaved honorably . . ."

"You terrify me," Irma shot back. "I suppose you're one of those people who rushes to the police when there's a crime to report too? *Oh, officer, save me!*"

"Another shocker: I've been known to telephone for an ambulance when there's an emergency," Leah revealed.

Irma grunt-chortled, but Leah couldn't quite tell if she'd actually been heard over the orchestral pyrotechnics the gramophone was hurling across the room. Wagner had everybody betraying each other and themselves (or was it that they were being true to each other and themselves?), and they were howling and rumbling about it; their songs sprang out of the open bedroom window and landed on pedestrians below. There were dots of hush when the gramophone stylus skipped the grooves it always skipped—micropauses that disclosed the response from listeners on the street: lusty cheering. Leah couldn't bring herself to take this as an indication that the Ring cycle was exactly what people wanted to hear on their way to work dawn shifts; she didn't allow herself to forget that, here more than anywhere, satirical acclaim was often indistinguishable from the euphoric kind. She kept asking Irma to choose different music for her exercise routine, but Irma maintained that there wasn't anything else that inspired her to bend her knees to their full extent. "Now, if jazz was allowed, it'd be a different story . . ."

Pre-1939 Leah had been a sheltered belle whose biggest

challenges were the wording of her editorials for the *Josefstadt Gazette*. Not that those were minor trials. The matrons, governors, and other good burghers of the Jewish Quarter held their press very firmly to account. Leah's paper went to press every ten days—she didn't agree with seven-day cycles for the reportage of neighborhood occurrences . . . what was the rush? For two consecutive afternoons following distribution of the latest edition she'd serve coffee and cake in the front parlor as she fielded pitches for exposé articles, most of which couldn't even be considered because they touched upon the affairs of the businesses whose adverts were framed by the *Gazette* contributors' paragraphs. Between bouts of pouring and slicing, Leah personally responded to requests for clarification of meaning, took down suggestions for zingier puns, and did not neglect to note factual refutations alongside demands for her immediate resignation. She cared because Josefstadt and its offshoots in wider Prague cared, but hourly she was moved to remind one of her guests that they were getting carried away with their expectations: "So it's no *Prager Tagblatt*. *Aber besser als ein Stich ins Auge, oder?*" Better than a poke in the eye . . .

Wartime Leah was somebody else. Someone she doubted any *Josefstadt Gazette* readers would recognize; her parents least of all. They'd died of old age, bedbound by so-called natural causes. Both had been overly animated mere moments before passing away; unnaturally so, she had felt, though her brain knew otherwise, and the doctors had explained. The doctors hadn't been the ones beseeched and berated. *Out of the question, that's absolutely out of the question*, her father had panted, a furious rejoinder to a suggestion Leah had had no inkling of even having made. She'd agitated Bedřich Loew while he strove so hard for rest, and she sought no mitigation of her guilt. She sometimes tried to be grateful to him and to her mother for not having been done away with by other people, as Irma presumed her own family had been. But gratitude doesn't come easily to brats like Leah. Selfish as it was for her to miss her parents as she did, in the back of her mind she still ran to them and snitched on everyone.

The querulous voice she thought she'd grown out of had returned:

Mama, Fritz went east—he didn't say "Pardubice," but there's nothing their chemists like better than cooking up explosives, so "Pardubice" is what I thought when he whispered in my ear that he and some friends of friends were going to kick the Nazis out by hook or by crook, even blowing a few of them up if they had to. I told him, I did tell him, Papa, that I simply couldn't understand his thinking. When has more violence ever improved a situation? Fritz had a mock epiphany and said: All right, the plan's changed: we're just going to go and play football with the fascists; we'll secure a gentlemen's agreement first, so that whoever loses the match has to do what the winner says, how about that?

Fritz Loew, the schoolteacher most students tended to develop a crush on, excelled at making youngsters feel listened to. His little sister lectured him, he asked for further advice, nodded receptively, and all in all conveyed the beautiful illusion that she had an opportunity to influence his decisions. Thus encouraged, Leah went so far as to tell him that if he really felt he had to go somewhere, he could go to their father's university friends, the ones who lived in Somethingshire—she still didn't know what shire, even after she and her brothers had spent a summer there once. Fritz and Emil were mad about that woolly, hilly shire and always remembered the name of it. Fritz still demurred; he would go east first, he said, and "be back in a jiffy": he made that promise in the posh English accent he put on to make her laugh. A year had passed since she'd waved to him from the platform at the main station; he hadn't written or sent any word at all, and nobody seemed to know where he was. Leah had written to everyone she could think of, excepting the Somethingshire friends, who weren't listed in her father's address book. Pages had been torn out of that: Was this a good fact, a bad one, or irrelevant? Fritz no longer appeared in Leah's dreams: Was this a good fact, a bad one, or irrelevant . . .

She hadn't yet stopped dreaming of Emil. Leah's twenty-nine-year-old brother, younger than her by a year, had dug his naïve little heels in and insisted on his rights as a natural-born citizen living in his own property. Growing up, Leah had always turned to Fritz with her secrets and schemes; Emil was almost tiresomely trustworthy; a letter-of-the-law type who usually spoiled the fun. Nobody should have been able to do anything to him, yet he was eventually arrested on charges that left them all speechless. The men who led him away thought the baby-faced butcher was crying at the thought of the hardship he would face; but Leah knew that it was about their name, their good name and the reputation for decency that had been entrusted to him, now mangled by a few typed sentences. After fourteen months of silence, he'd managed to get a letter to Leah from Theresienstadt. A very brief letter, not addressed to his siblings, wife, or sons, but To Whom It May Concern (as if he no longer dared to write their names): *Emil Loew has reason to believe he will soon be moved on to another camp*, the letter read. *He sends all his love—all—and hopes to write more soon*. No hopes of seeing them soon, only of writing.

Seven days after Emil's arrest—so, about a year and a half after the regime change—Leah took food and a change of clothes to the prison she'd been informed he was now an inmate at. It had taken her that long to find someone who actually knew something and wasn't just sending her on a jaunt to hand over the things she'd prepared for her younger brother to some other confused and exhausted-looking man who only said, "Thank you, whoever you are . . ." That day she was at least shown Emil's name in a register, though she wasn't permitted to see him or pass on a message. Later she learned that he'd been transferred before she even arrived at the prison; perhaps he'd already been sent north, to Theresienstadt. It simply hadn't been deemed necessary that Leah be informed; why tell her anything when more likely than not she'd see it all for herself soon enough? She returned home to find the front door ajar, its lock smashed. She asked three neighbors to accompany her into the house, and they did, making a point of going in unarmed, holding the items they'd been dealing with when Leah had knocked on their doors. A watch and a pin punch, a year-old edition of *Vogue Paris* that had only just arrived, a tin of cat food. Hardly fighting accessories: well, maybe the cat food. They found a small gaggle of people looting the Loew residence.

("So, five, six people?" Leah's mother, Hana Loew, would have asked. Family-wide consensus decreed that there were nine to a gaggle.)

Leah only recognized three of them, at most—three members of the small gaggle chattily separating her family's belongings into piles of things to sell and things to keep. They had never spoken to her before, these traders, though she'd sometimes heard them say "Good morning" to her jewelry, her clothes, or her boots.

Leah had asked the intruders who they were and what they thought they were doing, and they'd asked who she was—though they knew—and she knew that they knew. A few of these people had bought meat wholesale from her father and younger brother; decades of trading had come to this. With a vigilant neighbor on either side of her, Leah walked in arcs that circumvented the intruders and their indistinguishable mounds. She moved around the house putting important things into her handbag—dowdy-looking items the intruders overlooked because they didn't know the Loews. A couple of times one of the intruders pushed Leah's neighbors aside, cornered her, and shouted at her to put something down, put something back. They tried shouting at her in Czech and in German, but she just stared blankly, as if they weren't speaking any intelligible language. She stared and went on collecting the last few bits and pieces that only she could take proper care of. If it was bigger than her hand then it could fend for itself; it would have to.

"What's she staring at," the intruders said to each other, and to her: "Memorizing faces, are you?"

It was still early days; there wasn't any clear guidance on what to do with people whose names weren't on arrest warrants. The intruders weren't yet bold enough to decide that they didn't have to allow this miniature neighborhood watch to leave uninjured.

Leah and her three companions could feel things going that way, though, and they left before they got frightened enough to be turned into a test case.

Leah went to stay with Mrs. Fischerová, the grandmother who was only just getting around to looking at the pictures in last year's *Vogue Paris*. But first she marked the occasion in the manner accustomed to her, crossing over to the street corner where the Jewish Town Hall stood. She turned her face toward the black-and-gold faces of the two clocks up above and asked: *Did you see that?*

Years ago, too many years ago now, Pavel Hennig, the second-brightest jewel in their school debating-team crown after her best friend, Olga, had come up to her, said, "Hold still, Leah," and hung a stem of dark-red cherries over her left ear. Right in front of her house, where anybody and everybody, including these two clocks, could see. Pavel had backed away, laughing and saying, "Don't move . . . I'm going to look back at you in a minute, and if the cherries are still where I left them, we're soul mates!" She held her breath, but Pavel didn't look back. Which was fine, because her mother had told her that when it came to boy-girl things, it's the girl who chooses, always. The boy gets angry about that sometimes, and does things like not looking back just to show that he's his own man. Still, Leah had asked the clocks if they saw what had happened with the cherries, and they replied, *Yes, we saw, and in twenty minutes' time it will be four o'clock in the afternoon.* They'd seen Leah's best friend's iniquity a few months later too—that lumpy porridge morning when Olga had ignored her and linked arms with the new girl instead. The town hall clocks were sorry to report that a person really could be that fickle at half past eight in the morning. And their latest message for her was that it was ten minutes past three p.m. and as of now she had no fixed abode. She watched from Mrs. Fischerová's window as the locks on her front door were changed. A few days later it was Mrs. Fischerová's turn to take a few things of her own and try to reach some distant relatives abroad—they agreed that it was better for Leah not to know anything about her intended route . . . and so it went . . . Leah grew accustomed to thinking a lot about where she was going to sleep—usually a different place from the night before—and how to assist Sara and Růžena with the upkeep of her growing nieces and nephews.

And now she was an old woman. Not in any chronological sense; she'd fallen prey to the belief that today was not for her, that *her* day was long over. It used to be possible for wrongdoers—genuine wrongdoers, not born transgressors of Aryan ideals—to be . . . well, stopped. Leah's temples still smarted whenever she allowed herself to recall such things. Those were the days. Like living inside a scroll of Scripture. There was no prospect of any such thing now. Most of the intruders Leah had walked in on that afternoon were the kind of people Irma told her she sucked up to: men, some of them policemen. It was not impossible that a couple of them drove ambulances, nor was it impossible that she would not hear from her brothers again because of men like these. Leah didn't know, and tried not to think about that too much. A month or so before landing the taxi-dance job she dreamed that Pavel Hennig, her cherry-stalk soul mate, came to see her. He seemed all right. Older, but weren't they all? Dream Pavel told her he wasn't dead; he said he and his family were living in the Netherlands now, that he'd married a woman he loved dearly—someone dedicated to the Allied war effort body and soul, he said. And now Dream Pavel was a house-husband in charge of the home front and the children. He seemed shocked by how happy Leah was to hear him say all this . . . he blushed (something Leah had never seen nondream Pavel do), and suddenly she thought: These are lies from start to finish; he knows it's only right that I receive confirmation we're no longer engaged to be married, but he can't face telling me he's gone, he'll make any and every excuse except that one.

Pavel Hennig was the worst fiancé in the world. When she told him she knew that he was dead, he went even redder: "A fine thing to say to your first love! You feel like crying . . . you're just in a weepy mood, that's all." And he reminded her of the weeping-as-exercise sessions she used to lead as a schoolgirl. That was how she and her best friends had kept their figures looking so nice. Now Pavel wanted to know if Leah had any special motivation for keeping an eye on her figure these days.

"Ah, Pavel . . . not you too."

If Leah had thought that Irma and Vojtěch talked to her the way they did because they were worried what would become of her, she would have told them it was OK, she was in no danger of befriending anyone or of allowing anyone to befriend her. Leah, too, was turning inward and padding the drab cushion of prolepsis so that it could bear her up when her very bad news arrived, whatever it was.

Leah had no choice but to tolerate these patronizing little chats with her fellow taxi dancers. There were degrees of physical beauty that she was too shallow to withstand; her ego disappeared as soon as Irma or Vojtěch made eye contact. Her trusting mannerisms in the presence of authority figures remained . . . they were habitual. Leah could see how she looked like a huge joke to Irma, a Bratislavan who described her own family background as "riffraff" and preferred the company of women because she felt she had a better chance of swiftly overpowering another woman at the inevitable moment when goodwill proved to be a facade. Girl-next-door Leah was preferred by younger officers and awkward but mostly agreeable tourists who interviewed her on the topic of "things Czechoslovakian women like and dislike." Irma got the visiting grandees and the high-rolling businessmen.

"Well well, here's Hedy Lamarr researching her next role," the big shots would say—or send their go-between over to say. Irma's "Who, me?!" made it impossible to tell that she had only just finished eating some barfly's martini olive while they slurred that she looked more like Hedy Lamarr than Hedy Lamarr did.

Irma didn't ask for gifts, was offered them anyway, and accepted them even though she wasn't supposed to. If the gifts were wrapped, she didn't open them, just found room for them in the suitcase that she'd left in the corner of the bedroom and never fully unpacked. She and Leah should have been too tired to talk when they finally did make it back to their bedrooms. In fact they talked their heads off. Irma's Wagner-aided calisthenics forbade rest, so what else could Leah do? Vojtěch and Dušan thumped on the wall until the gramophone was switched off, then they came in to rebuke Irma. Which led to quite a cozy klatch. The coziness mostly came from Dušan, the resident rough goods. He was most popular with the women who fancied a dance with a big, bald berserker who handled you with the utmost delicacy. Dušan's valor was not in question like Vojtěch's was—he'd lost the use of one arm fighting in Galicia twenty-six years prior, before Irma and Vojtěch had even been born. Dušan could have taken a fatherly attitude toward the two youngest taxi dancers, or established himself as disciplinarian of the group, but he'd have had to be settled down inside himself first, and he wasn't. He told them he'd gone from an itinerant life along roadsides to army conscription, and from there to Czechoslovak Legion, diving headfirst into his career as a defector without any real faith in the prospect of the Legion getting the independence they were fighting for. "I was nineteen, had no education, no prospects, didn't know how to do much or even what I wanted to do, had nothing to say for myself, really. I was the guy who can only make reactive noises while his mates talk about the things they've seen and done and heard and thought about. I could sense that I was sort of a waste of space . . . and . . . you know, since I'd been drafted and my neck was on the line anyway, why not burn a few more bridges between me and . . . I don't know, ever getting the chance to take things easy . . ."

He'd been married a couple of times, but hadn't been able to prevent either spouse's eventual realization that he was the opposite of a provider. He'd only realized just how low he stood in his friends' and acquaintances' estimation when, a few years ago, the police had taken him into custody on suspicion of having slaughtered Otýlie Vranská. Dušan was told that they'd had multiple tip-offs that his plethora of unexplained absences and his overenthusiasm at the barbecue grill of a summer afternoon meant that he could quite easily be the ghoul who'd chopped Otýlie up with a meat cleaver, separated her body parts into two suitcases, and taken a train to Bratislava, where he'd left one suitcase at the train station before traveling on to Košice station and leaving the second suitcase there. The police officers didn't like the look of Dušan, or his imprecise account of his deeds and whereabouts along the timeline they were asking about. But in the end they'd had to release him. He'd come home from the police station to find that his most recent wife had dumped his belongings onto the pavement outside their house. A few of his friends might have offered shelter, had they not been married to hard women who called him a parasite . . . so he'd had to sleep rough for a while, a long while. And now here he was at the Silver Złoty, making the most of his talent for taking. He admired Irma's almost as much. "Come on, Irma . . . get it out . . ."

Irma snuggled up close to him and laid her head on his shoulder. "'It'? What exactly are you asking, Dušánek?"

"Your offering of the week, Irmička! Or was the worship feeble this week?"

"Oh." At a certain point in the evening when it seemed as if they were drunk enough to make confessions, Irma liked to ask her dance partners if they were villains. If they said that they were, she'd ask how bad a villain, and she'd also ask them to prove it. "I am the goddess of villains," Irma would say. "Worship me, and I'll reward you with invincibility."

Usually Dušan was the only one who took Irma's demands for tribute seriously. But that morning she actually did have something to show the others. She got up and wandered over to her suitcase. "It's from the gargoyle who's been in every night these past couple of months. Yes, that's what he is—a gargoyle—though you wouldn't know it from looking at his supremely average-looking face or listening to his forgettable voice or the things he says. One thing that always made me wonder about him, though: this man doesn't smell of anything. I mean, no odor at all, not even laundry soap. It's as if my nose goes numb when he gets really close . . ."

"Oh, him," Vojtěch said. "The psychologist . . ."

". . . who specializes in Germanizing the orphans of Czech undesirables," Leah added. Both her and Vojtěch's regulars had mentioned this man at some point, and had sounded as if they felt lucky that he was with them rather than against them.

"There's a certain reaction that children seem to have to him," Dušan volunteered.

"Well, they can probably tell he's part of the . . . er, procedure that makes them orphans. He probably scares them to death," Vojtěch answered.

Dušan set his head at a tilt as he thought that over. "Not fear, exactly. It's . . . they seem to adore him but also find him . . . shocking? I don't think I've managed to describe it correctly, but that should give you a general idea." And he told his colleagues what he'd observed a few weekends ago at Letná Park. The Sunday kids usually galloped up to the merry-go-round horses and whinnied at them, nostril to flared nostril, as they waited for tickets to materialize. But one day the odorless psychologist was there, standing right in front of the pavilion. He was the very picture of drollery—partly due to the gormlessness of his grin, but mostly on account of his preposterous purple beret: it slouched across his head like a fat grape befuddled by its own juices. The children halted several feet away and stared—at the friendly wooden horses and at the fresh-faced jester figure standing beside them—and a few of them tutted slightly, a few shrugged . . . the general atmosphere was one of being faced with two wholly incompatible escapades and deciding not to decide. "I was there with—a friend, and her son. I say to the boy: Hang on, what's going on here! Do you know that fellow? Have you met him before? The boy doesn't really like me—thinks his mum can do better or something like that—so he doesn't always answer when I speak to him. OK, that's up to him. I start to ask another kid, but then my friend's son whispers: *Yeah, I know him.*

So I look at my lady friend, and she looks at me as if this was very big news for her, and *Oh, really?* I say. *Mind telling us where it was that you met that man?* says my lady friend. Now if I recall correctly, the boy said: *Somewhere. Just somewhere. The trouble with him is, he wants to play all the time, and his games don't have any rules. Everything's allowed and nothing's . . . fair . . .* That was it. I think he might've told us more if some friends of his hadn't grabbed him and took him aside. It was obvious they'd warned him he'd said too much, because when they let go of him he'd changed his tune—kept muttering that it looked like it was going to rain and he was ready to go home. Which possibly bothered me more than what he'd already told us. I mean, a kid of eight or nine pretending to give a shit about the weather? It isn't natural."

"Sounds like a mix-up to me," Irma said. "The kids probably mistook that gargoyle psychologist for somebody else."

"Someone else . . ." Leah shook her head. "Irma, if that was meant to be reassuring . . ."

Irma made a face that confirmed she'd intended no such thing.

"No, of course not," said Leah. "I don't know what came over me. Because how could we possibly be reassured by the question of who the children could have mistaken the psychologist for. Three cheers for the other menacing games master whose existence you've just implied."

"Pfft. The kids were just being their completely unreasonable selves, that's all I meant. You know how abrupt the imagination is when you're little. All it takes is a purple beret and *Ooooh, it's purple hat man . . . we know all about purple hat man.* I don't know about you, but . . . making it seem as if I knew all about things adults were very much against me knowing . . . that was a childhood specialty of mine. Now then—here—"

Irma returned to their circle holding a gnarled lump of gray wood. Or metal? Or . . . felt? It filled her arms, yet she carried it as if it didn't weigh much.

"I buried it in clothes, and for a second just now I thought it had disappeared and felt . . . betrayed? Amazed? Both and neither. But here it is."

She set the object down on the floor and sat back as the other three tapped it, pushed it around with their feet, cautiously ran their palms over it. It had been—was still—a box. Leah surmised that before this box had been assailed with bullets, hammers, at least one explosive device, and every other bright idea that had been hatched to open this thing in a hurry, it would have been an oval-domed coffer—more or less the classic symbol of a treasure chest. They couldn't decide what material it was made out of. Something that was simultaneously very hard and lightly . . . furry? An iron hide with a touch of rubber, for flexibility?

"Irma," Vojtěch said. "Never mind what this thing is . . . where's it from? Don't tell us your gargoyle brought it from his hometown?"

"No." Irma folded her arms across her chest. "He said he'd found it in a house in 'one of those L villages.' Lidice, Ležáky, one of those, he said. His saying it like that was a strange moment because it gave me the idea that he carries the exact memory of where he found the box, and what happened—what he did, or what he saw done—before and after the owner or owners of this box were prevented from challenging him. When he described it like that it was . . . I mean, how disgusting words are. How disgusting that that's what can be done with them— remembering something and destroying that memory by speaking in impossibilities, making the event play out in two places at exactly the same time. He didn't need to say any more than that, really. The activity—no, the overactivity, of those few words were so malignant that all he had to do afterward was smile and let them go to town on me. So then, in those silent moments, I heard what it was he meant to tell me, which was something along the lines of: You, little simpleton, had an idea Lidice and Ležáky were two places, but they were the same nonplace. And everything that was done in Lidice and Ležáky was done to the same nonpeople. He wanted to make me believe that the razing of every building to the earth, the killing or kidnap of every living being in those towns, all of that was a comparative exercise: *How many hundreds and thousands of you add up to the one man of ours who was killed in these lands?* Just an exercise. A hard one for the likes of me to learn from, but for him it was fucking easy. I was dancing with a man who is not 100 percent real to me—I could see him and feel his body and hear him, but no scent at all . . . and he's making the mildest mention of a couple of trips he took last year: 'Ah, yes, the chest—I got it in one of those *L* villages . . . Lidice, Ležáky, one of those,' giving me to understand that he had participated in the complete destruction of both. And do you know, my feet didn't falter at all. We kept dancing and everything was puffy and fluffy, my skull was full of soufflé . . ."

"As if the things he was telling you somehow induced a kind of sickness? One that was beginning in your head?" Vojtěch ventured.

"More or less," said Irma. "My head or my soul. My soul! I don't always think that I even have one of those. But actually, when this gargoyle fully showed himself to me, for the first time since this whole Protectorate business started, I felt like I wasn't going to be here anymore. I don't mean—what I'm saying is, I'd still be alive if I could possibly help it. Just not in the way I—we, all of us, been trying to be this whole time. To blazes with all the brave things that sane people do; I was ready for the boldness of those who aren't really able to be here with the rest of us and can't escape either, I was there, at that part of my story, I mean my own life story, where nothing holds me back anymore, and I just start yelling like crazy without stopping until the world finally ends."

"So," Leah said. "Something was breaking. As for what it was—we won't quibble. And then?"

"And then I opened the box," Irma said.

Dušan pointed at the malleable yet seemingly impermeable gray shape that lay between them looking like a squashed hat: "This thing?"

"Yes. That thing."

The psychological gargoyle had styled it as an offering, but really he was just getting rid of it. That was Irma's opinion. Didn't they share it? ". . . I mean, look at it. It's obvious that he's tried everything he could think of and still couldn't open it. But when he shook it he must've been able to hear that there was something inside . . ."

They could all see that he'd grown less careful of the contents as his frustration increased.

"And you just popped it open," Leah commented.

"I wiggled a hairpin around inside the lock for a bit. Which felt somehow like clearing earwax? Then, yes—it opened. I was by myself up here. And I took a look at what this box has been working so damned hard to guard and . . . I laughed . . . and whatever was breaking went on breaking, but I'm carrying on too . . ."

Irma's colleagues had been inclined to leave the box closed until they heard that. Now Vojtěch lifted the lid and took out a stack of envelopes, each card emblazoned with a village school crest. There was a wall calendar in there, too, and in an additional envelope marked "Cubist Ball," twelve paper pentagons, a matchstick, and a sketch of a star-printed ballgown, the shape of which adhered as closely to that of a dodecahedron as it was possible to get once allowances were made for the emergence of limbs, a head, and a neck. Finding that each paper pentagon had been supplied with two flaps, Vojtěch tucked and folded until a small replica of the sketch stood before them. Forehead wrinkling with amusement, he picked up the matchstick and dropped it into the neck opening of the paper dress. Now they could see something of how the gown would look on an upright form. The lines and lines and lines of a twelve-pentagon dress, crashing loudly along until they collided at the corner of a blank space. Alone again, then together again, alone once more, together. It was a locomotive dream just as much as it was a dress design. Leah longed to put this on and dance. Irma was thinking about that, too, and so were Dušan, and Vojtěch. The pattern would rotate perfectly with the motion of one's shoulders. Eventually they snapped out of their gown-induced trance—it wasn't as if any of them could fit into this minuscule paper model, though there may have been a heated dispute if that was an option. They looked to the calendar for anything it cared to tell them about this schoolteacher who wrote and kept long letters to the parents of her pupils when she wasn't busy preparing a hypnotic entrance to a mysterious Ball. The letters declared themselves as supplementary to the simple list of grades the pupils' report cards provided. But the calendar seemed to have been homemade well in advance—it was for 1943. The owner of the calendar didn't have many plans. January to March were pristine, then in the box allocated to April 1 were the words PRAGUE: DRESSMAKER, with fat asterisks inked all around them. The rest of April, May, and June were blank aside from the usual printed Saints' Days, but the last two weeks of July 1943 teemed with notes. In Prague the schoolteacher would visit the hairdresser who always brought her bang up to dress, see two plays and attend two concerts, copy passages from rare books, visit the observatory on Petřín hill IF sky-viewing were suitable, and end with . . . the Cubist Ball. The dates she'd marked out were already in the past—well, in their past, not hers. This calendar could be an elaborate prop for a village dweller's castle in the air, but if it wasn't, the Ball that had been looked forward to for so long had taken place somewhere in this city about a week ago. Leah already knew that this was going to be all she asked her dance partners about for the next few evenings. In the highly unlikely event of there being a shindig that was unknown to the taxi dancers of the Silver Złoty, they must know someone who knew of this Ball. Leah and her colleagues continued their lives in this city without asking themselves why they didn't try some other place where they could find stability instead of perpetually losing it. But most places have movable and immovable parts. Perhaps, Leah thought, this city of theirs was a needle that every thread passed through at least once, and she, Vojtěch, Dušan, and Irma were living out their own lives in the very eye of this needle—unable to see, of course, what patterns the stitches were pulled into. There was a gown that had not been made, a Ball that a whole calendar had been made to hold anticipation of, there was some crotchety personage turning in the direction of their city and reaching out to it, both patient and impatient at the thought of the two weeks when she'd finally, finally be there.

The taxi dancers heard her as they read her report card supplements aloud, Irma leading with her favorite excerpt:

Mr. and Mrs. Hampl, please be assured that your daughter is not the only pupil I describe in these terms; this has got to be the most disobedient class there ever was! Punctuality is an issue, polite conduct is an issue, almost any question asked of these children receives a reply that bears no relationship to the original inquiry . . . as a matter of fact, retention of the places, date, and names provided by textbooks is a problem in and of itself . . . the veracity of our history and geography textbooks is constantly contested and revised by these pupils . . . it seems they have compiled their own textbook, but when I asked to see it I was airily told, "You can't; it's an oral textbook." The only things your daughter has learned this year are advanced catapult skills, jousting with bicycles in place of horses, and participation in schoolyard conspiracies of a complexity that rival those of the Ottomans. Last November Mr. Sedláček brought his most prized possession in for Show and Tell: he hoped it would be an eye-opener for our pupils, and I don't see anything inappropriate in that. Who wouldn't be inspired by solid evidence that the school caretaker has found it in himself to become an ornithologist in his spare time? Not just any ornithologist, but one who receives a certificate of Merit and Expertise from the Kladno chapter of the National Ornithology Society . . . ? Well, we'll probably never know who made off with Mr. Sedláček's certificate, and why. If this cold-blooded criminal and their accomplices have benefited from the theft in any way, they've kept it to themselves. Months later there is no sympathy for Mr. S to be had anywhere, only heartless remarks such as, "Oh, so he's still going on about it . . ." and "Is it possible to be an ornithologist of merit and expertise without a document that says you are? Time to find out."

Your daughter and her friends say that in the next decade or so there'll be role reversal in the classroom: pupils, they say, will write reports on their teachers . . . however, your daughter assures me that she and her classmates will do their best to delay this transformation. She says she doesn't fancy sitting around writing reports; she's got better things to do. O ye Hampls, heed this voice in the wilderness. My atheism has been challenged by the youth of this village. Exorcists are required here, not teachers!

In a postscript to another letter—an evaluation of the conduct of a pupil who came bottom of the class when completing assignments on his own behalf but earned high grades for his best friends when he did homework "in character" as them, Leah discovered the reason these letters had been stored away:

This afternoon I presented each pupil with these notes and explained that I would be stapling them to the corresponding report cards and sending them together. The response to this was efficient and near immediate—the class split into two groups. One group, drawing on the texts of historical speeches I thought they had completely ignored, presented sophisticated arguments against my proposed course of action. The second group petitioned with such pathos that my heart is wrung in all directions. Your son has told me you will lock him in the barn without food and water if you are ever told the truth about his behavior this academic year. I am not sure if I believe your reaction would be that extreme; it also seems to me that some time spent in an asocial environment (WITH food and water) might help him understand that he and his friends are separate entities who ought to attend to the work that they are accordingly given. Your son and his classmates seem convinced that submitting these notes will ruin everybody's summer. They say I will worry you, and that you already have more than enough to worry about. They say they'll be all right, they're fourteen and can choose to be serious scholars or not later on, but for now it's best for you to think they're doing well. Allowing their grades to speak for themselves will start summer off nicely—it could even save summer. Such a small thing to do for the greater good . . .

And as the savior of summer, I have been promised that I'll see a complete change next year. As matters stand, I am most doubtful that these vows will be honored. But I shall do as I promised. I somehow don't have the heart to destroy these report cards altogether, especially after all the time and trouble that has been taken over them—but I'll hide them so well they shan't be found until there's no longer any risk of them adding to your worries. Looking over the new report cards, which I've rewritten so that they only include very brief mentions of misbehavior, I think I've done the right thing. The disobedience harrows me less when I think how there isn't a single student in this class who lacks a confidante or an advocate. I also note their willingness to work hard to defend their jousting championship titles and other accolades that hold meaning for them.

Since September I've been furious with my pupils because they wouldn't have liked me when I was their age. I always did what I was told without really thinking about why or whether I wanted to. That's how I was, and nothing unexpected has come of me. I do not think that will be the case with this class, and it was stupid to be envious of that, but it's all right because I'm not anymore. I'm looking forward to them. Almost as much as I'm looking forward to Prague!

Everything was allowed and nothing was fair. "Prague" and "1943" were locations that didn't intersect with any of the seemingly infinite number of pathways diagrammed across that Cubist ballgown. One route was missing: the one that brought the teacher and her band of tearaways into the time looked forward to.

Irma said: "About time. Is it passing in this place? Is time passing or not, that's really all I want to know . . ."

She might actually have said something else.

The four taxi dancers were rarely able to hear each other properly when they talked like this; the music was so loud and they spoke quietly—they were so afraid of being overheard, of hearing their own thoughts and discovering each other's. These factors were both conversational handicaps and a saving grace: had those four heard each other clearly, they may well have realized that they couldn't stand being together.

Still, this is what Leah heard Irma saying: "Our gargoyles—including the ones we dance with and laugh with . . . especially them, actually—they never stop trying to smash and scare and bribe their way into our heads. And I know it's not working—nothing they try is working . . . but what else is happening? They're just as determined as we are. This is . . . oh God, this is permanent warfare . . ."

"I know what you mean," Dušan said. "I'm waiting for the ones who swore they'd be good this year"—he tapped the report cards—"I don't think it can be over for them. None of this can ever be over. So I'm expecting these kids to pass through. When? Now . . ."

"Except that now never actually got here either," Vojtěch said.

Leah dismantled the model of the paper gown and slid each piece back into the envelope, one after the other. A slow restoration that allowed her to take note of the paper that had been used. Rubbing it between her fingers, she grew fairly certain that these paper hexagons had been cut out of some sort of ceremonial document. A certificate that had been issued to: ah, here was the name: P. F. Sedláček. Filling in a few blanks as she examined other slivers of print and cursive script, she came up with "Kladno," "Ornithology," "Society" . . .

"Time isn't doing anything different," she told the others. "It's passing just as it always has. We're not as we were—the years have changed us. And them too, probably. Take your gargoyle, Irma. Are all offerings made to secure invincibility? What about the ones made to disperse uncertainty and confusion? The guy is used to success, he's well known for his Germanization. But the view from here denies him that. We saw that Lidice and Ležáky were lost . . . and we see this bulletproof, bombproof chest that can be opened with a hairpin, and we can see something that the fellow who gave this to you has probably already noticed—his people aren't in control either . . . they're losing too . . ."

"Come here, you," Irma said, crawling across Dušan's lap to get to Leah. She cupped Leah's face in her hands and stared into her eyes. "OK, so you tell us time is passing, and that we're moving along with it. Are we going forward or backward? If . . . and I don't need to tell you that that's a gigantic 'if' . . . if anyone throws us a lifeline, isn't it true that we'll find ourselves tied to something equally disgusting, if not more so? And as for you, Leah Loew, isn't it girls just like you who'll make those guaranteed-piece-of-shit liberators feel just great about themselves? You'll be throwing your arms around them and saying, *Thank you, thank you so much, we never stopped believing that those dark times would come to an end and you'd get here at last!* Stop lying for once, and tell me that you understand that we're all damned to hell."

Leah listened to all this without allowing herself to block any of it out. Irma's terror. Irma's revulsion. Then came Leah's own: for a moment she felt a clammy phosphorescence on her skin, then under it. Some germ or scrap of gore that swerved straight into her guts and was extinguished there. Had that sensation stayed with Leah for a second longer, she would have been emboldened to strike Irma, or to grab something sharp and punch a hole in that bitch's chest. The urge left her almost as soon as she'd noticed it, so all Leah did was stare back at the other woman and mumble that time was passing in some way that didn't seem to be about going forward or going back.

The look in Irma's eyes was awful; her pupils appeared to simultaneously drift and thicken, just like spots of activated charcoal. "Show us," she said.

Horrible, horrible. But Irma was beside herself, that was all. Who wasn't these days?

"Did you hear me, Leah? I asked you to show us that time is passing."

Leah fumbled for an answer, but grew more confident as she spoke: "If we get hold of a ladder, I'll try."

A visit to one of the hotel's storerooms yielded the showiest ladder possible; two golden palm trees with broad rungs running between them. It folded up nicely into a peacock-blue carriage they dragged out from under tarpaulins. There being no horses about just then, the four bound themselves to the carriage with long ribbons and marched across Old Town with the gilded ladder rattling around in the seat of honor. This procession caused no more of a public disturbance than the Ring cycle did. It stopped at the corner of Maiselova and Červená streets. Leah and Vojtěch held the ladder steady while Irma ascended the stuccoed facade of the Jewish Town Hall until she was level with the first of the two clocks, the one that marked the hours out with the letters of the Hebrew alphabet.

These were the clocks that had convinced Leah that she, Irma, and everybody were in perpetual motion, moving at such breakneck speed that it felt like staying still. These clocks had always told Leah that yes, they saw what she had seen—and they had always refused her real request, which was that they stop. Whenever Leah chose to address time, she tried to make it sound as if she were larking about, yet she was sincerely beseeching: *Don't add anything, don't take anything else away. Please. Please, I'll do anything.* The clocks listened and then told her the time, which was already a moment later than the one she had begged to have immobilized—and this was exactly the same as notifying her that her appeal had been unsuccessful.

Irma touched the hour hand as it moved from Yod to Kaf. And Dušan pressed his finger very lightly to the minute hand as it glided between Bet and Gimel.

Next Vojtěch mounted the ladder, but a polka-dot-aproned figure threw a window open and poked him in the thigh with a mop handle before he could get past the first floor. Guessing that it was only a matter of time before other Defenders of the Clocks arrived en masse, they made a run for it. Their head start was dependent on leaving the ladder and carriage behind . . .

Leah and Vojtěch had to content themselves with asking the other two what it had been like to touch time. Dušan told them it felt like breath—it was as if the clock breathed out into his palm. Irma described a memento that was much more concrete: there had been no warm mist for her. She'd been nipped. Bloodlessly, though she definitely felt a tooth go in.

Good grief; look. Yes, at the time.

It's time you were leaving.

Undeterred, Thea turned a page—then marked her place with her forefinger, sniffed the air, and scrutinized her surroundings, which included her benchmate, a sallow-skinned and elderly personage in a red tracksuit. Thea stared at the parting in her neighbor's hair for quite a while; it was the cleanest two-to-eight parting she'd ever seen.

So. No more chair on a night-shaded hotel balcony. The reading of this chapter of *Paradoxical Undressing* had proved to be far from a sedentary activity for Thea. While reading she'd got dressed, she'd put her shoes on, she'd breakfasted (she brushed a flake of croissant off her bottom lip), and she'd taken a seat in some sort of glass tube. There were flask-like lamps overhead, and flora all around—foliage that grazed the roof. She turned her head and saw the green steeples of St. Vitus Cathedral imprinted on the pallid sky . . . ah, she'd made it to Castle's Orangery. Nice. She'd read about this place, but hadn't known that she knew how to get here. This felt right. The balmy temperature, the mellow luster of the morning sun—she felt as if she could grow now. She closed her eyes for a moment, not caring if doing so activated another switch of scenery.

She could have done without the reek and the munching sounds, though. Both were coming from the woman in the red tracksuit: Thea stared straight at her, no longer able to dissimulate. The woman held a peeled yellow onion in one hand. In the other she had a pair of dentures, and she was snipping at the onion with the dentures; her lap was full of mashed vegetation. The look on the woman's face correlated with consumption of an especially spicy meal; a wincing smile, mouth closed for modesty's sake.

"Seriously?" Thea said in Czech, dead certain that she'd be understood. "Is this seriously how you're starting your morning, ma'am?"

The woman in the red tracksuit nodded forcefully, as if to answer, *Yes, seriously.* Against all olfactory predilection, Thea leaned closer (Would the woman mind if she held her nose? She probably would mind. Thea didn't hold her nose.) and confirmed that the onion eater wasn't elderly. The wrinkles were stage paint. The jaundice too, probably.

Thea had to ask: "Ms. Mole? Is that you?"

The woman didn't answer, but guarded her personal space by raising her hand and clacking the dentures in them like a castanet. One hopes that would've been enough to make Thea mind her manners, but I'm sorry to say that it might not have been had Emma Barber, Thea's client for her Prague job, not phoned. A call that had to be taken.

Quoth Ms. Barber: "You're at the spot, yes? Or on your way there?"

Thea pointed at the un-elderly lady with her eyes narrowed, then speed-walked out of the curvilinear door and down a stone walkway: "I'll be there soon. Not to worry, it's all on schedule."

It was only after she'd bought and drained a bottle of beer and stowed it away in her handbag that she realized she'd left *Paradoxical Undressing* behind on the conservatory bench.

7.

HERE'S HERO AGAIN—the one who wanted to leave "before things got out of hand." Under what circumstances would Hero concede that not only were things already out of hand, but they'd been like that for ages? Let's explore.

She phoned Jean-Pierre before she set out for the bridal party breakfast. An aberrant event: the surfeit of pain she and J.-P. had caused each other precluded even the semblance of chumminess. Worse—the fact that neither side promised never to do it again exposed J.-P.'s penchant for giving her one more opportunity to break him, and vice versa. After an extended period of trial and horrendous error, they'd settled on communicating in writing. Or, if there was something time critical and Jerome-related, they addressed that in brief phone calls that never deviated from the matter at hand. That particular morning broke their agreement for the following reasons:

1. *Paradoxical Undressing* was J.-P.'s recommendation.
2. Of the two of them, he was the academic, and she thought it might settle her nerves to hear what he had to say about it.

"Well . . . how far in have you got?" J.-P. asked. He was typing on a laptop keyboard; she could picture him using his shoulder to pin the phone to his ear.

"Hmmm. Did you or did you not recommend this book to our son?"

"I did . . ."

"Well, don't fall over yourself to elaborate or anything."

"I'd actually love to. I just want to make sure I observe thriller etiquette here. I know I hate it when people spray spoilers all over the place, but it does make discussion so difficult. Why don't you just read it first and then we can fangirl over it?"

"A thriller," Hero said. "You consider this—*Paradoxical Undressing*, by Merlin Mwenda—to be a thriller?"

J.-P. got defensive: "Well, all right, maybe the pacing throws it out of that category, but the machinery of it, you know. The ingredients, Hero! The Charles Square sniper and their accomplice . . . that kid who helps the sniper confirm that he's hitting the correct target by screaming out the victim's name. Goose bumps, Hero, goose bumps. Standing in Charles Square I didn't just imagine hearing my name screamed like that, I heard it, it happened to me . . . it was Jerome screaming DAD! And there he was, a newsboy with all the day's unsold papers flapping from one of those slings across his chest. I ran to him, but something was off. Jerome just stood there with this stare of malignant anticipation, and there was this fizzling in my chest. Then pop, pop, no more sight, no more hearing—"

"I don't think I've got to that bit yet. The sniper gets going in the first chapter, you said?"

Increasingly frenetic flipping through the pages of the book on

Hero's lap proved unsuccessful; not a single mention of a Charles Square sniper. It was, however, brought to her attention that Chapter One had changed again. No more fearful 1950s High Court judge; now the book opened in February 1342; the Vltava had lain beneath a heavy slab of ice since December, and on the morning the ice thawed, the river engulfed every item on the wish list it must have compiled while it hibernated. Livestock and lapidaries' workshops, guild houses and market squares, homes of every size and description swamped from basement to awning. The list was topped by the Judith Bridge, the only bridge between New Town and Old Town, which the floods tore down into a sandstone raft, so creating two separate cities—or so it seemed to the nurse and the Franciscan doctor, one stranded in New Town and the other in Old Town, each of whom could only pray that those patients the water had wrested from their care had somehow been placed within their lover's reach . . .

She'd left the book on the window seat while she took a shower; that's what had happened.

"God, it must have been a decade since my one and only visit to Prague," J.-P. went on, as if she hadn't spoken, "but the first thing I did was walk a little way around Charles Square—didn't have time to get that far around it since it's so massive. Once you've finished *Paradoxical Undressing* you have to take a look, Hero! I don't know how it will be for you, but the book created such a crazily tangible unhistory for me . . . I saw the Square just as it was right at the opening of the book. Nineteen thirty-one, everything grayscale, and it's like your eyes are reels of analog film . . . there's this light drizzle making the air jump. Someone behind you shouts out HOFFMANN, or some such name in a terrified voice, as if HOFFMANN is their last chance of escape. And upon hearing that name, a figure to the right of you, a man who was already walking fast, sets off at such a hard sprint that he almost brains himself with the briefcase he's carrying. He doesn't get far before he keels over—in ten seconds flat he's just a paint-spattered body in a trilby hat and tightly cinched trench coat . . ."

"Paint-spattered?"

"Like you wouldn't believe," J.-P. said. "Curdled yellow and electric blue and a writing sort of red . . . you get the message. Bucketfuls of color! And you're just like . . . fuck. So this is where I am. These are the exact coordinates of the spot where answering to my own name gets me shot with lethal paint pellets. That Hoffmann guy answered to his name by running away. I mean, maybe if he hadn't reacted at all he'd have been spared . . . maybe if he'd just kept moving like a nameless person you could've lived . . ."

"J.-P."

"What is it, Hero?"

"We're talking about this Merlin Mwenda book?"

"Yes. *Paradoxical Undressing*!"

"Describe the cover. Actually, no—never mind that. Did you . . . put the book down at any point while you were reading it? I mean you must have . . . or did you carry it around close to your body or something?"

"What d'you mean?"

She began to tell him precisely what she meant, but he talked over her.

(J.-P. knew, she thought. He KNEW that there was something tricky about *Paradoxical Undressing*—or about its subject, anyway. No, that was transference. Hero was the one who did eldritch things with what she knew; J.-P. was a sharer. She wedged herself into J.-P.'s shoes for a moment: OK . . . from where he stood it was most likely that his ex had decided to fuck with him today and was using a book that she knew he liked as a goad.)

"So how's the hen weekend going?" he said. "How's Sofie? Still heinous?"

"And just like that, we've run out of civility. Enjoy the rest of your day, J.-P. . . . thanks for answering the phone . . ."

"I can be happy for Sofie without liking her, Hero."

"Is that so?"

"It is. I'm over the moon that she's making an honest woman of Polly."

"Over the moon? What are you going to say next; many a mickle makes a muckle? Go easy on the English phrase book, J.-P."

"Seriously . . . give them both my best. Claudine's, too."

All was indeed in order: this was the zombie hostility that was only temporarily quelled by some mention of their son. And now it was supposed to kick in, the realization that there were far less precarious ways of checking. She should've just emailed after all. On the brink of hanging up, she went out into the corridor, and— stayed on the line. There was a sheet of paper stuck to the door of her room; at each corner, a sticker imitated a nail driven into the wood. Her diaphragm buckled; there could only be one reason for this 95 Theses–style presentation. Someone from that dastardly courier company had found her; this was the letter she'd refused to sign for four times already. The letter was from a man she had written about; his name was Gaspar Azzouz. J.-P. had sent her Gaspar's obituary years ago:

The impact of appearing in a widely read character study (Dorothea Gilmartin's *Faiblesse*) took its toll on Azzouz, most unmistakably in his later use of social media as a means of making his life "transparent"; an approach that was by all accounts excessive. It is doubtful that Azzouz would have chosen to live stream his suicide had Gilmartin not taken her scalpel to the untruths he told in his search for self-respect.

Gaspar had made arrangements for this letter of his to reach her that summer. There was footage of him writing it and entrusting it to a friend who neither spoke nor appeared on camera. The footage captures Gaspar Azzouz telling that taciturn friend: "This is for the one who wrote all about me and was too cowardly to say a single word to me afterward."

Each of the couriers told Hero the company would keep making delivery attempts until she accepted the letter. She could only assume that this was financed by Gaspar's friend, who she'd probably have to sue for harassment (though this would involve finding out their name and address and mundane things like that). Only one sender was identified on the envelope the couriers presented her with: Gaspar Azzouz. The dead man. Once at the supermarket, once at the post office, once outside Jerome's school, then in the waiting room at the dentist's . . . that desecration of the waiting-room frame of mind had tipped the entire state of affairs over into the chimerical. She'd run away to Prague without delay, and here the letter came regardless.

Hero unpeeled the stickers, took the sheet of paper down, and drove her sight along it—that was how it felt, heavy wheels turning in the place where her eyes usually were. But it wasn't a letter! She might have guessed as much, actually, since there was no envelope, and no courier pressing for her signature. This sheet was covered in Czech, so she made neither head nor tails of it. But it looked official—it had been stamped, signed, and dated with that very day's date. She squinted when she saw a certain name—Hero Tojosoa—and a signature. Her signature.

"Hero?" J.-P. was still on the line. (Why?)

"Yes."

"Are you OK?"

"I'm great. And you?"

"I don't know . . ."

"While you're deciding, J.-P., could you use that DeepL thingy to translate something for me, please?"

"All right—spell it—"

She spelled out the document heading: Oddací list, skipping the diacritical mark, and he said: "Czech, right?"

"Right."

After a second or two, J.-P. said: "It means 'marriage certificate.'"

"It can't mean that. Try Google Translate."

A click and a few keystrokes: "'Marriage certificate.'"

Hero spelled the words out again, describing the diacritical mark. J.-P. offered the words to the translation algorithm again. "Sorry—it sounds like you really want it to mean something else, but it really does seem to mean marriage certificate. What's up? Whose paperwork have you got hold of there?"

She checked the name and signature planted in the column that ran alongside hers. Wendell Wechsler. The certificate was claiming that she, Hero Tojosoa, had got married to one Wendell Wechsler today.

She got off the phone without any goodbyes, folded the marriage certificate in half, stuck it in among the pages of *Paradoxical Undressing*, dropped the book into her handbag, and went downstairs, cheered by the superlatively ordinary sound of vacuuming coming from behind the closed door of the room that she'd half dreamed another, earthier Malagasy speaker was staying in. The proprietor of the bed-and-breakfast, Mr. Surname* was out on the pavement having a smoke and shaking his head at the sky—denouncing its cloudlessness, perhaps. Sweat molded his hair to his cranium.

"How do you do, Ms. Tojosoa," he said, when he saw her. Daunted by the courteousness of his memory, she blushed and praised her room, the building, the neighborhood. And she showed him the marriage certificate.

"Congratulations!" he said, after studying it for about five minutes—maybe longer. "But where did you get this?"

"It was stuck it to my door."

"Huh," said Mr. Surname, blowing smoke out of the corner of his mouth. He channeled it upward, to amiable effect. He was like a steam kettle that didn't screech its teatime manifesto.

"You wouldn't happen to know who, would you? Or who this Wendell Wechsler is?"

The blue light from Mr. Surname's eyes was a bit . . . could the

---

* "Surname" is the stand-in for a name with so many more consonants than vowels that Hero could neither pronounce it, remember it, nor find a gracious way to ask him to repeat it one more time. He'd already told her ten times!

blueness of eyes be like tablet screens, disrupting the circadian rhythms of those subjected to their gaze?

"You're the one who's marrying him, Ms. Tojosoa, so if you don't know, you'll soon find out, won't you? Don't worry about it. Just enjoy."

Hero would normally have bridled at being told "not to worry about it" (it was too much in the vein of "calm down" when you weren't yet upset), but Mr. Surname's English accent veered toward Cockney, and when an East Ender tells you not to worry, you don't.

"Whose wedding? Polly and Sofie's, or"—Hero smiled; an intimation that she was an excellent sport—"or mine?"

"Yours," said Mr. Surname, running his index finger across the words *Bazilika svatého Petra a Pavla*. "That's a smashing little Basilica to get married in of an evening. Lucky you."

"But Mr.—I mean, sir . . . I—I have no intention of—"

"Maybe you would have preferred nuptials at Notre-Dame de Paris or some such place, but I assure you our Basilica really isn't bad at all," her host said. "It's not just for Catholics, you know. They've got St. Valentine's shoulder blade on display there—it's been here since the 1300s, but mostly sat around in the Basilica basement until—well, the second millennium. And why hurry; after all, we can take our time with St. Valentine. He's here for all lovers; there's no expiry date on his support, is there? Yet you seem to be telling me you don't want to see his shoulder blade."

"No, I don't. Why should I? There's nothing between me and that saint . . . never has been. I'm actually hoping to stay in with a book tonight, thanks."

With a "suit yourself" shrug, Mr. Surname pocketed the

marriage certificate: "Nonetheless, Ms. Tojosoa—I don't think you were meant to see this yet, so I'll take it off your hands for now."

He offered Hero a cigarette. She took one and walked to the nearest tram stop with it despite being a nonsmoker.

BREAKFAST WAS HELD AT a café with a French name and brocaded dollhouse feel; all Hero had to be was a lady in waiting, and she took to the role quite happily. Self-effacement was a master key that unlocked all benevolence that had been held in reserve. Sofie's mother, Denisa, smiled dotingly upon her. It was most strange and most marvelous to experience this instead of the screaming *Oh no—no no no!* expression Denisa usually donned whenever she crossed paths with either Hero or Thea. Polly's mother, Veronika, smiled dotingly upon Hero, too, even though she had probably heard all about her from Denisa. They were good to look at, the mothers of the brides, in their matching sage-green tea dresses and sparkly nude eyeshadow. This was either a demonstrative approach to familial blending, or fodder for a restricted audience "who wore it better" Facebook post once the wedding photos were available. Hero looked forward to seeing what the fathers of the brides were wearing when they arrived later on.

"This is your first time here, no?" Veronika asked. "So how does Prague compare with Mount Olympus, Hera?"

"Hera" began to answer that the city had inspired her to square up to whatever jeopardy awaited her at home, but Sofie, seeming to anticipate this answer not being the right one, elbowed the dashing cavalier to the left of her. Conor was so much more than just the Humanist Registrar who'd be officiating Polly and Sofie's nuptials in the morning; he was a good grandson, and some kind of bard as well. In a low, County Cork–accented voice, Conor told the bridal party of the time he'd taken his eighty-year-old nan to a peat spa in Třeboň. The mud baths had done wonders for his nan's arthritis, and they'd decided on a spur-of-the-moment trip to Prague; it seemed a shame to visit Bohemia without seeing what the capital was like. They'd done the royal procession via boat and horse-drawn carriage: Old Town, the New Town, the Lesser Quarter, the Castle District. Light took on trancelike incarnations, clinking off cobblestones and lining alleyways with velvet—in short, Prague really worked a number on them. Freya, Conor's nan, had resisted for as long as she could, sullenly biting back the gasps that the vistas before them demanded. "Yeah, it's all right," Freya Healey had mumbled. "Nothing special. Not that different from Budapest, actually. Except that you get more for your euros in Budapest." But at the main train station she'd burst into hacking sobs. How preposterous this star-crossed lover feeling was. At her age! She was just so terribly sad that this place had been here all her life and she was only just seeing it now. It wasn't as if she hadn't been anywhere picturesque; she had, she was one of the lucky ones, she knew that . . . but this was like being in a moving picture. And now Freya Healey felt . . . burgled, bereaved? It didn't do anyone any good for her to feel like this, or for her to protest against it, but there it was.

"Yeah," said Hero, as the mothers of the brides drew Conor to their bosoms with extra loud *awwwwww*s. "What he said." Conor winked at her and Sofie, Sofie winked at her and Conor, and Hero resigned herself to liking one of her replacements.

("But seriously," Conor said to her later, as they walked over to the salon, "a place can live in you without letting you know about it for the longest time. That could be why you don't like it here. Who likes being thrust into their own insides without a word of warning?")

A heated discussion between a waiter and another customer drifted across the room: the customer had ordered and consumed a BLT without bacon, and had just discovered that this would cost her twice as much as a BLT would have. And now she was raising her voice about it.

There were no apologies forthcoming from the waiter: "Was the sandwich to your liking, ma'am?"

"It was all right, I suppose. I mean, it wasn't terrible. But . . ."

"If it was to your liking, then what is the problem here?"

Having been called for, the manager advanced an explanation: "As I'm sure you appreciate, ma'am, when you eat out, you're paying for a lot more than just the food. Knowing how to make someone happy with just some lettuce, some tomato, some sauce and some bread—this kind of knowledge costs more than bacon does."

"Sorry, but NO! That just doesn't sound right . . . I really want to tell you why, but it's too hard in English. Let's get this crispy clear: Even if what you say is true, that 'knowledge' wasn't in the menu, it isn't on the bill, and you can't charge me for it all on a sudden!"

Michaela, the bridesmaid seated to the right of Sofie, jumped up to mediate, yanking the exchange out of English and steam-pressing it into dual threads of Vietnamese (for the thoroughly incensed LT eater) and Czech (for the waiter and manager). English was restored when the LT eater very, very begrudgingly agreed to pay the price listed on the menu for a BLT.

The mothers of the brides approved of peacemakers. "You worked a miracle there, Míše," Denisa said when the impressively brawny vegan took her place among them once more.

"Not me! All that aunty needed was an incentive to pick sightseeing over infinite war. They needed her to make that choice, too, and by budging just a little bit, they made it so."

Veronika tutted: "I would've held my ground forever. Half the price or nothing at all. Then again, I've already seen all the Prague sights a zillion times over, so I wouldn't mind arguing for hours. Actually . . . I would've just ordered the normal BLT! This craze for self-deprivation is going too far. Just think how nourishing meat is—think how it strengthens the body . . ."

"So does ethically harvested semen," Michaela replied, flexing her arm muscles. "I'm not going to talk about protein from legumes; everybody talks about protein from legumes. But semen's like a turbo-boosting supplement . . . you get your vitamin C, protein, zinc, you get a jolt of positivity—"

"Yeh, nothing more uplifting than the taste of all those almost-babies who won't be adding to your existing share of sleepless nights," a bespectacled blond a couple of seats down from Hero (Niamh?) agreed. "No offense to the parents and wannabe-parents . . ."

None was taken. Regardless of what went on at the other tables, affection presided over theirs; the whole group was demonstrative, everybody instinctively reaching out to hold hands with the nearest person. They hadn't had anything to drink yet, so it must have been the stories. Over daintily pleated crepes, Denisa asked them to discuss Polly's and Sofie's lesser-known virtues and to share happy memories. Everybody had a tale or ten. Polly's hangover soup saved lives. The annual spring parade in Sofie's hometown had only ever had a Kolache Queen riding the lead float until Sofie, intent on making 1990 the Year of Unisex Purple Pantaloons, had successfully campaigned to be Kolache Prince. Polly would think nothing of staying on Skype for seven hours rehearsing and re-rehearsing your paltry lines with you on the eve of your audition for a small part in a soap opera. Sofie was the Scissr date who told you off for using profile photos that didn't do you justice and took enticing new ones across the duration of the thirty-six-hour phone-karaoke-augmented urban hike that was only cut short by the fact that you had patients waiting for their dental checkups. Hero's Sofie story revolved around the hedgehog café the two of them had run together in early-aughts Ménilmontant, and how hedgehogs, fairy lights, and grena beer had proved such a winning formula that after a year they'd attracted the attention of a Tokyo hedgehog café owner who was interested in developing a portfolio of locations across the globe: Hedgehog World. Chinatsu's mission was to look after the needs of those who were unable to commit to pet ownership but couldn't do without a hedgehog in their day. Hero told the bridal party that if Chinatsu hadn't taken over, she and Sofie would probably still be in Ménilmontant, running the café and filming season 10 of the reality show they'd been in talks about just before they sold up. Not that there was anything regrettable about moving on. Chinatsu made them an offer they'd have been mad to refuse . . . plus she was a vet and had far greater understanding of hedgehog physiology and psychology than they did. Last of all, her concept was hedgehogs plus soufflé pancakes, and they didn't really want to have to deal with cooking on the premises, it was too much to have to think about.

Michaela gave the bride-to-be little push. "Sofie, I didn't know you'd been part of something like that! You never said . . ."

Sofie told her that really it had been Hero who'd done most of the work: accounts, stocking supplies, handling anything that required more than rudimentary French, etc. There was a bit of pouting around the table: this was meant to be a Sofie story! So Hero took over once more: "I knew we were going to be a success the very same evening we opened. Our first customer was the most frazzled-looking man in the world—apparently middle aged, though he could also have just been a super-stressed-out adolescent. And he came in to ask about the sign she'd put up in the window: CÂLINS ET HÉRISSONS POUR TOUS. Was it true that anyone could get a hug here? He was asking for a friend, he said. And Sofie said to me: Quick, get Millie—Millie was our most . . . I don't know, each of our hedgehogs had their strengths, and I'd say Millie's was her depth, wouldn't you agree, Sofie? Right. She wasn't a laugh-a-minute buddy like Patrice, say—but Millie could go under the surface with you; that wasn't a problem for her. So I got Millie, and you hugged the frazzled guy like he was your long-lost brother, and when you let go I sat him down at a table with Millie and he was so . . . to say that man was 'thrilled' is too mild . . ."

"I remember," Sofie said. "He asked us: Is this expensive? Do you have a loyalty scheme? He told us he didn't have a lot of money, but he'd come here every day."

"Which he did, until he found a new therapist," Hero added. "We were happy he had his priorities straight, of course. Hugs and hedgehogs can keep you afloat for a while, but yeah."

She closed her mouth around a forkful of buttery, lemony crepe, and Sofie flushed with gratitude for her contribution to this oral history—or relief that Hero had finished speaking without revealing anything untoward. This was the sort of thing that reminded Hero that she'd spent most of their friendship in a state of uncertainty as to whether Sofie actually liked her or not. Maybe Sofie didn't know either.

"And after him, the deluge of daily customers, right?" said Dominik, the clean-cut, lantern-jawed fellow sitting opposite her. He was also the author of the play Polly currently had in rehearsal at the National Theater, if Hero had correctly interpreted some of the banter that had been exchanged as they'd taken their seats. He had a Polly memory for them all, but first he wanted them to picture an almost unreasonably shy boy from the countryside—he rarely took the trouble to mention the name of the village he was from; it was a place you were only likely to have heard of if you came from the neighboring village. Dominik had come to the capital for Pride Week—not because he was a homosexual, you understand, he'd never had such urges. No, the young country boy was open-minded and wanted to party with some homosexuals—he'd heard that they were more fun somehow . . . plus, art and music were the country boy's thing, and what would those worlds be without the gays? He had to show some appreciation.

"Spoiler . . . similar reasoning can and does apply to others I've met at Pride, but Dominik just happens to be the gayest life form at this table," Polly called out.

Dominik threw his napkin at her. "Could it be that Apolena and Sofie share a hatred of having nice things said about them? It seems that Apolena in particular will interrupt with any old thing. Perhaps she'd prefer to be trashed instead?"

Polly waved her hands: "No, Domek, she wouldn't. Please excuse her—she won't interrupt anymore."

She remained true to her word as Dominik relived their first encounter, on their steps leading up to Letná Park from Edvard Beneš embankment . . . just a couple of levels below the Metronome, and the spiky red of its stationary pendulum. He'd been leaving a fancy-dress picnic in a huff, slinking away as more revelers poured in. Some of the new arrivals called out to Dominik in glad voices, but none of them *got* him, nobody could see that he'd come dressed as a jewel of the avant-garde. It was Polly who ran after him, saying that she'd always wanted to meet Toyen. She told him she was on her way to meet friends who felt the same way, one of whom made excellent quiche . . . Dominik had asked her why she was bringing quiche into it, and she said she didn't know, she was just saying anything in the hope of scoring an afternoon together.

And how do you know an afternoon together would be a good idea, Dominik had asked, unsure if she was hitting on him or what. And Polly said: Come on, you're Toyen!

Polly led Dominik to a picnic unit whose members set aside their feather boas in order to arm wrestle for the right to sit near him and cool his brow with pocket fans.

"I was there," an apple-cheeked member of the bridal party piped up (Hero hadn't caught their name). "So was I . . ." said Michaela. The fancy dress lunch had turned into supper . . . they dawdled on the grass, talking by the light of solar lamps that had been charging all morning. The view from Letná put Dominik on tenterhooks; even now he can't get used to the face the city shows when it looks up at its central plain. From where he lay the meetings and partings of (and on) the streets looked like a rotary dial encased in plumed plaster. Each minute rotation pulsed and growled, registering input of a preposterously long telephone number, and this Pride Picnic was being held on the enormous cradle where the handset would've rested. Unless assuming a position on Letná Plain turned you into a handset . . . his head was ringing and so were his ears; half to the view and half to Polly, the open-minded country boy said: "Hello . . . ?"

It was the summer after the floods of 2002, and Praguers had not yet reached the end of the evaluations the water had made mandatory. Dominik listened and listened—now the Praguers who'd adopted him for the evening were speaking of the records that the water had erased, and the miscellanea they'd found floating, intact but so long forgotten that it seemed they'd only got in among the other belongings by mistake; it was only some doggedness on the part of such oddments that forced you to do your duty by them. In the morning, he went back to the hostel he was staying at and wrote down everything he could remember being told. He began to set the recollections down in verse—or something like it—then caught himself. These were true stories; he hadn't any right to them.

Dominik had phoned Polly and asked her to get in touch with everybody who'd been with them that night. And he phoned them, one by one, asking for their blessing while expecting to receive an injunction on making a play out of things that had happened to them. He still could not understand—none of them could—how it was that none of the things he'd written down bore any resemblance to what the picnickers remembered telling him. Over and over again he was told, Those aren't my memories. Then whose? They definitely weren't his own. After a few days Polly had called him and said: "Domek, are you sitting down? I'm going to ask you to consider something. Is it possible that you're . . . a playwright?"

Hero kept between Conor and Dominik as they strolled out of the café and along a main road where palatial facades clattered against each other. The King of the Immortal Jellyfish lived next door to the Queen of Parakeets, whose nearest neighbor was, well . . . the Burger King.

She found herself asking Dominik the playwright if he'd read a book called *Paradoxical Undressing*.

"I haven't. A novel?"

"I think so? A Prague book. My son got it for me." She took the book from her bag and showed it to Dominik. He took it into his own hands gently. "Looks like outsider art . . ." In his opinion, she was unlikely to meet many people who knew it.

"*Paradoxical Undressing*?" That was Denisa, behind them. And Veronika said: "Not the Merlin Mwenda book?"

Hero snatched the book from Dominik and walked backward until she was in step with the mothers of the bride. "The very same. You've read it?"

"I tried to, for book club a few years ago," Denisa said. "When you said Prague book, that rang a bell. I believe the title alluded to, ah, what the coldness of the Cold War made people . . . do? And the story followed a misinformation agent, this super-ambitious Czech gal, who accidentally leaks accurate information. Her bosses kinda like her—or they like messing with her head—so they give her twenty-four hours to completely discredit and invalidate herself in the eyes of the British contact she usually feeds misinformation to. But it's really hard because the misinformation agent's one of those gals, she's—well, the type of sports fan who not only roots for a team that winds up at the bottom of the league every season but starts the next season all rah-rah-rah like 'I've got a feeling this is gonna be our season!' Endearing in a way, I guess, but also sorta 'Oh my God' . . . " So the misinformation agent's contact has this unbreakable trust in her even though she's gotten stuff wrong so many times before. And even though the contact keeps getting in trouble with her own higher-ups for channeling such crappy intel. And . . . you know, *Paradoxical Undressing* is just callous. Every bone in that story's body is a mean one. All it wants is to make you watch someone pulling out all the stops so as to wreck what's maybe the sweetest thing she has in her plain, pinched life—somebody else's unconditional acceptance of her. The book wants you to want that mission to be successful, so that both the liar and the lied-to can live. But something told me the book was definitely plotting to kill them both off anyway. Like, maybe it'd have them forgive each other first or something, but it definitely wasn't going to let that friendship continue. Well, all of THAT was draining my life force so I, ah, donated the book to one of those phone-booth libraries and just kind of waited until the next book club read was announced . . ."

"Well, I'm all right with mean stories," Polly's mother told Sofie's. "I would agree that *Paradoxical Undressing* is in that vein. A mean vein. And yet its attitude is not at all as you've described it. Our book club read it, too, and I can't speak for the others, but I must say I got such a rush from it. Just like candy! Hero, the book is all about a feud between two of the greatest sixties pop singers in this country . . . how to describe their style? A little bit jazzy, swingy but sort of . . . light and up here, you know, not down-low-type cool. Maybe like those Yé-yé singers they had in France and Spain. So, in

Paradoxical Undressing, it turns out the groovy goddesses Helena Blehárová and Jarmila Veselá are both enthusiastic beekeepers. They practice their apiculture mostly in secret, but it's everything to them. Only when they're in among their bees—the celestial singing and the dancing of the bees—only then can they get a true buzz from being one with the masses! Well, somehow Alena Tichá finds out about their secret love—ah, Alena Tichá and her cover of that 'Sugar, Sugar' song"—Veronika executed a wavy kick and pushed down imaginary layers of crinoline with her hands—"Sorry, I'm afraid the action involves too many singers you don't know . . . OK, here's one who was big internationally: Alena Tichá forces Karel Gott to help her with her plan! What? You don't know Karel Gott either? I suppose he was more of a hit with the German speakers. But believe me, all the people I'm mentioning are *very* big stars. . . ."

A supercilious-looking brunette came up to them and stood in their way for three or four minutes; she was waving a handwritten, Czech-language picket sign: the lettering was red and pointy and all in capitals. Veronika read the sign and stuck her tongue out at its bearer; the brunette returned the gesture and moved on.

"What did that sign say?" Conor and Hero asked.

Dominik was laughing. So were Denisa and Veronika. At last, Veronika answered: "It said: 'Czechs who speak a lot of English are not real Czechs' . . . But where was I . . . right, *Paradoxical Undressing*. The fabulously wicked Alena Tichá decides to pit Helena and Jarmila against each other, and thus clear the field of rivals. She comes up with an idea for a documentary on beekeeping that will draw parallels between the archetype of the bee and the ideals of womanhood: you know, fearsome beauty, community spirit, hard work, sweetness, and dedicated cultivation. Alena's plan is to do completely separate pitches, so that Helena and Jarmila both get the idea that they'll be the one and only presenter of this show. But Helena and Jarmila already know what Alena's like—so they never return her calls. That's why Alena has Karel Gott's voice coach kidnapped. Karel G. has to cooperate with her in exchange for his coach's freedom. Karel G. says all right, all right, and he makes the phone calls to Helena and Jarmila. He gets them both hooked on the idea of filming this documentary, gets his coach back, and disappears back into superstardom, leaving the two beekeepers to fight it out. Which of them will appear on-screen as the personification of Czech honey? Who will survive the cloak-and-dagger machinations they set in motion? Smear campaigns, poison-pen letters . . . and oh God, the scene where Jarmila locks Helena into that walk-in freezer and goes home, and she's in a great mood until she visits her bees and they all scream out JARMILA, JARMILA, YOUR REAL TROUBLES HAVE NOW BEGUN as one, in Helena's voice. Iconic . . ."

"Maybe my spy book had a different title," Denisa conceded, after a long moment. "Though I could've sworn—I have total author-photo recall, Veronika. The monocle and the handlebar mustache . . . I couldn't get enough. He's a retired Bengal policeman, I believe—that's what the author bio said. There's no way I could forget that guy's name."

"No, that was some other author and some other book. If you'd read Merlin Mwenda's *Paradoxical Undressing*, you'd know," Veronika assured her. "It's totally 'out there,' as I believe Americans used to say. And, you know, that's just how a lot of us wanted the sixties to be, after so many years of, let's say, introversion . . ."

Hero thought: Oh, if I could swap my life for the life of any other being, Denisa isn't the one I'd force to be me while I'm being her—I wouldn't want to do that with Veronika either, I wouldn't even want to be this book they're telling me about. I'd swap with whatever it is that's happened between them and the book. The process so personal it's a person . . .

Aloud, she said: "No, please. You hold on to the book. I . . . don't have room for it."

But Veronika insisted on passing it back to her: "Like I said, I loved it, but I already have a copy somewhere. Besides, I don't really reread novels. Furthermore: it doesn't seem as if you've read it yet yourself?"

"I'll take another crack at it," Denisa said, holding out her hand. Moments later, she opened the book and read the first line aloud—and Hero ran ahead of them and into the salon, stuffing her fingers in her ears so that she didn't hear it.

The ponytailed receptionist in the navy-blue shift dress looked familiar in a post-makeover sort of way . . . she recognized Hero, too, and reached across the desk to smack her on the shoulder. "Heroine!"

"Jitka!" Hero said, not bothering to correct her. (Heroine, Hera, what next?) "Where's the wheelbarrow?"

Jitka thanked her for asking: her cousin was watching the wheelbarrow for her. She added that she hadn't said bye the night before because she really hadn't felt it was over between her and Hero. She hadn't expected Hero to find her at her day job, but this was very lucky for Hero: "My hands are like Botox shots . . . I need to share the gift, you understand. Listen, Heroine, I'll get everybody settled down first, but you're my client today. Go on up and I'll get all those wrinkles out of your forehead, OK?"

THEY WERE ONLY on the second floor, but the room felt higher up than that, as if it were teetering atop a stem. The bridal party was swathed in shades of beige and apricot as gauzy linen curtains swayed in the breeze—no. No breeze. That was the air-conditioning. Hero had her eyes closed anyway. She was undergoing facial massage. They all were. Nine pairs of hands pinching, patting, and kneading nine faces. She could feel Jitka's focus fluttering across her face, pressing down in the same spots as her fingertips did. She snuffled when Jitka pressed the heel of her hand down on the bridge of her nose . . . was that standard procedure? She heard herself sigh, heard a few of the others sigh, too, as if in response. Denisa and Veronika were bickering about *Paradoxical Undressing* as quietly as they could, but eventually Jitka chided them in Czech, and they took to sighing at intervals too.

Eventually Hero's face was left alone, the settings on her reclining chair were adjusted so she could sit upright once more, glasses of unsweetened iced tea were brought around, along with tiny wooden forks and dishes that held hearts composed of strawberry slices. The forks stabbed into the hearts with a satisfying squish. Sofie must have requested these; the gruesome romance of them was right up her street.

Jitka tried to get Hero to look into a mirror. "See how much better your face is!"

"Incredible, thanks ever so much," Hero said, ignoring her reflection and impaling heart after heart. Jitka mimed throttling her; she did see that, and caught her hand. "Truly, Jitka. You're right that I got lucky today. My face feels great. Like it managed to fit a couple of weeks of genuinely happy smiling into just a few minutes."

She checked on Polly and Sofie, and made the awkward discovery that both brides-to-be were checking on her. All three looked away, then looked back at each other. Hero mouthed: "What?" and Sofie noiselessly gestured toward the door. She was frowning. Was Hero being told to leave? No. It was a "look at that" gesture.

There was a tenth, nonreclining chair in front of a mirror on the other side of the room. It was occupied by someone with outsize curlers trundling all over their head, a phone in one hand and an empty beer bottle in the other. The person under observation didn't turn around: she watched the bridal party in the mirror as, one by one, its members took note of her and asked each other: "Who . . ."

Dorothea Gilmartin was crashing the party she'd been invited to, and she was going neon blond while she was at it.

Once everyone had fallen silent, she congratulated the brides-to-be. "Thanks," they mumbled.

The stylist who'd been attending to Thea looked nervously to Jitka and the other beauticians: "Was I not supposed to . . . I thought . . . sorry, she said she was with you?"

"She is, I think," Polly said, upon receipt of a very slight nod from Sofie.

The mothers of the brides whispered to each other, then, at almost exactly the same time, they both said to Thea: "Well, what do you want?"

Hero stayed sanguine as she met Thea's reflected gaze; there was no need to shrink down into her seat or try to hide behind Jitka (who was a full foot shorter than her anyway). She re-remembered what Thea had said to her when she was moving out: *If you ever contact me again . . .* well, she hadn't. So Hero took another sip of iced tea and swallowed another strawberry heart.

"What do I want? Well, for starters, another five minutes to let this dye do its stuff. And then . . . Denisa, it's good to see you, by the way. You're looking well! Hello to you, also, Polly's mother—I don't believe we've met. This isn't a social call, unfortunately. I'm on a job. I've got a message for you, Sofie. From Emma Barber."

Hero tried her utmost to think fast; Thea's being here "on a job" was not good—Emma Barber would be someone who had a grudge against Sofie. But the name rang no bells.

"Emma Barber used to be married to someone named Mark Colby," Thea said, her tone mild, calm, and encouraging. "Mark Colby. It'll come to you. He was a client of yours a couple of years ago."

"Oh, he's in theater?" Polly said hopefully; sense now seemed to be within grasp for her and for all. She laid a hand atop Sofie's hand: "You did some set design for this Mark Colby?"

"Set design . . ." Thea leaned forward, pointing the beer bottle at Polly. "Sofie wasn't a set designer when she met you, and no more playacting that she was unemployed until then, Polly-Anna, my girl. We were employed, weren't we, Sofie? Hero? We were active."

Quivering with displeasure, Sofie stood up and went to the door. "Join me outside, Thea. Now."

"Well, we already know about the hedgehog café," Veronika offered, clearly hoping that Thea would decide against delivering the message in private.

"Oh good, so Hero's dredged up the one story about Sofie that's rated Universal," said Thea. "Nicely done, Hero. But that's not the Sofie story that Emma Barber knows."

"I'll see you out there, Thea." Motioning for Polly to stay where she was, Sofie stepped out into the corridor. Thea checked her watch, requested a rinse, and said she'd be out afterward.

"Hero," Jitka whispered, with her hand over her mouth. "Is this really a friend of Sofie's? Just say the word and we send her out."

The door opened again and Sofie poked her face back into the room. "Hero," she said.

Thea could be heard sighing with annoyance even as her head was thrown back into the washbasin. "She wants you to go out and wait with her, I guess," she said.

Sofie nodded, and Hero went out into the corridor, where a row of potted plants ended with the two of them stood next to each other with their hands behind their backs and their fingers fidgeting away at their thumbs.

After a few moments, Sofie took out her phone and began texting. Hero readied her own phone, familiar with this method that removed the risk of their discussion being overhead from the room where the others were.

Sofie:

> This could be about the photos you took. I mean, the photos we took.
>
> Those three months or so when I was pictures and you were words?

Pictures and words: a side hustle they'd discarded when their bond with Thea had turned an anonymous and dissolute duo into a trio with a name and a code of sorts. Hero sent a shrug emoji.

Sofie:

> Hero. Don't be like this, please
>
> I'm racking my brains here
>
> I didn't know the names of anyone who was asking for pictures, I just posed

Hero:

> And took half the money.
>
> You posed and took half the money, Sofie.
>
> It was not peanuts.

Sofie:

> Right. I know.
>
> And I actually felt like you should've taken more

Hero blinked hard, typed a reply, and then deleted it.

Sofie:

> Because you were the one corresponding with them and you were doing most of the thinking about how to set up the photos so they turned out nice and natural looking & all that jazz
>
> tbh I kind of checked out once you started snapping

Hero:

> Liar. That would have come across in the shots; we'd have had unhappy customers. Believe me, you were all there. Maybe even more so than you are in person.

Sofie:

> Oof. Look, I'm not trying to push anything onto you. We did what worked for us at the time.

There was some commotion in the room they'd just left; they heard raised voices, then Denisa hurried out to join them. She addressed Sofie in Czech—Hero listened as closely as she could, expecting to hear something about Thea. Thea didn't come up (not by name, anyway), but there was some repetition of the word masáž, which must mean massage . . . apparently not missing out on the bodywork segment of the day was foremost in the mind of Polly's mother. Sofie said some words that sounded soothing, and Denisa gave a couple of not entirely convinced nods before leaving Sofie and Hero alone again.

Sofie:

> The shots I felt strangest about were the ones where I was mostly clothed and the requests were just like: "Look virginal. And a little scared, look a little bored, not a lot, not a lot. Just enough to show that you don't want this but you're doing this because I want you to and you can't say no."

> You remember the ones I'm talking about, right?

Hero:

> Would hardly forget the ones that brought in the most cash

> Could have been because you were superb at looking virginal? Not an easy one to pull off, even for actual virgins

> The real value was in the Mucha inspired nudes, I thought

Sofie sent a heart-eyed emoji.

Sofie:

> The marvels we achieved with pink & blue fairy lights & daisy-marigold garlands! Sometimes I think they were wasted on the customers.

They both looked up as Denisa emerged from the facial treatment (and hair dyeing) studio. "Honey," she said to Sofie. "As always, I'm trying to keep it in mind that poor Dorothea has been unhappy for so long that she has no idea how to be happy for other people. But I just . . . I mean, does she really have to be with us today, of all days? Is there anything you want to tell me?"

No, nothing. Sofie kissed her mother and shooed her back into the gathering of strawberry eaters. Hero sent a thumbs-up emoji as the door closed behind Denisa. Then she replied to the message she'd received just before Denisa's outburst:

> No greater way of showing aesthetic appreciation than just having a really good fap

Sofie:

> But the "routine teen, with a sprinkling of repulsion" pics
>
> Weren't those the kind this Mark asked for? Mark Colby?

Hero:

> Maybe? Sofie, I had to jettison a lot of the names so that I could pick up speed and grab all the bags of gold
>
> That's what running that website profile for you was like. Being in the most basic video arcade game imaginable. Bags of gold popping up everywhere.
>
> The thing about doing the words while you did the pictures was that there were just so many messages to read and respond to, and
>
> The simple, sensual and comprehensively bogus Eastern European girl persona that they were all looking for—she took up so much more headspace than I thought she would.

Sofie shook her head, then typed for a few minutes, her brow creasing as she reread each sentence before continuing. Hero found that switching her gaze between Sofie's deliberations and the message-in-progress dots on her phone delivered a heady sensation that was, oh no, but this was true, it was not unlike going up the staircase of a silent house toward a book that was waiting only for her. Hero crossed and uncrossed her eyes in the hopes of fending off another trance, and for the moment, that seemed to work.

Sofie:

> Yeah, super down-to-earth E. European chick who just loves a roll in the hay and never makes an issue out of it. Fucking like a champ is just something she does before and after putting her apron on and getting on with all her other womanly stuff. She's a tenacious model, ain't she.

> I guess she was created by the drunk guys in bars who tell me that the only "kinda Western" women who still know how to fully appreciate a man are the ones from the East of Europe. They're hot, but not stuck up. I'm still hearing this shit! I just used to say OK, well enjoy your night. But now, just in case the record never changed because we boudoir photo selling, Central European bar frequenting femmes let it play, I'll say: "OK, look, that's a personality type for sure, but can you confirm that this is the rule with Central European females? If so, can we talk about the methodology employed?"

> Then, with this "huh, I thought maybe you were from here but I guess not" look thrown in, I usually get some variation on "Central, Eastern, tomaytoes, tomahtoes, you know I'm talking about women who grew up in the lands once covered by the Iron Curtain, and don't try and turn this into a fucking scientific study, sex and sexiness aren't lab work . . ."

> So yeah, that little sex kitten's creators are probably the only ones who can banish her. But

she's got them so they don't want to; they've fallen
in love with her!

Hero:

Every time I received a confession of love from
someone I was chatting with as "Sofie," I knew I'd
have a sleepless night fantasizing about finding
that person and giving them the most savage
beating of their lives.

Then there was this kind of zone I kept going into
where there wasn't really a me but there was an
"us," and "us" wasn't even me and you, it was me
and the you I'd made up to gratify the bags of gold.

Sofie:

You think I didn't notice?

Once you said to me, "What if Sofie is right and
feminists really are just the boys and girls who are
so saddened and angered by their lack of natural
charm that they start acting up just to try to get
more attention from men in one way or another?"

Hero sent a coffin emoji.

Hero:

And you were like "Sorry, what? You're telling me
that this is what SOFIE thinks? Which Sofie? I
don't think we know any Sofies like that . . . ???"

"I missed you," Sofie said suddenly, flinging her arms around
Hero, who didn't and couldn't submit to the hug. Their greetings
just before breakfast had been nothing like this. This was too
exactly what Hero wanted, and yet she was most palpably *not in it*.
The declaration and the embrace were occurring because Thea was
around. In fact, this entire scene was taking place between Thea

and Sofie. Hero had watched from the sidelines with enough frequency to know.

The invocation must have been performed correctly; Thea came to them, still carrying her phone and empty beer bottle. She came with her hair still drying . . .

While the dye had been setting in it had looked like a metallic shade of blond, but the end result was mineral, as if each strand of her hair had ossified. Sofie stammered hello. Hero said nothing. She and Dorothea Gilmartin weren't speaking; Thea's behavior would almost certainly worsen if she heard so much as a word from her. Hero perceived that this was the case without understanding why it was the case; nor did she believe that Thea understood it herself.

"Hero can go now," Thea told the ceiling.

Hero would have very gladly gone, if not for Sofie's look of being rattled out of her mind. She put an arm around Sofie's shoulders, squeezed, and planted herself on the floorboards.

"Sofie. You're a big woman now, and you can stand alone. Tell her to go," Thea said to Sofie. Sofie replied to her in Czech, but Thea didn't answer, just kept her eyes so firmly trained on the ceiling that both Sofie and Hero looked up, too, on the off chance of there actually being something worth staring at up there. There wasn't. After a long moment, Thea drawled, "All right then . . ." and dialed a phone number. Her call was answered immediately; it was a FaceTime call, and Thea turned the phone around so they could see the caller.

"Hi," said a woman about a decade younger than them. She was of mixed ethnicity, her skin a few shades lighter than Hero's, her wavy hair cropped pixie style. A slackened scar jerked the entirety of her right cheek up toward her eye socket, draining her aquiline features of their equilibrium.

This was Emma Barber. "Go closer," she said, and Thea moved the phone closer to Sofie's face, walking forward every time Sofie and Hero stepped back.

"Look who's been aging well," Emma said, after a few seconds of intense scrutiny. Her diction could mostly be placed in West London, with a hint of the West Indies.

"I—sorry, do we know each other?" Sofie asked, accessing and exhibiting the oh-so-amicable smile of a former Kolache Prince who could fix any misunderstanding.

"No. I only saw you in photos. The photos where you do a fairly good impression of—let's say, an unwilling teenager—remember those?"

Sofie didn't dim her smile by a single lumen: "Yes, I do. It's weird, Emma: I keep hearing that body confidence comes later on, if at all, but I feel like I had more of it in my thirties than I do now."

Please, Sofie, Hero thought. *Please don't try to nudge this woman into camaraderie with a "how about you," please please.*

Emma didn't give Sofie time to try that, anyway: "Body confidence isn't all you had! I read the messages you wrote to my ex-husband. Well, as many as I could—he deleted a lot of them, but he was in too much of a hurry to be able to get rid of them all. Do you feel proud of your little role-plays with him, Sofie?"

Very carefully avoiding eye contact with Hero (whose memory remained fuzzy to say the least—the correspondent Emma seemed to be referring to had been one of hundreds), Sofie said: "Firstly, Emma, I wasn't aware of the relationship status of anybody I was chatting with at the time."

Emma gave a bitter laugh. "And secondly?"

"Secondly . . . it sounds like finding those messages was, ah, wasn't the very best introduction to your ex-partner's sexual fantasies you could've had. Especially since—I'm guessing they aren't fantasies you connected with at all. So now you're pissed at him and pissed at me, right?"

"Our daughter's best friend," Emma said. "You couldn't have known this, and he wouldn't have told you, so this bit I don't blame you for, but in those naughty snaps or whatever you called them— I think you wrote 'here are some naughty snaps for you!'—you looked like our daughter's best friend. Our thirteen-year-old daughter's fucking twelve-year-old best friend, Sofie. You didn't look her age, of course, but the resemblance was just enough if you wanted to imagine . . ."

Thea, maintaining a stalwart grip on her phone, was shaking her head, her eyes no more readable than they would've been if she'd been wearing opaque-lensed sunglasses.

Sofie pressed her hands together. "Emma, whatever you want to tell me, I will hear it. I'm not disowning the part I played. I know I can't."

"Sofie—" Hero said.

"Who's that?" Emma asked sharply.

Instantly, both Thea and Sofie answered: "No one," which stunned the no one's mouth shut once more.

"In the role-plays he told you how old you were supposed to be, and you played along. What was the harm in being twelve only in this very specific scenario that vanished at the click of a button, right?"

"I guess I must have been thinking that the role-plays would stop him from bothering, you know, an actual twelve-year-old," Sofie said. "And what I want with all my heart right now is for you to say that it worked. You're not going to say that, though. Are you?"

"Our daughter's best friend, Sofie. He went after her. And she went absolutely tonto on him. While we were waiting for the ambulance she said to me, 'I did hit him, Mrs. Colby,' in a way that made me . . . God, she said it like she was expecting to be told that's why he—fuck. I suppose she'd been afraid for a while. That girl was onto Mark long before anybody else was. I remember her and my daughter having a huge falling-out when they were nine and ten because she'd told another girl that my daughter's dad was creepy. I was worried when they made up—I remember hoping that it was a definitive split, because being such close friends with someone who said things like that could backfire on my daughter big-time. What could this girl end up saying about my daughter, or me?"

"And then it turned out she wasn't just stirring shit," Sofie said.

"Well. I still don't understand why she had to say it to that other girl, who went on to tell EVERYONE—but yeah. She was saying what she saw. She saw—felt—that he was going to try something, and when he did, she went straight into combat mode—and he switched too. A child going tonto on an adult is—nothing— compared to the reverse. Do you understand, Sofie?"

Sofie gulped. As did Hero. But as per instructions, only one of them answered: "I do."

"That fucker cut her with a bottle." Emma turned so that they were faced with her scar in full profile. "Just like this."

"And you—?"

"And me?"

"How . . ."

"I've been on a really long road, Sofie C. Going from being sure that some small but important part of what happened to that girl was my fault. She was lured into our home by her closeness with my daughter, after all."

"Did—ah, you didn't copy her scar, did you?" Sofie (almost) pleaded.

"I was so convinced that she was jealous of our family, of what we were, what we had, whatever—that I treated her like . . ." Emma bit at her nails, spat off to the side, then continued more briskly: "Your pen pal's in prison. With any luck he'll be killed in there. And I've worked hard to get my daughter's mother back where she's supposed to be, you know? Reflecting, researching—I've had his email accounts hacked, for instance. As soon as I found your messages I knew the portion of blame I was trying to bear actually belongs to you. You can take it, and I can just—I need to—I thought I'd be happier about this."

"Emma," Thea said. "Do you still want to go ahead?"

Emma nodded.

Thea looked at Hero and Sofie: "She nodded, didn't she . . ."

They, too, nodded.

"Understood," Thea said. "Just as I practiced, then."

There was a quantum quality to what happened after that; all three of them would agree, I think—it was like trying to track waves that were also particles. But a rough summary: Thea gripped Sofie's shoulder to hold her steady as she broke the beer bottle against a wall. A needless hold, since Sofie, tears lingering on her cheeks, only closed her eyes in a kind of assent while Hero head-butted the bottle, which Thea immediately tried to drop—she'd raised her hand against Sofie and no one else. Besides, this was the first time Thea had been scared in years: she'd never seen someone go toward a jagged edge like this, driving on wide-eyed as wounds sprung open. Hero kicked the broken bottle a little way down the corridor before picking it up and pursuing Thea all the way out of the salon's front door and halfway down the street with it. Then Hero collapsed, or so she thought. In actual fact when Jitka ran down to reception she found Hero sitting there, confusedly holding her head. "No one," Thea and Sofie had said, trying to gloss over her, but she was the no one who'd most merited this cut and she couldn't have allowed Sofie to bear it in her stead.

She couldn't even claim that the role-plays Emma had spoken of had seemed like a good idea at the time—they hadn't at all. There were hundreds more exchanges where the Colby ones came from too. If even an eighth of those had had side effects, and the sufferers found their way to Dorothea Gilmartin, Ms. Gilmartin would be dropping in on Hero and Sofie with who knew what manner of weapons week after week for the next five years or so. And even that estimate was based on Thea's deciding to pace herself.

8.

PRESENTED WITH A CHOICE between a cleanup and suture administration by Jitka and attempting to describe the circumstances of her injury to someone at a hospital or clinic, Hero placed herself in Jitka's hands.

"Oh, so now you can't take your eyes off the mirror," Jitka grumbled as she stitched. She was quick, and sure—and— . . . "Did you heat the needle? You didn't, right? I'm trying to figure out why it feels like it's burning," Hero said.

"You saw me going wild with the rubbing alcohol, Heroine. No heat treatment; it's less reliable. I guess this is the borovička saying a big hello? Have some more and let me know if you cool down or get hotter."

"No—no more. But thank you. And not just for the booze."

She eyed the stack of cardboard boxes behind them; it was shifting, and they'd soon be submerged in a spray-tan lagoon.

"*Tak*—it looked worse than it is. Just try not to get your face dirty or wet for a day before you next wash. Everything I know about People was screaming, kick this gate-crasher out, she's definitely going to hurt somebody," Jitka said, completing and checking the third suture before reexamining the other two. "Next time I'm going to listen to what I know about People instead of listening to the 'she's a friend, she's with us' stuff."

"Jitka—"

"What? Jitka what? What is it you want to tell me? That I don't know the story of you and that woman? Do you yourself know the fucking story of you and that woman? You're the one who finishes living early, Heroine. And that woman is the finisher, in case I'm not making myself clear."

"And Sofie?"

"Your Sofie gets finished early, too, for sure. But you first."

"I was actually going to say that those boxes are going to fall on us any minute now."

Jitka glanced over her shoulder. "No. The boxes are not moving."

"OK. I'll take your word for it. As for Thea: How would you fix things so as not to be the one who finishes living early, Jitka? Involve the authorities? Bump her off first? Go back in time and refuse her friendship?"

Jitka took a seat on a stool beside her. "Use your head, Heroine. You really don't have anything on her, anything that can keep her at bay? It's usually like that when somebody brings out the worst in you at the same time as you're bringing the worst out of them. Even spicier if for a while there was some kind of . . ."

She mimed pulling a rabbit of a hat: "What do you say that is?"

"Trick? Illusion?"

"Illusion, illusion. Some kind of illusion that it's the best that's being brought out instead of the worst. If not the best, then at the least 'the real you' and 'the real them' . . . "

Hero began to grimace, but Jitka's taut needlework prevented her from finishing.

"What about this, Jitka: What if the chemical reaction you're describing is what goes on between you and your best friends, you and the person you have a child with, you and anybody you get interested in? I just want to . . . should I just go away from everybody? I'd miss my son, but he'd actually be all right. That boy's in hiding from me all the time anyway. I tell him we're going to have a talk and he's like, 'Sure, Mum, ready when you are. Maybe when you get back from that wedding? Didn't you say you were looking for something to read, Mum? Here's something for you to take a look at while you're away . . . ' And the book my son gives me? That book is like . . . you know in movies, when someone's being chased and they're throwing down all kinds of obstacles to multiply the distance between them and the person chasing them? That's what this *Paradoxical Undressing* book is like. The book my boy gives me when I try to have a talk we need to have."

"So your kid isn't stupid," Jitka said. "At least there's that."

"Oh, he's tragically smart. Smart enough to have worked out that as I'm a mother, I'm a bit . . ."

"A bit what?"

"Mmmmm, I expected parenthood to transform my mentality. It's changed the way my son's father thinks, for instance . . . or maybe just the way he talks. My son's father talks about his need to set the right example for our son, and how he's more serious in his work because he needs to provide. I could just be hoping he's bull-shitting because that's not my thought process when it comes to choosing what to do and what not to do. But no, it makes sense that he really feels it. Parenthood's that huge step that pulls your brain out of a lake of other people's brain juice . . ."

"Brain juice???"

"Other people's lives and thoughts, I guess. When my son was born I thought I'd just be his mother, I thought I'd only really want to know about him, he'd be my entire life, you know? So somehow . . . yeah, I don't feel great about the fact that my son's— my son's *plan*, I guess—his plan to distract me with that book is working. Was working. If Jerome really had become my focal point, wouldn't I be like 'Book? What book?' Well—I got rid of it, I think. The book's gone. He can't escape me now."

Hero's phone buzzed; Sofie was calling. Hero and Jitka watched the phone jangle around on the counter until Sofie gave up.

"Well, you are away from everybody," Jitka said. "I'm not even sure I know the way back to the main door from this storeroom."

"Maybe your wheelbarrow knows . . ."

"You're going to stand up slowly, Heroine, and we're going to walk slowly, and I'm going to put you in a taxi back to that place where I left you last night, OK?"

"OK," Hero said. "I don't know how to thank you, Jitka."

"It's simple," Jitka said (the customary precursor to an impossible task): "Don't waste the efforts of my golden hands! It's fine if you don't want to do anything to that woman, but you shouldn't be helping her to do things to you. And that's that."

Sofie called again. And again. Then she sent a couple of text messages. And called three more times. Finally she left a voice-mail message that Hero listened to in the taxi. She listened with a sinking feeling: she was going to have to cut Sofie loose. Sofie was talking about resurrecting Florizel, i.e., getting back together with her and Thea. She was talking like this in spite of Polly, in spite of the friends she'd made since finding her way out of Florizel, in spite of the work she'd found—work that suited her far better than any project since the hedgehog café. None of that was "really her," Sofie was saying. But where was the evidence that Florizel was?

Hero felt her brain gyrate every time she tried to type, so she dictated a text message:

> Really hope you weren't hurt at all, Sofie. That glass jumped around a bit. Someone helped me, so I'm OK, though shaken up—I can hear that you are too. Listen: I've been best friends with all of the yous. The ones that are really you and the ones that were less so. Just like you've been best friends with all of the mes. I was ready to read and write messages as you back then. And you were ready to take blame for me just now. Let's call it even

"Dot dot dot," Hero said,

> . . . no more trying to protect that "us," OK? So now you know what I think you should tell Emma and Thea next time. Which will be a lot sooner than either of us would like, I guess.

Hero stared out of the cab window, trying to decide how to sign off. The taxi coasted past a pub with a violet-colored latticework facade that took up the entire length of a side street, Hero's eyes met the all-too-memorable eyes of a figure standing outside that pub, she abandoned her draft message, squeaked out: "Stop, please," paid up, and was out of the taxi and at that person's side before she'd thought of a conversation opener. Perhaps she didn't need one. He was holding out an empty glass—raising it above his head, actually, and appeared to be waiting for the sky to fill it. He gave her a nod, then shook his glass, muttering what she presumed was the Czech for "Come on, come on . . ."

"Er—ahoj . . . ka," Hero said, once she'd come to the realization that he wasn't going to greet her first. He didn't reply, seeming to assume that she was talking to somebody else. It was as if they'd never met. But it was him all right, the earthen-toned man who'd popped out of a room at the bed-and-breakfast the night before, asking her if he was . . . not even a golem, but *the* Golem.

"Ahoj?" Hero tried, initiating direct eye contact. His gaze was much less shocking in the afternoon light. Perhaps it was the five o'clock shadow, white linen, denim, and straw loafers he wore that settled him into the mundane. They didn't establish him in the mundane for good, though; he somehow showed her exactly half of a smile as he said, "Hi yourself," and in a flash she was off balance as she tried to catch hold of the veiled remainder. The half smile was all the more enticing for not having been tactically executed, or not striking her as such. It felt like half a smile actually exceeded the amount of smile he had to spare just then, but he dispensed it anyway, banking on the chance that more would come in before too long.

"How—so, how's it going?" she said. (What was tying her tongue here—was it the marriage certificate? Or the fact that she looked and felt like she'd engaged in fisticuffs with a windowpane? That was probably it. Either way, she'd misjudged her ability to hold this particular conversation, and she was going to walk away in 3 . . . 2 . . .)

"It's too hot," Mr. Not-the-Golem said, moving the glass back and forth one more time, then lowering his arm with a sigh.

Hero shrugged. "Is it?" The sweating and wilting and

mumbled protests against the heat hadn't escaped her notice—she'd been seeing and hearing them ever since arriving in the city—but she ran cold herself, and could've stood to layer a jacket over her long-sleeved dress.

"See you in the beer garden?" she said, halting at the door to trail her fingers over the wooden fretwork—a plump quadruple-leafed pattern, like shamrock, only purple. She looked back at him over her shoulder in a manner she hoped was intriguing, then went straight to the gray-brown, root-cellar-reminiscent bar and asked for a small beer, a bag of ice or frozen peas, and some ibuprofen. The bartender gave her a giant tankard of beer she had to transport with both hands, two packs of frozen peas (balanced atop the tankard), and no painkillers. The change she received seemed to add up to more cash than she'd handed over, but it was probably just that she didn't understand the coins yet. She took her beer and peas through to the walled garden at the back, and lo, the frozen peas section summoned: everybody seated there was pressing peas to their heads, arms, necks, etc.

Twenty minutes passed; Hero placated her chin and forehead swelling as best she could, exchanged rueful nods and shrugs with her counterparts at neighboring tables, and acquired a beer-foam mustache. Sofie tried to call again, then Jean-Pierre, and she dashed off messages to both callers. The trees crackled hoarsely when birds rearranged their branches, but were otherwise still. Which somehow made Hero think of the Not-Golem standing there all parched, waiting for rain to fill his beer glass. She went back to the entrance of the pub. He was still there. "This drought . . ." he said to Hero. Then, looking at her again: "Oh, hello. What's your name?"

"I thought you knew," she said.

He rubbed his chin. "And you thought so because . . . ? Stop, don't tell me—let me guess—are you well known?"

The Not-Golem didn't sound as he had the night before; his voice was less tuneful and his accent more clipped. The Not-Golem was a much-beleaguered individual who'd momentarily halted in the middle of his life span to give himself a few ulcers while he considered all the commitments he was trying to balance. He had nothing for her and she didn't have anything for him, except. Except that she'd just said "I thought you knew" in Malagasy and he'd answered in English. That was probably the most she was going to get by way of concession that this was their second meeting and not their first.

"Got anything that kills pain?" she asked.

"You'll tell me your name if I do?"

"Yes."

He stuck his hand in the pocket of his jeans and pulled out a fraction of a blister pack of ibuprofen: the last two pills, still sealed into their plastic pockets.

"I'm Hero," she said, taking them from him. "And you?"

"Leander," he said. "Oh, but not really. I always thought he was a simpleton. There can't have been a shortage of fetching women on his side of the Hellespont, or even a shortage of fetching women who'd go for a drink with him. So his motivation for that nightly swim across the strait was lost on me."

"Until now?" Hero prompted him, laughing.

"Until now," he said, neither solemnly nor cheerfully; he wasn't flirting, he . . .

"Oh no. No, Wendell. I'm . . . not available," she told him, mainly so they would stop swapping twitterpated gazes.

"In general?" he asked. "Or just to me? Also: Who's Wendell?"

"You. You're Wendell."

He mulled that over for a moment or two. "Wendell what?"

Very well; let him joke around: "Wechsler! Isn't that you?"

"Certainly. I mean, why shouldn't that be me?" He squared his shoulders. "I'm Wendell Wechsler. And I'll drink a beer with you now, Leander's lamplighter. If you don't mind."

She took the ibuprofen in the beer garden; itemizing the list of things that were wrong about this aloud: asking a stranger for painkillers, taking those painkillers with alcohol she'd left unattended—

"And those are only the things you're aware of," Wendell said, as he got stuck into his second pint. "I've found that once I've done my housekeeping in those areas, the stuff I didn't even allow myself to notice I was doing circles back around and then: well, chaos again. You almost don't want to bother tidying up in the first place."

"Stuff you didn't know you were doing," Hero mused. "Like sticking marriage certificates to people's doors?"

Another chin rub: "That doesn't sound like me. Which is not to say that it couldn't have been."

Beyond that point Hero was steered by the befuddling factors of painkillers plus beer plus Wendell (Wendell being the greatest befuddler of the three).

This is what was unforgettable for her:

1. That Wendell Wechsler proposed to her twice. His first proposal came shortly after he'd asked her what she loved, and she'd told him. Hesitantly, because he might not have believed it, might have thought she was just saying that because she'd seen how much he wanted it to rain.

"So that's the way to your heart, is it? Thunder and lightning and misty sheets of rain? In other words, nothing that just any Jean, Pierre, or Gaspar can offer . . ."

"How about you, Wendell? What do you love?"

He scratched his head. "I am finding out," he said. "Even though almost everybody I meet seems to want to stop me from finding out."

"Well, all right—let's hear it: How would I go about stopping another person from finding out what they love?"

"By making that person a donkey or a cart—by loading them up with all the things you think and feel and telling them that those thoughts and feelings are for them. By telling them—and I have been ambushed in this way when I pass through graveyards, Hero—that you died for them. Or if you're still living, you can coo that you're living for that person. I will find out what I love irregardless, Hero. Listen"—she laid her cheek against his, and he draped an arm around the back of her chair—"I'm not busy this evening, are you? Have you ever been married?"

"No."

"I have. I mean, I'm not anymore. But I do think it's a worthwhile experience, and I think we could make it really nice for each other, and, the long and short of it is, Hero, that I'm advising you to accept a marriage proposal from me."

Hero laughed a laugh of general unavailability. To her own emotions as well as to the emotions of others. It wasn't as if Wendell hadn't noticed this; he'd acknowledged it aloud with his remark about rainstorms being the only love gifts that were acceptable to her. Hero's version of unavailability wasn't as dependable as she'd have liked, though. Unavailable, too available, which one was it?

She googled "How to tell if you're being truthful" three or four times a year but had never found any answers that helped.

"I'm going now," she muttered. Her body was annoying her, nestling into this man's warm, compactly hewn shoulder and inhaling his scent with intemperate enthusiasm.

Her stitches were smarting . . . she really was leaving. "I've got my own housekeeping to do."

Thea . . . she was probably going to have to contact Thea after all. There were those words she meant to have with Jerome, as well.

"Down with housekeeping," said Wendell. "Stay."

Hero was not available. And yet to Wendell, who was now suggesting that they get married that evening, she answered: "Only if you know a nice Basilica."

"Well, now that you mention it, I do. It's mosaics on mosaics."

"And what about the shoulder bone?"

"Ah, that's right—I almost forgot—they have St. Valentine's . . . but why do you look as if . . . ?"

She was being wooed as wife of the day; that was what made it all right. Just a day, nothing to be anxious about. This reminded her of reading one of those online articles that are accompanied by a clear estimate of how long it'll take to get through it with your gaze moving at average pace.

Wendell proposed for the second time as he led Hero up moss- and ivy-layered steps that took them to the edge of a steep bank. There was the city they'd just ascended, curling and curving and growling and beneath them like a great supine bear cub with the sheen of youth still on it. "It's harder to get her to do this without rain, but, let's see," Wendell said. He pursed his lips and blew. The rooftops rose, each tile and gable an arrow that split the night. "Live with me, here, please," he asked her, above the blazing river and beneath the sky that sparkled with newly sown stars. This had to be it, the unreachable place that reached you after you'd set every other place aside. It made her laugh when he hurtled away in the direction of the Basilica, pulling her along with him as soon as she'd told him yes.

"Wendell! Why—are we—running?"

"Hero—I'm—overjoyed—that—you—will have—me! Thing is—it might not—have been me . . ."

"Might not—have been—you?"

"The—Wechsler! That—certificate—under—your—door! It—might—have—been—me—but—if—it wasn't—oh—I couldn't—let—some—other—fellow—be your bridegroom now—"

Neither could she; they were on the same page there, and made yet more haste in order to be wed before the other guy arrived. Wendell drew her head down a little as they ran; at first she thought he was trying to form some kind of wind shield for her with his hand and arm, but really it was to keep her from looking up. There were hefty feet running alongside them—feet that shifted about a bucketful of soil with each tread. *Stone feet.*

"Wendell! Who—are—we—running—with?"

"Just—some—well—wishers—who want to—be—there—too . . ."

2. Hero and Wendell were wed just after the Basilica's bells rang out eleven o'clock. At the pub he'd mentioned that some friends of his reliably frequented the Basilica at that time of night

("Doing what? Praying?"

"I don't know . . . maybe that's just where they go to take things easy . . .")

and one of those friends opened the Basilica doors upon hearing Wendell's special knock. She was a sun-weathered fifty- or sixtysomething, was of a similar height and build to Hero, and insisted on their switching clothes, as her gown—a floor-length muslin affair with tiny, capriciously chiming brass bells in place of buttons—was much more bridal. Hero did not permit her thoughts to loiter around the fact that this lady only seemed to speak what sounded like Latin and was accompanied by two fair-fleeced goats. Nor did she turn a hair when she saw that one of her and Wendell's witnesses, the only one who beamed at them but kept to his pew without a word of greeting or congratulations, was a well-built older gentleman with a white man bun and an eye patch . . . a carbon copy of Merlin Mwenda, the author of *Paradoxical Undressing*. The pew behind him was overrun with a gaggle of church mice (she felt she had to call them that, since they all had tonsured heads). A bald man in a modrotisk tailcoat made copious notes on the proceedings. There were tens of other guests—as a matter of fact, the size and the variousness of this congregation touched and alarmed her. A couple of statues closed the doors once they'd received Wendell's signal that it was time to begin.

Their officiant wore a red bow tie over his clerical collar, and the ceremony wasn't particularly Christian. It was more of a handfasted pledge. Hands, eyes, hearts, shoulder bones, lips to lips, shattered singing from the belfry and from the chiming cordon that ran from her chest to her waist to her knees. There came a truly dreadful pounding on the Basilica doors. The sound could have been that of fists, if each fist weighed as much as a full-grown man. "IT'S HIM," shouted one of the onlookers amassed in the pews. "It's the Wechsler! You kids had better get a move on—"

Still as they were, rapt in their mutual regard as they were, Hero and Wendell had not ceased to run—toward each other, in a way—toward a road where they crossed? They reached it, and their breath bled outward, painting the two of them into the very murals that overlaid the Basilica walls. Together they crisscrossed the ceiling, too, smudging the wings of seraphim and the green wreaths that had been thrown up between the naves lifetimes before; the oils in the paint had not yet dried. The pounder of the Basilica doors slunk away.

It was a union not adequately described by the document that was handed to them once the vows were concluded. All it said was that the marriage of one Wendell Wechsler and one Hero Tojosoa had been recorded in the parish register, along with a date and other small sundries. That's Pragensia for you. Their officiant looked far from pleased with dents the late-comer had left in the Basilica doors, but murmured that it couldn't be helped . . .

9.

THEA'S HAIR HAD ALREADY DRIED. This caused her substantial disquiet; she kept patting her scalp as she went through the motions of setting this triple-jinxed job back on track. There was a barrage of text messages and phone calls from Emma Barber. None of which Thea engaged with. She'd hurt Hero: she had to know how badly. She bolted, and was reassured by the speed at which she was followed, and the distance covered. She turned back when Hero turned back. She went into the café on the roof of the building opposite the salon, ordered a beer, and called Sofie, who actually answered the phone. What was going on with Sofie; was she having cold feet or what? The woman was just too receptive to being lured to a new location where she could be bottled without interference. Setting that up should have been at the forefront of Thea's mind, but, watching as Sofie and Polly's friends left the building in nonplussed dribs and drabs, looking very much like a search party unsure of what they sought, Thea ended up asking if Hero was OK. She crumpled air between her fingers as she asked;

her way of praying for forgetfulness. *May I forget the crunch of glass against skin and bone . . .*

"I don't know. I don't know where she is. I called and she didn't pick up." Sofie was choke-crying.

"Call her again. And again. Text me when you hear from her, please."

"OK. And then what? Business as usual?"

Thea watched Polly leave the salon, texting at warp speed. Her mother and Sofie's mother were hot on her heels, their grim expressions undoing all the facialists' fine work.

"You take this up with Emma, Sofie. It's going ahead unless she calls it off."

"Fuck. Can I have her number?"

Thea took out her work phone and texted Emma: Permission to give S your number?

Emma: NO. Proceed with this job as discussed!

"Sorry, Sofie, I'm not able to divulge Emma's phone number."

Sofie exited the salon and stood on the street, swiveling left, then right, before looking up at the rooftop Thea stood on. Thea took a couple of steps backward and resumed the patting of her hair. It hadn't seen any blow-dryer action. How could all the moisture be gone already? Was there something this insane heat was wanting to *say* to her, and if so, what?

"I could come back to Florizel," Sofie said. She swiped the back of her hand across her face a few times, frantically removing evidence of her tearfulness. "Hero, too. Just like before."

Thea took a swig from the beer bottle. "That might be your best bet. Failing that, see you at the airport in the morning."

The "see you in the morning" was misdirection; Thea was going to have to strike before that. She drank as slowly as she could, waiting, waiting, for Hero to reemerge from the salon. That took an hour or so . . . OK, so Hero was out, and she didn't look too bad, considering.

But the woman who waited for Hero's taxi with her . . . what was it about the way she gesticulated? Those were the gesticulations Ms. Mole had made last night. Ms. Mole last night and the un-elderly lady at the Orangery that very morning.

Once Hero had been whisked away there was nothing stopping Thea from approaching her companion and picking up where they'd left off. Well, nothing except for a premonition that this woman would tell her to fuck off, just as Ms. Mole had, and her Orangery benchmate (with deeds, if not with words). *See*, she said to herself, *see, I'm learning! Going away without being told to!*

THEA ASKED A GARDENER at the Orangery if they'd found a book on a bench, and the gardener told her they'd only just got there, and that she should ask about her book at one of the counters where you could buy tickets for St. Vitus Cathedral. The fellow at the counter wrote down the address for the city's Lost and Found Department and told her to go there.

"Have you ever handed a book in at a Lost and Found anywhere in the world?" Thea asked him.

"I have never found anything that anyone would miss," said the earnest young man at the St. Vitus Cathedral ticket counter. "But if I had, I would definitely have handed it in. And you?"

"Oh, I've stumbled across some important-looking stuff in my day. Stuff I didn't, you know, take, but didn't hand in either. I just left them."

The ticket clerk sympathized: "It's a time-consuming procedure, isn't it, handing things in. It can be hard to find out where you're meant to take them . . ."

She was sure that if he had any thoughts on this matter at all, the thoughts were that she should just buy a new copy of her book instead of wasting her time trawling an ecosystem she'd never contributed anything to. But the missing book wasn't a book that Thea could buy, so she went to the address he'd written down.

The exterior of this city's Lost and Found Department fit her notion of a boutique police station so closely that she almost didn't go in. But she overcame the antipathy, only to be handed a form and asked to leave her contact details . . .

Thea wandered out again, consulting Google Maps. It was a library she needed, not Lost and Found. And there was only one library likely to have an otherwise unobtainable book: The Klementinum. This would be her seventeenth visit, the other sixteen being readings of the Borges story "The Secret Miracle":

> . . . *God is in one of the letters on one of the pages of one of the 400,000 volumes of the Clementine. My fathers and the fathers of my fathers have sought after that letter. I've gone blind looking for it . . .*

It was the only interior so far that maintained a perfect disregard for the heat outside; she was washed through a prism of brown and black and musky gray. Her sight dimmed and her skin cooled. Fragrance polka-dotted the doorways she passed—not the smell of books, not exactly. A by-product of bookish labor, the creaking of chair legs and the cracking of spines. In a room that was like a flotation tank lined with baize, she walked up to a cubicle and spoke to the librarian standing behind the counter.

"*Paradoxical Undressing?*" he said, his glasses sliding down his exceptionally shapely nose as he entered search terms into the system. "I think we actually just received a copy."

"A new edition?"

"I doubt that. I think there was only one."

"You know the book?"

"I do. It's an interesting one for me; ninety-five percent of me was calling out to Quentin Tarantino to come and adapt this to the big screen. The other five percent was really conscious—possibly too conscious—of what comes with being a post eighty-niner. You know . . . I get to wondering: What would it be like around here if justice was a thing? I mean, what if it was more than a concept that we mostly act like we're too smart to try to live out?"

Thea stared at the librarian for such a long time that, seeming to believe that the terminology he'd used was beyond her, he began to rephrase what he'd just said, using simpler terms as he switched from Czech to English.

"No, I understood you. I'm just . . . I mean, sorry, what? The 1940s taxi dancers—theirs is a tale that gets you in your post-Communist feelings?"

The librarian's reply was tinged with hostility: "Taxi dancers? What are taxi dancers? Anyway, I think you mean a taxi *driver.*"

"No. I know what I mean, and I mean—"

"Excuse me, Ms. . . ." he waited.

"Hladíková," Thea supplied.

"Very well, Ms. Hladíková—I know and love that Borges story, too, by the way—before I fetch this book for you can we please get it clear that the novel *Paradoxical Undressing*, which takes place in December 1989, concerns a Prague taxi driver whose neighbor hires him to drive all the way to Bern, Switzerland, keeping refueling stops at the absolute minimum?"

"That's the book you're about to give me, Mr. . . . ?" She waited.

"Toàn," he supplied. "And yes, that's the book you're getting."

"What's the author's name?"

"Merlin Mwenda."

"Hmmm. And why does this taxi driver's neighbor want to go to Bern?"

"So . . . OK, I guess the author was imagining the winter of 1989 as a time when all the pieces of shit who'd somehow made it through the previous forty or fifty years finally got what was coming to them. He takes the taxi driver's neighbor as a case in point: a guy who's been an absolute pain for years. When any difficulties cropped up in the taxi driver's life, seven times out of ten this particular neighbor was at the bottom of it. The neighbor wasn't a Party bigwig, per se, but big enough to make everyone around him dance to his tune. Until the change in political climate, right? So now the way people look at this asshole has completely changed— so has the way they speak to him . . . and he can feel that sooner or later someone is going to assault him, or worse. The asshole actually hears people talking about it, outside his door, but they disperse because they can't agree on the most fitting way to execute him. He's got to get out, and he doesn't feel safe taking public transport to the train station, even. He begs the taxi driver on his knees . . . the taxi driver just goes *Ah, get up, get up*. He's not on any power trip, but he does want to get paid. That's why takes the job—it's a fare, and a big one . . . half now, half when they get to Bern. But as they drive across the city, word gets out that the asshole is escaping, and everyone who hates him but never dared show it—and it turns out that was a lot of people—they all come out to try to stop the taxi. Or to try to get the driver to crash it . . ."

"But the main character's not a Prague taxi driver for nothing, right? He knows how to get his fare?"

"The strength of the taxi driver's antihero game is just—" The librarian kissed his fingers. "But you'll see, Ms. Hladíková. And we'll talk. You will need to talk about that standoff with the pancake thrower of Holešovice. I know I did . . ."

A few minutes later, Mr. Toàn handed Thea a book that was near identical to the one she'd left behind in the Orangery that morning. She thanked him, found a desk seat in the reading room across the hall. Tuning out the murmuring of what sounded like multiple amorous couples amid the adjoining bookshelves, Thea opened the book to Chapter One and read:

Remember how uneasy all the long-haired bus and tram passengers were the summer of 2016? That was the summer no user of Prague's overground public transport system could count on arriving at their stop with their tresses unmolested. The violations were small but mighty; just enough snipped off to make your head look . . . different. Bad different. "Potential candidate for study of phrenological defects" different. These little cuts bamboozled the city's elite hairdressers, who'd cautiously snip around in a few different directions and cast appalled glances at your reflection and theirs as the attempted remedy aggravated the situation beyond repair. Then the electric razor had to be brought out. Still, it wasn't so very terrible, was it, having to start all over again—better than a poke in the eye . . . *lepší než drátem do voka, že jo . . .*

A load was taken off a lot of people's minds when the Uglifier—well, a Prague rascal isn't a Prague rascal until they've been nicknamed—was caught and taken into custody. But the suspect was released the same day; he swore on all the Bibles that it wasn't him, and proof was lacking. Yes, extra-sharp styling shears were found in the suspect's bag, along with a steel-colored curlicue freshly snipped from a nearby Babička's bun. This was how the police knew it was a real sicko they were dealing with: loose-hanging hair made some sense as a target, but what sort of person lacerates the smooth tidiness of an old lady's updo?

There were no fingerprints on the shears, though. And bystanders corroborated the suspect's tale of being body-bumped by a masked and hooded stranger who must've left the hair and the scissors in his bag.

The real Uglifier remains at large. We know who she is, and we know where you can find her. On Tuesdays and Thursdays, she's in Prague 12, at a little café called Rocking Horse Spa (loads of beanbags and wall-to-wall saltwater tanks populated with raffish seahorses) serving up the kind of iced coffee and banh mi that puts a smile on your face and keeps it there for a good long while.

On Mondays and Wednesdays she's in Dejvice, singing a hypermarket's list of daily specials into a microphone—she's in the choir's contralto section, and her voice is in perfect harmony with the spiritual succor that only shopping for essentials can offer. Overwhelmed by the miracle of needs that conform to an affordable price range, some of the shoppers join in without seeming to realize that they're singing too.

On Friday nights she's part of the night-watch patrol at the crematorium. More about that one later.

Ataraxia Pham, aka the Uglifier, works just as hard as you or I, whether it's waitressing, warbling, or watchfulness she's working at. So we can see why she wouldn't balk at Uglifying a granny's hairdo. She didn't get a sicko's thrill out of it; she was working. For the silkworms.

About those . . .

We can begin by informing you that for over a decade, Ataraxia had been saving up for something big. She'd been saving ever since she received the wages from her first three simultaneous stints of part-time employment. Twenty-one applications— three acceptances, when it was so hard to get even a single "yes"—it just seemed like the kind of luck she wanted more of. Her father pooh-poohed that. "Just take one job and get another if you need another," he told her. "The Czech Republic is just like all my cousins said it would be."

"Beautiful? Mysterious?" Ataraxia suggested.

"No . . . a small country with a lot of jobs. But you're right: a low unemployment rate *is* beautiful. Three point ninety-five percent unemployment! Lowest in Europe!" Mr. Pham kissed his fingers.

Disregarding her father's abundance mentality, Ataraxia accepted all three jobs and got quite good at remembering which uniform she was meant to be wearing, along with the when and the where of each dress code. Every now and again, a boy she was seeing gave her money to buy makeup or something (it was always very carefully posited as a sort of wellness bursary: *Hey, why not spoil yourself for once, Ataraxia*) and she added the cash to her savings, banking on the boy being too embarrassed to ask why she hadn't spent the money on making herself more attractive.

Ataraxia gave no gifts, and the gifts she was given were never seen again. Boys stopped asking her out and started joking about the mansion she'd be buying in a few years' time. At thirty-three (the age at which she became the Uglifier) Ataraxia continued to select the most economical version of everything . . . which wasn't the same as snagging the cheapest version in the short term, of course. Her priority was getting a great deal when it came to cost per use. This applied to meals too: Which ones would keep her fuller for longer? Her savings grew until she felt secure enough to make a single investment—a big one that paid near-immediate dividends—in a nightclub that rivaled the one her parents ran.

Ataraxia didn't hide this seemingly cold money-growing decision from her family, whom she shared a home with—and a heart too . . . she often visualized their closeness in that way, as four calm heads growing out of one violently lambent heart. Ataraxia, her younger sister, Phronesis, and their parents (a pair of Epicurean philosophers who'd absconded from Hanoi University posts to try Czech life) had a fairly civil discussion about the positive knock-on effect that they saw this nightlife upgrade having on Sapa Market as a whole. Ataraxia's rather disappointing input was a shrug and a remark that since she was saving up, all the extra cash would come in handy. Afterward, one by one, the other members of her family took her aside and asked what was going on with her. What was it she was saving up for? Was she in some kind of financial trouble? Was there any way they could help?

She thought for a second, and then asked her father for a Netflix Premium subscription, billable to him but administrated from her own email address. She wanted to watch some shows on the way to and from work, but she knew that any money she earmarked for that would only end up in one of her savings accounts.

Her father said OK.

He got her a couple of other subscriptions too.

"Anything for my firstborn," he said. "It's like you've arrived too early for your appointment with the present moment, and you're stuck in some kind of waiting room. Maybe while you're busy getting square-eyed you'll see something that lets you know it's OK to stop waiting for 'now' . . . "

Ataraxia and her family were right for each other. Their affinity was more than just habitual acclimatization to living together. The Phams were a team; four factors of free will, each relying on the others to cover what they had missed. Mrs. Pham addressed the items and qualities they possessed or did not possess, and the things that must or must not be permitted. She was the one most likely to say, "We can manage that," or "We don't have time for that . . ."

Mr. Pham was all about establishing and dismantling assurance: or, at least, distinguishing between it and actual knowledge with a spirited "Oh, really?"

Phronesia, Ataraxia's younger sister, had a lot of feelings that tended to arrive disguised as thoughts: she had made herself a mistress. Well . . . her married lover had some say in this matter, too, but on the whole Phronesia had been the pursuer. It was a relationship that meant they could both continue living with their families on more or less comfortable terms. But also—and this was the reasoning that surprised Ataraxia a little bit—Phronesia said she had decided to preselect a reason for the adversities that were bound to face her in life even if she didn't do what she wanted to do. She felt she could bear it all, as it could be viewed as an ongoing penalty for having fulfilled her desire at least once. Ataraxia was somehow reassured by these being feelings that had momentarily sounded like thoughts. This circling of Phronesia's romantic purgatory was laser specific; it could not be adapted for application to other scenarios . . . that was a key difference between feelings and thoughts.

As for Ataraxia . . . Ataraxia who had, according to family lore, screamed blue murder when, cradled in her father's arms, she'd been told her name and asked if she liked it . . . she was Phronesia's inverse. Or Phronesia was hers. Or both! Ataraxia was thinking her way toward . . . well, the point of her being. She saw that those around her found their answer in either the pleasure or the solace that their existence brought to other people. This seemed to center around the goods—not necessarily material goods—that they accumulated and gave away.

Ataraxia, too, wished to accumulate and to give. But not in a stable, sensible fashion, with everyday loving-kindness and charitable deeds and donations here and there. There was no way in which Ataraxia felt above that daily deepening of what it is to be a human in the world; it's just that she wasn't made that way. She was one of those for whom nothing digs deeper than peril. So she plotted an episode of catastrophic profligacy—trading absolutely everything for precisely nothing—and hoped to learn whether or not this particular iteration of altruism was her reason for being, i.e., the extraordinary thing that might not have happened if there had been no Ataraxia.

A lot of people who are happy to sponsor all manner of financially unprofitable endeavors don't want to give artists a penny. Especially the sort of artists you get nowadays. "What will you make with this money?" we ask suspiciously, and if we receive an answer, it isn't one we feel we understand. Maybe if it was a do-or-die decision between giving money to an artist or giving it to a drug addict who's just shared their full shopping list, we'd manage to choose the artist without feeling as if we're siding with some representative of the Void. Maybe . . .

At any rate—yes, Ataraxia Pham was saving up for the least trustworthy cause possible: art. She'd give up her stash when the right artist crossed her path. She didn't look around for artists—gallery visits would eat up time and money that had to go toward the aforementioned savings. Ataraxia felt she had no choice but to assume that when she was ready (that is, if or when she was no longer able to keep up all this working to save rather than working to live), that was when *the* artist, her artist, would appear to ask for everything she had.

It didn't quite occur that way. Ataraxia's artist first made himself known to her while she was on her way to her night shift at the crematorium. Settling into a bus seat for a nice wildlife documentary session, she opened one of her TV apps to find that her RESUME WATCHING panel was a long line of shows that she would never have pressed play on even by accident. True crime documentaries and reality shows. So Ataraxia's account had been hacked; it happened to everybody sooner or later. Her passwords weren't as unguessable as she'd assumed.

But the more she thought about it, something about this violation—the peculiarly well-mannered limitation of its scope, perhaps—didn't seem so humdrum after all. She changed all her passwords for all her accounts, and changed her email password, too, just to be sure. Most of these changes were made after work: Ataraxia couldn't be on her phone at the crematorium, where she and her patrol partner walked the simple lines that led from the ceremonial halls to the refrigerated storage, and on to the preparation suite with its weighing scale and the marble slabs that appeared to blush in the light. They checked the cremation chambers, too, and the furnace room. And when they finished their round they checked again. They had to keep checking, but in all these years nothing had been amiss so far. Ataraxia's patrol partner said this must mean they were doing a good job; the dead felt well protected, and so they didn't bother making a scene. Ataraxia couldn't tell if he meant what he was saying—the only thing her patrol partner ever seemed somewhat in earnest about were the endless improvements he made or considered making to his cottage in the countryside. ("A million miles away from this shithole, thank God," he'd say.) Which tile would she say was more . . . him? This one or this one? etc. Even then, it seemed to Ataraxia that those who spoke only Czech always seemed to reserve the option of denying their passion. Not out of fear, but because they knew that the faithful sometimes had to forgo laughter, and that wasn't something they ever wanted to do. Ataraxia thought (but didn't say) that there was only calm at the crematorium because the living knew there was nothing here for them.

On the bus home, Ataraxia reopened the TV app she'd most recently changed the password for—a different one from the one she'd opened on the way to work. She found that a new user profile had been added in the ten minutes or so between her changing the password and reopening the app—

Politesse again: Gunzelin (that was the name on the new user profile) seemed to be signaling that though he had no intention of discontinuing use of her accounts, their divergent tastes didn't have to be an issue: he'd have his viewing section and she'd have hers. Teeth gritted and heart pounding, Ataraxia changed her password once more—but why hadn't this Gunzelin changed it already?—logged out again . . . and repeated this over the course of the following day. Whenever she got a moment alone with her phone, she was busy changing passwords, all of which Gunzelin guessed.

The next morning, tired, perhaps, of taunting her with this omniscience, Gunzelin sent Ataraxia an email. From her own email address.

Want to hear something wild? "Ataraxia Pham" wrote to Ataraxia Pham. My last art project was called **What's the Password?** I created a character—a woman who's very private— kind of like you, maybe. Well, not maybe. Obviously. I'm not sure which of us lacks originality here . . . all I know is that I created a character who's just like you, Ms. Pham. A character who doesn't have any major secrets but there isn't really anything she wants to tell anyone either. I got a friend to play her and filmed her in various scenarios: she'd refuse to give out any information at all until the person requesting interaction with her gave the correct password.

All the passwords I made up for this character—extra random passwords, I thought at the time, just waves of numbers and letters, really—every single one of them are passwords you use.

I'm finding this really crazy, Ataraxia.

I'd been struggling to move on from that password project. As you can tell, since I've been testing the passwords out in the (un)real world.

But seriously—for months I've been feeling something like heartbreak. Was I in love when I was working on that thing? If so, what with? God, I don't know, I'll think about it later. Yeah, boo hoo, life's tough for us sensitive ones!

Would you think about helping me move on? I have an idea and some silkworm eggs but I'll need the right space to hatch them in, I'll need bushels of mulberry leaves from the Central

Bohemian Highlands, I'll need moral support and who knows what else.

Just so you know: this is no seduction attempt. Quite aside from my preference for masculinity, even I understand that hacking your accounts would be a bad start.

Gunze lin Suchý

Ataraxia replied immediately:

When can we meet?

Two evenings later, at the Church of Our Lady Victorious and the Infant Jesus, the pair stood before the child who held the orb of the world in his unsullied hand. They examined every doting stitch of his garb as best they could through the glass case, and they could barely guess at the work and resources that had gone into just one of the Holy Infant's robes. Their beauty—the fineness of their texture and hue—was the kind Ataraxia dreamed of; it took and held everything that had been given to it. To her this labyrinth of fabric was just like the inner mass of those figs that absorb the wasps that pollinate them.

Gunzelin showed her sketches he'd begun since writing to her. He would hatch silkworms, draw silk from them, dye the yarn, and learn to weave with it—they would learn together, he told her, fingers darting, sinking, flicking their way across a manual loom that only he could see—and then he would sew outfits for a profane Infant. Brocade booties and taffeta tracksuits for the brat of all brats.

OK, Ataraxia thought. Sacrilegious as he was (Praguer as he was), Gunzelin was the something big Ataraxia had been saving for: he was her artist. Her savings were at the ready. She mobilized them over the weeks that followed. There were crateloads of fresh mulberry leaves to be paid for and couriered in; the rest of her patrol team at the crematorium had to be paid for their silence: "Seven weeks, just seven weeks—eight at the most," Gunzelin told them, showing them the silkworm eggs. At first glance they looked like blanched lentils, but there was something precious, something venerable, in the brittle balance of their form. The crematorium had the cold air the eggs needed, and it provided the humidity they needed too. This house of the dead was the silkworms' mother, and Gunzelin Suchý was their father. Quite a few of Ataraxia's fellow security guards said they wouldn't take any of the money she offered; they were happy to keep quiet about this out of respect for the daydreams these eggs induced. But Ataraxia didn't relent: the payments were about implicating them in this project, making it their project too, for better or for worse.

When the silkworms hatched, Gunzelin spread mulberry leaves all over himself at feeding time; the worms lay on the leaves, munching contentedly.

The worms closest to the artist's head acquired a taste for his hair . . .

. . . they ate it all, and then they ate all of Ataraxia's . . .

. . . and then the worms went off their other food, the very expensive mulberry leaves that Ataraxia was having brought in from the Highlands.

So Ataraxia had to find them more hair. She had to. She went out with the styling shears and brought back the choicest tidbits. It surprised her—maybe also pained her a little—when she heard her nickname. The uglification of the hair donors was wholly unintended. Was she doing the right thing? Could this really lead to . . . art? Gunzelin had begun to say he wasn't sure that the silk from silkworms who ate hair was going to be up to the Holy Infant's standards.

Really he was warning her that he wasn't going to be able to carry out his original plan. How could he harm the silkworms? He wasn't that kind of father. He read poetry to his children:

"All right, it's time for a bit of Vrchlický . . . listen to this one, kids:

Za trochu lásky šel bych světa kraj
šel s hlavou odkrytou a šel bych bosý
šel v ledu—ale v duši věčný máj,
šel vichřicí—však slyšel zpívat kosy,
šel pouští—a měl v srdci perly rosy.
Za trochu lásky šel bych světa kraj,
jak ten, kdo zpívá u dveří a prosí.

Or:

For a little love I'd go to the ends of this earth
I'd go bareheaded and barefoot
In January—with May forever in my soul,
I'd pass through hurricanes—and hear the blackbirds'
    song,
I'd pass through the desert—with pearly dew at heart.
For a little love I'd go to the ends of this earth,
Like those who sing at doorways and beg.

"Wouldn't we all, eh?" Atraxia muttered afterward. "Wouldn't we all?"

And she saw to it that his silkworms—their silkworms, really—were kept fed until they cocooned. That's why it's not so scary that the Uglifier is still at large; she only needed to do what she did for those three weeks when the silk moths (that unrepeatable eddy of spectral lace that hatched more or less en masse from hundreds of cocoons) were still moody little worms who wouldn't eat their greens.

That's all you're getting: now begone.

Begone, I said.

10.

"C losing time," the librarian whispered (loudly). He took a seat at the empty desk beside Dorothea Gilmartin's chair, and he held out his hand out for *Paradoxical Undressing*: "I'll hold on to it for you."

She laughed at him as she returned the book to his keeping. "You haven't read this book," she whispered back.

"No, YOU haven't read it," said Mr. Toàn. He pressed the book to his stomach and folded his arms over it, projecting mother-hen energy.

Now it was Thea who switched to English: "No, YOU, you shameless scallywag."

He retorted: "No, YOU'RE the one who hasn't read it! Do you even read, bro?"

"I've literally just been sitting here with my face in this book, 'bro,' and an account of a high-octane taxi driving mission it is not. It's not the book I lost earlier today, either. Here's what I really want to know, though: Why would you tell me you'd read this book, and why would you give me such an involved summary of it, when you could've just handed the thing over and gone about the rest of your busy day?"

"But I'm telling you, I have read it. None of my friends have, or want to, and it felt good to talk about it for a minute or two, all right? I thought I might never get another chance . . ."

"Open the book, Mr. Toàn, read the first line aloud and then look me in the eye and tell me that this is the book you read."

"Right now?"

"Right now."

Mr. Toàn opened the book, took a deep breath, and read: "Er—*Chapter One: Very early one morning on the Gobi-Manchurian steppe, Kublai Khan went walking alone with hopes of clearing his head.* What?? No, this isn't—"

Thea liked the librarian's reading voice—that or the alarm she heard in it. "Let's hear a bit more, if you don't mind."

He nodded:

> Before long he encountered a city where no such city ought to have been. The city itself seemed to realize its impropriety. Blown along by a mild, yet stalwart gust of air, it made the greatest of haste across the plain, appearing to hope that if it moved fast enough it could evade comment. But this was not a sight the Khan could forget or ignore. This was the longest longboat he'd ever seen, sailing across the grassland as if earth were water. Each boat dweller was blindfolded, from the very eldest to the youngest. Before the Khan's astonished eyes, livestock was reared, meals prepared and served, fabric woven and laundered, pottery spun and public debates held and recorded—and it was all done blindfold.

Running alongside the longboat, the mighty ruler cried, "Stop, or at least slow down, and tell me where I am—I mean, where you are. Where we are. Is this still the East?"

One of the boat city's astronomers laid down her planisphere, got to her feet, and began: "Most magnificent of all Majesties! Even as my people feast upon the august tones of your voice, we strive to be worthy of this largesse. Oh, peerless regent, you govern the vastest spaces of this world. You are the supreme leader of innumerable peoples, you—"

"Yes, yes. I know," said the Khan. "But where are we situated at present?"

"Unparalleled Sovereign, the lowly mortals before you have been asked this question many times. Our reply has either been ignored or outright corrected by our questioners. But you—you know all! In short: we are wherever you say we are. We beseech you to declare our location first; once you have spoken we will finally understand how to answer."

The emperor was disturbed by the degree of passive aggression with which he'd just been addressed; shouldn't he exert some discipline here? Even as he considered the implications of nonretaliation, he intuited that this spokesastronomer both dreaded and wished for his wrath. That settled it; he would not perform for her. Besides, he was Kublai Khan, divine thought burned in him; there was no need to be shy about thinking aloud.

"This is an Eastern vision," the Khan declared. What else could it be . . . ?

The boat people made no dissenting motions; they kept their heads perfectly still. Why did he now feel that he'd blundered? He realized he was waiting for those blindfolded heads to nod, and that they weren't going to.

The Khan changed tack: "I've reached the West, then. It wasn't as difficult as everybody keeps saying it is. But then all things are possible for those of my bloodline."

The silence of the blindfolded ones grew even more contemplative—and Kublai Khan was not fated to hear it broken . . . he could not keep pace with the longboat, and he had to let it glide onward.

A few days later, feeling that he must either express his concerns or go mad, the monarch mentioned this incident to one of his own astronomers, who told him that what he'd seen was a lunar phenomenon called "Praha." Not a terrestrial matter, then . . . this was all the Khan needed to hear; he motioned for his physician to close the topic. He had other plans. Big ones. Shengdu awaited.

The librarian scratched his head, tossed pages this way and that, soundlessly read a little from the middle of the book and then a few lines from the last page, then gave Thea a saucer-eyed stare.

"Oh, but . . . this must be a publisher's prank, or a printing error. They've printed different books and accidentally put the same cover on," he said, after a moment or two. "Anyway . . . this is what I meant to tell you—some people were here looking for you."

Thea pointed at herself, silently asking: *Me??*

"They were showing both staff and readers a photo of you . . . it looked like one of those dingy ones they make you take at passport control sometimes. You weren't blond in the photo, but aside from that it was unmistakably you."

"And who were they, do you know?"

"There were three of them. One of them was in full Krtek costume, one of them had all this stage makeup on, and the third . . . the third was a raven-haired beauty . . ."

"High ponytail, eyes like fig halvah and smile like a saber?"

"Yeah!" So, the woman Thea had seen putting Hero into a taxi.

And—what, appearing in tandem with Ms. Mole and the lady in the red tracksuit was meant to press the point that they were different people? Somehow it wasn't doing that for Thea. It was a little too on the nose.

"I wasn't sure what tone to take with the first two . . . I mean, I wasn't sure if they were having a laugh, or if this was actually legit, or what," the librarian continued. "But they had these belts on, and very real-looking handcuffs hanging from the belt. Are you"—he looked down at the tabletop as he selected his next words—"Are you—ah, I mean . . . are your papers not in order?"

"I thought they were, but perhaps not. Then again, maybe that's exactly what these people want; they're pro-insecurity. Did they tell you I'm not here legally, Mr. Toàn?"

"You can call me Vinh," he said, transferring to informal address.

"And you can call me Jaromíra."

"No, I don't think I will call you that, Dorothea Gilmartin."

She sighed. "Well. Thanks for not telling them we spoke, anyway. They've left, I take it?"

"Yes. But they had a message for you. They said that Florizel is not a name that just anybody can pretend to. They said I should tell you that you and your friends are not the Prince of Bohemia—they are."

"Oh yes? Anything else?"

"No, that was it."

Thea swallowed hard, but tried to look coolly amused. Vinh rose from his seat and gave her a featherlight tap on the shoulder with the book in his hand.

"Oh, is this your first time getting summarily rebuffed by some unfathomable Bureau? I would suggest that you don't get accustomed to that. Outsphinx 'em! That's how Praguers handle such things, right? We wouldn't still be here otherwise. Now—I have to get home myself."

If that trio could come to the Klementinum asking after her, they could pay similar visits to her hotel throughout the night and morning until they caught her and double-handcuffed her or whatever it was they had in mind. "Could I . . . sleep here?" she asked.

Vinh announced that he had a better idea. "The shortcut tunnel . . ."

The librarian led her down so many staircases that she lost all understanding of what floor they were on—three?—five? Good. Both her phones were quiet now; no signal, no more messages. This was how Thea wanted to be in and with this city whose name was said to mean "threshold"; she wanted to sink into it so profoundly that Ms. Mole and company would never be able to get her out. She thanked Vinh for showing her this way beneath the below. The darkness was tensile where they were, and tapestries of dust hung in its many alcoves.

"You've gone above and beyond your librarian duties, Vinh. I owe you one."

"Oh, *není zač*," Vinh said. "I'm the one who owed you, for letting me go on about *Paradoxical Undressing*. Aha . . . here we are . . ."

Vinh halted at an iron-planked, copper-hinged door, unlocked it, and showed her into a cellar that might have been musty if there'd been enough room for mustiness to circulate. The cellar's only occupant was a stone whale. It lay on its belly and looked up—straight up at the moon, she imagined. Vinh threw open a smaller door behind the shingled tail and shone his flashlight into the shortcut tunnel he'd spoken of. It led to a trapdoor on Petřín Hill; he'd made use of it himself in order to spring a romantic surprise on his girlfriend on May Day, the Day of Love. It was quite a long walk in murky conditions, though—he hadn't accounted for that, nor for the fact that if you were taller than four foot seven you had to walk slightly hunched over and scramble over the occasional mound of debris that marked the spots where the tunnel was crumbling from above as well as from below. But then you popped up with a rainbow of roses hovering just a few steps away . . .

"Anyway, it's so much drier these days . . . you could sleep in there if not being disturbed by the No Bureau is your priority. Have you got enough phone battery?"

"Yeah, I reckon so," Thea said. "Goodnight, Vinh."

"Goodnight," he said. He didn't close the tunnel door on her, and the difference that made was mainly psychological (after five minutes the gloom of the open doorway was swallowed up by the far greater blackness of the tunnel), but she kept thinking: *I can go back if I want to, I can come out of the tunnel and into that room and mount steps until I'm walking around under the light of the moon that stone whale had its eyes aimed at.* She didn't do any physical looking back; all that returning only happened in her mind. Thea bowed her head, breathed deeply, and trained her light on her feet. She watched her feet. And tried to breathe without listening to her breathing.

The shadows ahead of her were so firm in outline . . . she almost didn't want to cast light on them, in case they were fed by it. These couldn't be the piles of debris Vinh had mentioned; they were altogether the wrong shape for that. More statues? She raised her phone and brought the flashlight beam beating down on the silhouettes. Which were more than mere silhouettes. It was the trio Vinh had just dubbed the No Bureau: Ms. Mole, the un-elderly lady in the red tracksuit and the ponytailed beautician. Ms. Mole was in front, with the un-elderly lady, and Ponytail behind her. The impression of their being somehow light-activated was probably just one they were putting on to disconcert her, but it was effective. Having been authenticated by lantern beam, they blinked, implemented a few neck stretches, and broke out into chatter among themselves:

"Good old Vinh."

"Knew we could rely on Vinh to send her straight into our clutches!"

"I was so worried we'd be left standing here all night while she just went and smacked her friends around again . . ."

Dizzy, nonplussed, tiring of keeping her head low but not wanting to sit at their feet in order to raise it, Thea went for a half measure, squatting with her back against the tunnel wall. After about ten seconds this began to feel like Pilates, and she just let herself drop into the sludge.

"Just let me stay," she whimpered. "Why not go and harass some overzealous bachelor party? Let me stay. Come on. Please. I'll be good."

"We'd be imbeciles if we actually believed you, Thea. Besides, it's not about being good, bad, wanted, not wanted, liked, disliked, or any of those things," Ms. Mole said. "This simply isn't a place for you, and you've got to go. You can't say you didn't have fair warning, Dorothea. I tried with you, didn't I?"

"That's a lie. You never gave me a chance."

The crayoned crone gave Thea a thumbs-down.

"Don't let her make you feel bad," Ponytail said to Ms. Mole. "We know you tried. You gave her a parting gift; she took it and didn't . . . well, depart . . ."

"Hang on, hang on, hang on—if I give the parting gift back, I can stay? If I find the book—"

"No," said Ms. Mole. "You're going. Look at the way you came here, Dorothea Gilmartin. You didn't come in like a person who can stay."

"It might've been different if one of the first things you'd done was go to your mother in Vinohrady," Ponytail said.

"Vinohrady? That's not where my mother is. By the way—why are you giving me shit about this, whoever you are? Are you a Dagmar Dlouhá fan? A fan of the Progress Girl series?"

The No Bureau bent toward her and jeered as they jostled Thea with their shoulders; it was obvious that they felt no reluctance about being bullies. They didn't have to include this bit, they just wanted to. She looked up into their faces. Ms. Mole's was the only one that was venom-free, but then the face of Krtek is always encouraging. Part of the secret of the cartoon mole's success is the way his grin keeps saying *Hey you, you're young and strong, you can still do it, you can make the world a better place today.* Thea kicked Ms. Mole's shin. Not hard; it was just a starter kick.

Ms. Mole jumped back. Not without a lecture, though: "That's not where my mother is," she said. "Sorry, but the cemetery at Vinohrady is exactly where your mother's ashes are interred. It's a fact that I'm very sorry about—nevertheless it is a fact. Why don't you take a good look at yourself? I mean, what are you doing? You're meant to be going on an emotional journey here, woman. But instead of paying your respects at the cemetery, you give your all to persecuting your friends . . ."

"They're not my friends," Thea said. "If you know anything about the three of us, then you know they had it coming to them. But look—I regret hurting Hero. That I never wanted to do."

"Oh yeah? What makes you say so?" the ponytailed beautician asked, with a look of limitless skepticism.

Thea got to her feet—slowly, with her hands up; she was showing them it wasn't necessary to even think about making use of the handcuffs that swung from their belts. "I'll tell you on the way to Petřín, OK?"

"Who says we're going to Petřín?" said Ms. Mole.

"Well, that's where I was going, and you were in the way. We could go back to the Klementinum, whatever, it's up to you . . ."

With a curt and authoritative nod, the lady in the red tracksuit turned on her heel and led them forward, to Petřín. She also grabbed Thea's phone, to light the way.

This is the order they walked in:

Red tracksuit

Thea

Ponytail

Ms. Mole

Ponytail poked Thea in the back: "So you've got a thing for the Heroine?"

Deciding that she must be referring to Hero, Thea replied: "In a manner of speaking. I need her."

"What for?"

"You know in spy stories, when the spy's cornered and knows

they can't withstand torture so they unstick this little pill from behind their earlobe . . . ?"

"So your friend . . . is your cyanide pill. What a lovely thought."

"Improve your listening skills, Ponytail: she ain't my friend."

Ponytail answered calmly: "Yes, so you said. You're an arrogant one, thinking that's something you can decide for her."

Was this supposed to be the part where Thea asked what Hero had said about her? Fuck that; she didn't want to know.

She stuck with her side of the story: "That woman—Hero Tojosoa—she makes stories untrue. It's havoc she plays a really fucking deliberate part in. And then she's like: What? No, that was an accident. Or—when she's feeling especially cruel, I guess, she's like: No, you did all that . . . it was you."

"Our deepest sympathies," said Ms. Mole. "We know someone like that."

"Wechsler," said Ponytail.

"Yeah," said Ms Mole. "The Wechsler."

A long exhalation from all three of Thea's companions; she might have found it informative to see their faces just then, but all she could half see was the back of Red Tracksuit's grizzled yet immaculately parted head of hair.

"And you'd hurt your . . . er, this Wechsler?" Thea asked. "Or not?"

Nobody answered her.

March, march, march, and then Ponytail said she wanted to know how Thea had found out that Hero made stories untrue. Did she learn this by talking with her for a long time, or from befriending her, working with her, living with her, what?

"None of those; that's how I know that what she does is

deliberate. I mean, she can choose not to do it, and mostly she does. But when she splurges . . . well, I learned that from book she wrote. *Faiblesse*. It's all in there—what she did to Nadezhda Miteva and Gaspar Azzouz."

"Hero made the stories of Nadezhda Miteva and Gaspar Azzouz untrue?"

"In Nadezhda's case, not really . . . or . . . actually, maybe? I don't know. What's salient here is that that lady died of what Hero did to her. She lady-killed herself a few months after the book came out, and left an annotated copy as a kind of suicide note. People were boycotting the book because of that, which is how it came to my attention, I guess. Gaspar survived a lot longer, for some reason, but in the end . . . it was just too crazy. Listen: I read about the boycott, and then I read about the book, and I just didn't get how being written about could have driven this Nadezhda to her death. I used to be all Jane Eyre about that kind of thing: you are the only person who actually knows who you are, so everyone else can and will just say whatever they're gonna say about you, right?"

"Uh-oh," said Ms. Mole.

"Ha ha. Well . . . in this book *Faiblesse*, 'Dorothea Gilmartin' meets two liars and exposes not only their lies, but the reasons they give her for telling them. Which are also lies, I guess. This leads to three allegations: the first, that nothing anybody says about themselves can be trusted because nobody knows who the fuck they actually are; the second, that everybody is aware of the first fact but doesn't know what to do about it so prefer to keep lying their heads off until the bitter end; and the third, that some people—people like Nadezhda and Gaspar—can be fed lies that they not only accept into themselves but present as themselves."

"Hero did that to both of them?"

"Not to Nadezhda, no—that had already been other people's doing. But Hero had been chatting with Nadezhda and realized: huh, this lady is lying the way Gaspar lies. Of course, Hero knew all about Gaspar's lies because she'd fed them to him. He was this former soldier whose Roma friends were closer to him than the people who called themselves his family—parents, wife, kids, those people. He spent most of this time on this Roma settlement in the Loire Valley, and he got deported along with his friends. A brown guy, who speaks Romani, hangs out with Roma, and says he doesn't have identity papers—he just got put straight onto a flight to Bulgaria along with the rest of the settlement. Hero had decided to spend a few days of her paid leave pursuing this story: What happened when the Loire Valley clique arrived in Stara Zagora?"

Almost everybody on the flight swore that as soon as the plane touched down in Sofia they'd be returning to France overland—they didn't care how long it took, they were going back. To piss off the authorities, if for no other reason.

Gaspar Azzouz had other plans in mind. He kept saying that he, for one, was OK with starting over. Later, looking into the probable reasons for his notably nonhonorable discharge from the military, and interviewing people who lived around the military base on Reunion Island where he'd been stationed (people who either froze or tensed prominent veins when shown his image), his eager absorption of the new life story Hero told him made sense. His old story was riddled with chapters he dared not recite. He did begin factually, but he faltered a lot, and Hero suddenly felt so much stronger than him that she told him that he was Roma, born and bred. Wasn't he? She told him where his family had settled before moving on to the French village he was now being deported from; she told him his parents had died, and that he had a younger brother who was always getting into trouble, and an older brother who was always ready to take the fall for him and their younger brother. She told him this life as if guessing it: "It's like this, isn't it?" And to everything she said, he replied: "Yes, are we soul mates? It's like you're psychic . . . how do you know me so well . . ."

They arrived in Sofia, and as promised, the majority immediately began to make their arrangements for the much longer, slower half of a round trip. But Gaspar and a few others traveled on to a mountain village, and Hero went with them, taking note of how Gaspar's traveling companions, all of whom had been Loire Valley acquaintances rather than intimate friends, began referring to the brothers Hero had told Gaspar she had (among other little details . . .).

As expected, the Loire Valley transplants weren't exactly welcomed with open arms; the established villagers were neutral at best. The least neighborly made their feelings known with fists and boots—there were clashes along the bucolic lanes, reciprocal blows delivered later on, there were town hall meetings and petitions, and Hero recorded as much of these events as she could. A great deal of her information came from Nadezhda Miteva, whose clinginess her fellow villagers cited as the reason for their dislike of her. Nadezdha was seemingly estranged from her grown children, who worked in Sofia. (These children were, of course, one of Nadezhda Miteva's lies—a neighbor had said to her inquiringly, "Won't your children ever visit?" and in an instant it had come to Nadezhda that she had raised selfish children who never checked up on her health.) Her reports on what her neighbors and their families said and did with regard to the new Romani villagers usually held up . . . she probably made sure her information was good so that the journalist from France would keep coming back to chat with her. For a time, Hero's interest in Nadezhda made her interesting to those who would never usually have made time for her; Nadezhda was invited to dinners—she wore her nicest jewelry in honor of such occasions—and she received visitors who saw that she was really quite comfortably off. She had been so lonely, but with her combination of truth about other people and lies about herself, she'd triumphed at last.

The night that Nadezhda Miteva was robbed and beaten, the quality of her information tanked. She told Hero that Gaspar Azzouz had done it. Hero asked her more details, and listened to three or four renditions of a story that Nadezhda had told herself to tell. Trying to think as she thought Nadezhda might be thinking, that this story was going to turn Nadezhda's real attackers into her friends and well-wishers—people who would laud her for saying what needed to be said in order to have the Roma removed from their village. Gaspar, innocent of the crime, but implicated by testimony from Nadezhda and others as well as planted evidence (planted God knew how, but everybody knows that villages are bloody terrifying places), was imprisoned. After that, Ms. Hero Tojosoa sat herself down to write *Faiblesse*, which began:

> Gaspar Azzouz has been wrongly imprisoned, and yet I cannot say that it would be right—or even possible—to release him from the cage he has built with his own hands . . .

Red Tracksuit pushed the trapdoor open and Thea clambered out into the grassy twilight, followed by Ponytail and Ms. Mole. Ponytail poked Thea in the back again.

"No more of this poking, please, Ponytail."

"I just wanted to be sure of what you're saying. You want to keep what was done to Nadezhda and Gaspar in reserve as some kind of contingency plan? Are there really that many things in your life you wish were untrue?"

"Yes."

Ms. Mole plucked a cloth square from her belt loop and began to unfold it.

"Have you ever considered believing Hero when she says she didn't cause what happened to them?"

The cloth square unfolded and unfolded and unfolded until it was the size of a tablecloth; Ms. Mole shook it out and gestured to Thea and the others to come and sit down with her. Thea did, warily, saying as she did so: "So you're taking the same line as her, that it was all accidental, or that they were the ones who did it?"

Ms. Mole nodded. "Precisely. What you've told us doesn't sound anything like what our Wechsler does. It was a link I was wrong to make."

Red Tracksuit pulled a thermos basket out of the bushes and unloaded three Tupperware boxes.

"Potato salad challenge," Ponytail said, removing the box lids and handing her a fork.

"We've decided to give you a chance after all. One of these potato salads was made by Viennese hands, another by Warsawian hands, and the third by Prague hands," Ms. Mole informed Thea. "If you correctly identify the Prague potato salad, you can stay."

Thea waited to be blindfolded. That didn't happen. She looked at Ponytail, who said: "You can look, smell, roll the mixture around in your fingers, whatever you need to make the connection, but get going, please. We haven't got all night."

The first potato salad was blatantly Viennese—tangy, herb fes-tooned, and mayonnaise-free . . . designed to cut sausage grease and the guilty sensations it left behind. The second was sweet and sour, oozed albescent white, and had a wondrous fluffiness to it. The third was quite a bit sweeter than it was sour, the potatoes were pebbly, and it was the kind of salad that could be a meal at a pinch. There weren't just eggs in there, there were carrots, swedes, and pickles too—

"This one. This is Prague potato salad," Thea said, and left her fork standing up in it.

"Wrong," Ms. Mole said, packing up all the paraphernalia. "It was the second one. I made that myself, then we took the eggs and vegetables out of it and added them to the third one. Now: downhill we go. You won't try to run, will you?"

"No," said Thea. "Fair's fair, I guess."

At the base of the hill, the No Bureau escorted her to a car parked on a side street. She sat in the back with her suitcase on her knees—they must have collected it from her hotel—and Red Tracksuit beside her. Ponytail was driving.

"Where to now?" Thea asked. "The airport?"

Ponytail looked at her in the rearview mirror. "You don't have to leave the country, Dorothea. Just Prague. We're taking you to Tábor. You should love it there, since you like tunnels so much."

Ms. Mole tried to lighten the mood: "Yeah, forget about this place, it's really not what you think it is. Take a nap, we'll be in your new city in two hours max . . ."

Dorothea Gilmartin did take the suggested nap, but she also made a pledge to herself that she'd take the train back to Prague in the morning. She'd repeat this until they gave up.

11.

T HE FIRST GIFT that turned out to be for both of them was the dress with bells for buttons; the shepherdess wouldn't take it back. The bells caroled when Hero drew her Wendell into her arms. When they kissed, glad canticles rang out, and there was a duet of sorts . . . a tumbling song of cries and whispers as the couple rejoiced each other (wet lips, slick knuckles, microdetonations in every hollow, pulse-quaking plunges that slammed them against the floorboards, shivers that swayed them like blossoms in breeze . . .)

These all but irresistible invitations to climax were interrupted by rapping at the door. Not just once; at frequent intervals. The first few times, Wendell said, "I'll go."

He ambled over to the door wearing their wedding dress as one would a housecoat, only back to front, so that his back and buttocks were all ajingle. He returned with the components of a feast: a couple of bottles of Cava propped up in buckets of ice, and a trio of platters piled high with melt-in-the-mouth lusciousness that he was somewhat cagey about, saying things like, "Let's just call it well-seasoned mystery meat," until, seeing that Hero had tasted and liked everything he'd brought, he gave in: "Those are roasted butterflies on skewers, that's scorpion ceviche, these chlebíčky are topped with . . . ah . . ."

Guessing that he'd saved the least palatable proposition for last, Hero dipped her finger in the velvety cream, crowned her left nipple with its riches, and melted clean away as Wendell's lips closed around both cream and point of delirium. "Yes," he said, once he'd fed her some more in a similar fashion, "this is hissing cockroach mousse . . ."

"And is this your everyday diet, or just for special occasions?"

"I do not accept any impudence from insects," Wendell said, seemingly unaware that this wasn't really an answer. "I simply don't care for it."

He told her he'd noticed various insects' flagrant crossing of lines when it came to participating in human life, and he was almost certain that he knew what their boldness was based on: an assumption that having the life squashed out of them was the worst that could happen. Accepting the body of another into one's own is so frequently understood as a gesture of the greatest love, isn't it . . . most insects never dream that those they encroach upon could think of doing such a thing. "They are, of course, forgetting their nutritional value and the fact that, when nicely prepared, they don't taste half bad," he concluded.

Hero proposed a toast: "Here's to being bigger and sneakier than insects."

"For now," Wendell Wechsler said, rattling his glass against hers. "I'm trying to remember what year it was—I mean, will be—the Revolt of the Fleas. Twenty ninety-three or thereabouts, I think. As usual, people see it coming from a long way off. They talk about the Revolt, they think about it, they write about it, they sing about it, create video installations about it, and yet when it arrives, they still aren't ready."

He tutted, and Hero grabbed his wrist: "What?"

"What," Wendell asked, transferring his glass to his other hand and completing the sipping action she'd just prevented.

"What was that you just said, Wendell, about the Revolt of the Fleas?"

"Hero: I'm not the type to raise such topics. The main thing is that your taste buds are not opposed to bug puree—that's the last remark I remember making."

It was true that the flavor of the mousse agreed with her—edamame crossed with lobster, a few short bursts of dill. But it was also possible that Wendell's kisses were performing feats of molecular gastronomics. *His mouth is sweetest drink* . . .

A fourth knock sounded at the bedroom door. A weightier knock than the precursors for the food and drink—it bore enough of a resemblance to the sound of the Basilica doors taking a walloping for Hero to jump up and lay hands on a Cava bottle to swing if she had to. Wendell didn't appear to be worried, but it was notable that he didn't get out of bed this time.

There was no second knock, so she decided it was her turn to put on their wedding dress and investigate. Back to front, just like Wendell. She whipped the door open to confront the fully illuminated corridor, all just as usual, with the addition of two silver platters. A slab of cake lay on the first platter, along with two

Neptunian-looking forks—tiny tritons that flashed silver beams as they were raised and set down. The second platter held a grinning heap of ivory pearls (pearls always looked to her like fangs that had been polished until they were blunt) and a pair of purple silk gloves.

"Was it the same when the other courses arrived?" she asked, bringing the trays in, donning the gloves, and placing her hands on her hips. Wendell nodded: "Room service."

Hero didn't believe him, exactly (Mr. Surname didn't strike her as the sort of bed-and-breakfast owner who'd indulge his guests in this way), but she rotated her wrist joints in the gloves and let it go. Everything felt more supple through silk. She brought Wendell along this conduit, too, her caresses persisting until he climaxed. Then, attempting to choose between pearls and cake and deciding on both at once, they unwound the string of pearls and, finding that it ran all around the room, from corner to corner, they made a skipping rope of it and jumped in between fluffy forkfuls of cake. Hearing the honeyed tumult of bells as they rose, and the staccato thud of pearls falling around their feet as they landed: "I remember this sound . . ." Wendell peeled a quince slice from the top of the cake, pleating it with his fork as he reminisced: "This is rain. Thinning the heat, rolling down tarpaulins, bouncing off flagstones—oh, rain."

"Hold on . . ."

Wiping sweat from her palms before wrapping sections of rope around them, Hero adorned her Wendell with pearls. "Say 'stop' as soon as you feel bridal, OK?" With the first loop, she held his hair away from his face so that he couldn't hide a single expression from her. Watching as the nacre rippled around his throat, dropped down his chest and stomach, and cascaded to his feet, she thought that he felt bridelike quite some time before he announced it. But at last even he had had his fill of the winding shell of splendor; abruptly shedding all the pearls, the bridal groom switched off the overhead light and crashed down among pillows, pulling her with him.

"Wendell," she said. Unnecessarily; they were already very close, and he was looking into her eyes. Even now there was something sidelong about Wendell's gaze. This man was sidelong always, his features both hawkish and lamblike: chiseled, but tenderly so. This effect had something to do with the way Hero was placed in relation to him. When they looked at each other, she thought this was how it might be if, having just skimmed the skin of a stream, it was possible for a stone to regard the most distinct ripple that arose. Or for the ripple to regard the stone . . . with perfect trust and equally absolute self-possession.

The night was a very dark blue, a dewberry stain on a black napkin. The main points of light in the room were two lamps, and their phones, which lay side by side as they shone with message notifications. They'd both changed their phone lock screens to a photo of them on either side of the rococo wavelets of the reliquary that displays St. Valentine's shoulder bone. In this photo the couple are forming love hearts with their fingers. Or rather, Wendell is demonstrating the effortless cuteness of the pose while Hero, watching him as if he's a how-to video, is making a highly unnatural imitation.

Now her left arm was beneath his head and his right arm embraced her. "Set me as a seal on your heart," she murmured.

"As a seal on your arm," Wendell replied at once, with considerable pep. *Now we're talking!*

Thus taken aback, she somehow managed to say without faltering: "For strong as death is love . . ."

They went on for a while, alternately teasing and comforting each other. The words themselves weren't of much consequence: within the name "Wendell" Hero had discovered a corybantic psalm to its bearer.

"Wendell" was a psalm and "Hero" a hymn; those two were just incredibly taken with each other, OK? Everything they said to each other boiled down to that. Listening to both their voices, the sharpest twist of something like distress led Hero back to the impression that she'd been trying to circumvent. She didn't mind that she was now saying the very same words she'd heard the night before, when she'd climbed the boardinghouse stairs without a clue that Wendell Wechsler existed. What bothered her was this: She was not hearing him as if his words were addressed only to her. She was attending the scene like a third party. And when she listened in this manner, it wasn't merely listening, it was listening along with . . . an otherwise imperceptible fourth party.

So. The bad news is that Hero's becoming conscious of us. Yes, I do mean you and me. The fourth party that not only calls upon her to be a third-party observer of her own exchanges but consumes the emotion and cognition at least nominally intended for her. And she hates that. Our advantage lessens as, realizing that there is access to restrict, she sets about it without immediate effect.

The good news is that she's not going to try to get back at us. She's just going to apply much more rigor to her stratagems for securing privacy. Especially when it comes to being alone with Wendell Wechsler.

Slipping her arms around him, she whispered a wish into his

ear. He laughed—her breathing was ticklish—and answered: "Yes, if I ever tell anybody about tonight, I'll fix this for you."

"How?"

"I'll tell it so that nobody overhears the beautiful things you've just confessed."

"Nobody?"

"Well, I'll know. But nobody else."

Smiling, she asked: "So I won't know what I said either?"

His nod wasn't so much of a yes as it was a skittish head wobble. Earnest, unsmiling.

Hero's problem with recalling what she herself had said always boiled down to the feeling that she'd been framed. In retrospect she was certain that she'd been deceived in the moments before she spoke; she wouldn't have said this or that if she'd understood that she could leave those words for somebody else to say. (Her conviction that anything that needed to be said would somehow be said was just as strong as the sense of having been framed.) Of course, being a person means communicating; there's no getting around that. Listening to almost anyone else was generally gratifying in one way or another; overseeing her own transmissions was quite a different matter . . . and so Hero longed for a particularly nimble form of idleness. That is, if there really were things she was unable to resist saying, she longed to do that without knowing what those things were. And now Wendell was offering . . . well, his offer spooked her a bit. In essence he was claiming that in any words he spoke about Hero, she would be as she wished to be. In speaking of her he wouldn't use her in any way . . . not even to repeat some adoring statement he wanted to hear again. She liked this—loved it, actually, but ego was an antagonist to such intentions. An overwhelming one, at that. She couldn't help asking: "Wendell Wechsler . . . are you sure this is something you can do?"

He shrugged. "I suppose we'll see."

And he allowed himself to be sworn to secrecy when they heard her—Hero—coming up the boardinghouse stairs. "All right, all right . . . I won't tell you I'm with you."

But she couldn't resist taking a peek at the Hero who set the staircase creaking with such apprehension. The quickest peek—a micropeek, actually. She saw no one. Everything happened as she remembered it anyway: "Oh—you—wait right there!" followed by the sound of an imperious hand striking the door of Wendell's room . . .

SHE WOKE UP just once before dawn. She'd heard Wendell's voice in the distance, snarling at somebody (or possibly at her?). But he was lying at her side, snoring industriously; it was a wonder that the snarling had woken her up and not this. After a moment or two the beautiful nail-grinder opened his eyes, asking: "What did you say?"

"I thought that was you," she whispered.

They listened again, not really expecting confirmation either way.

Which is probably the reason the sound recurred.

This time they felt it as something that had formed between their bodies. They felt it as they had felt the pearls and the pealing of the bells. The sticky air swelled with it.

Thunder.

12.

IN THE MORNING, husband and wife had no qualms about making a run for it. In opposite directions from each other, that is.

Hero woke up in a good mood: she had dreamed of Thea—some dream of retaliation. Hers and then Thea's, then Hero's again . . . both of them far too petty to leave things as they were. She left Wendell's room without taking the trouble to look for a note or checking whether he'd left anything behind. Those two being two of a kind, she (correctly) assumed he would have taken everything, including the wedding dress and the rope of pearls. She doesn't seem to mind us knowing that the final vow they'd made to each other at the Basilica had been a promise to break their vows as soon as possible; her only wish was that she'd beaten him to it.

In her own room, two floors above Wendell's, she pulled a sundress out of her suitcase and put that on. When she yawned, all three sets of her sutures twanged like banjo strings—she found some more ibuprofen in her hand luggage backpack and devoured it. Standing by the window, she snubbed the ludicrously pretty view one more time; she set her sights higher. The sky looked nickel plated, and the clouds were greasy thumbprints smudging its sheen. That assurance of the change in weather was enough for her; she looked no higher than the clouds, transferring her attention to the room around her. Wendell didn't seem to have come here. Nothing had been moved around, as far as she could tell. Nothing had been added to her belongings, and nothing was missing. Except the novel she'd arrived with and deliberately jettisoned: *Paradoxical Undressing*. Let Sofie's mother deal with it.

She reversed this opinion at the airport a couple of hours later. The check-in officer asked where she was flying to. With longing and relief, she answered: "Dublin." The check-in officer requested her passport; she supplied it. After a minute or two, the check-in officer transferred their gaze from the computer screen to Hero's face and asked to be shown her copy of *Paradoxical Undressing*.

"Just to confirm that it's in good condition," the check-in officer added, not appearing to understand this request as the catalyst for Hero's paralysis. Eventually, hearing a French speaker in the queue behind her lose their temper and narrating the process in the most graphic terms, Hero pulled herself together and said: "I don't have it."

The check-in officer decided to show some forbearance: "Well, who has it?"

"I gave it to Denisa . . ."

"And this Denisa is?"

"Er—my friend's mother, I think." (And now this book, this city, had Hero saying "I think" about something she knew . . .)

"Well, you're going to have to get the book back from Denisa, aren't you? Because you can't leave without it."

"I—but *why* can't I leave without it?"

The check-in officer consulted her computer screen, then said: "This is simply the departure procedure in your case, ma'am."

"This doesn't seem . . . legal," Hero said, and queued again, for the neighboring check-in desk, where she was informed of exactly the same travel restriction. When she reached the officer at the third check-in desk, he simply said: "Get the book back from Denisa."

Sofie finally replied to Hero's string of meek inquiries:

> Hi. We've cleared passport control—are you
> coming or what? As for your book: Mom says she
> already mailed it to a friend of hers back home

She sent another message while Hero was still composing a response:

> Nothing from Thea, though we may have barricaded
> a couple of doors last night, just in case . . .
> You heard from her?

Hero deleted what she'd been typing, and sent a simple No.

"Perhaps you can stand to the side while you finish your SMS conversation," the check-in officer suggested.

"Oh—sorry—I was just finding out . . . I mean, the book's gone," Hero told the check-in officer. "It's on its way to Oklahoma as we speak. There's nothing else I can do."

To Hero's wonderment, this check-in officer who'd just been snide about her texting suddenly picked up a phone that hadn't rung and began talking to someone. The conversation didn't seem

to be about the situation at hand; the check-in officer was simper-
ing, and from the sounds of it, so was his caller. While he was
talking, five people (representatives of the airline, the airport, and a
pair who didn't introduce themselves but had something of an air
of governmentality) approached and expressed their sympathies
regarding Hero's predicament. In due course the check-in officer
concluded his telephone dialogue and began arguing with the new-
comers about what could be done to help this passenger fulfill her
departure requirement. Eventually Hero was presented with the
option of tracking down another copy of *Paradoxical Undressing*.

She very briefly experimented with married-lady status: one
never knew, she might have made an alliance that impressed them . . .
but Wendell Wechsler wasn't a name any of these gatekeepers
seemed familiar with. Next, Hero phoned any and every good
friend who had a voice authoritative enough to frighten bored bu-
reaucrats. Hero's contacts shouted at the check-in officer, the airline
representative, the airport people, and the unofficial officials in
turn. All Hero and co. received for their pains were reiterations of
the "existing departure policy."

Sofie and Polly's flight departed on time. And the airport representative led Hero across the terminal and showed her where to
leave her luggage while she went book seeking. Hero Tojosoa paid
the luggage storage fee and headed back to the city, not in the highest of spirits, but knowing that things could have been worse. The
airport representative could have unbuttoned her blouse to reveal a
courier's uniform and insisted on her signing for yet another copy
of the letter the late Gaspar Azzouz had written to her. This was
one thing Hero liked about Prague: Gaspar Azzouz's letter was

unable to find her. It was as if the obligation to read a dead man's last (probably inculpating) words was robustly rebutted in this place.

Standing at the taxi rank looking at the Google search results of "Secondhand bookshop Prague," she didn't see a way for her search to take less than a year unless she had help from a local. Only one Praguer of her acquaintance was still within reach, and she didn't have his phone number. But wait—there was someone else besides her husband. He'd given Hero a cigarette: a token of goodwill, surely? She phoned the bed-and-breakfast she'd checked out of. A couple of seconds later the proprietor, Mr. Surname, was saying: "Ah yes, Mrs. Wechslerová . . . what's on the agenda for today?"

"Hello again! I need to see Wendell. If—er—if possible."

"Right. Well . . . let's see . . . Thursday's the day he drives that ice cream van. If my memories from around this time last week are correct, the van should arrive on Sulická Street in an hour and a half. I'm not sure if he'll start at the children's hospital or the nursing home, so you might have to do a circuit between the two until you catch up with him. Do you know Suzanne Vega?"

"Not personally . . . ?"

"Well, she has this song: 'Left of Center.' Wendell's van will be the one chiming part of the chorus. Ignore all the other ice cream vans: Wendell's is the only gourmet one."

⚘

FORTY-FIVE MINUTES LATER Hero was mooching her way up and down a winding and well-shaded street in Prague 4, refamiliarizing herself with "Left of Center" via YouTube. She found that whenever she walked straight ahead, the street name changed at the very next stretch of pavement, and she'd have to backtrack until she found a sign that welcomed her to Sulická Street once again. Clouds were forming above. Really dark ones, weighty shadows that seemed to bubble like churned batter. Hero attempted to switch to another street—for a change of scenery, or a distraction from some sense of being a desiccated balloon bobbing around beneath the trees. Having set off in three different directions and walked for around five minutes each time, she found that all three paths stubbornly remained signposted Sulická. She passed the nursing home at least six times, and the queue—for Wendell's ice cream, she presumed—snaked further and further along each time she passed. Each member of the queue waited with an opened umbrella stationed across their preferred shoulder. And the senior citizens were not conservative in their umbrella tastes: neon pink, ultramarine, buttercup yellow, and sparkly bronze. The gray of the sky had all these challengers and more. There was no queue near the slices of Art Nouveau gateau that doubled as the children's hospital complex, but doors opened as the chimes of Vega's song of edges, fringes, and corners began to sound. By the time the coral-colored van drew to a halt a few feet away from the hospital gates, there was a throng of customers exhibiting presugar hyperactivity, jumping up and down as if on pogo sticks.

Hero joined the back of the queue, rehearsing her request. *Wendell*, she would say, I'm *not here because I'm holding on to you. I'm here because I'm NOT holding on to you. If you help me track this book down you'll be honoring two freedoms we both cherish: the liberty to let yesterday be fucking yesterday and the liberty to leave . . .*

It was too lofty; he wouldn't go for it. Should she simply offer a finder's fee? Or ownership of a cricket farm? What would he like, what could she give him so that she could go somewhere that wasn't an adamant squiggle on the face of reason? She supposed she could always ask if there was anything he needed her for, but how scary if there was something, and how dispiriting if there wasn't. These were basically the same tenterhooks she was on with her son, and the same again with Sofie, Thea, J.-P., Yolande, Gaspar . . . everybody. She was resolute in her hook breaking, and the hooks seemed just as resolute in their almost instantaneous renewal.

Her face began to hurt again. She was now close enough to the ice cream van driver for him to acknowledge her with a friendly nod. He wasn't Wendell. Here, with his white crest of hair stuffed into a hairnet and a red-and-white apron draped across his burly front, was the lavishly bewhiskered black man she'd seen a few times now: on the back cover of the very book that was detaining her, and just once in person, at the Basilica last night. Merlin Mwenda. The children seemed to understand his Czech despite the uncompromising Australianness of his accent. As soon as their ice cream wishes had been granted and they'd exceeded an old man's expected earshot, they turned to each other and mimicked the ice cream van man's phrasing over and over with such wicked satisfaction that watchful hospital staff nagged them until they went back to their usual voices. Unable to decipher the nagging but picking up on a lot of rhetorical questions, Hero imagined that the kids were being asked how they wanted things to be once they'd received their medical test results or completed their courses of treatment: Did they want to go home better in every way, or did they want to go home with someone else's accent and/or shameful manners?

"How are you going, love?" Merlin Mwenda said, when she reached the front of the queue.

"I'm *not* going, and that's the problem," Hero told him. "What about you?"

"Can't complain," said Merlin. "Though it'd be good if you could tell your husband not to make me do things like this at my time of life." Instead of asking what she was having (or following her finger as she pointed at the vat of vanilla ice cream), before busying himself with scoop and cone he stared into her eyes for a couple of seconds first, seemingly receiving her ice cream wishes directly from her subconscious.

"Speaking of my—er, Wendell . . . where is he?" she asked, accepting the two-scoop cone he presented her with. "And what flavor is this?"

"Jasmine rice," said Merlin. "And he's got another job. Hang on a sec—he'll kill me if he hears I didn't do this for you—"

He placed a marshmallow of hockey puck dimensions on top of the ice cream, steadied it with a spoon, and flambéed it with a blow-torch so that her cone was topped with toasted gold.

"You know, I'm happy Wendell found someone," Merlin said. "It was starting to look as if he'd be a stand-alone unit for the rest of his life. I remember a few years back he tried to join a couple of cults and they just sort of said, you know, thanks, but no thanks . . ."

"Seriously?"

"Oh yes."

"Which cults? When?"

"I'll have to tell you some other time—" He nodded at the cone in her hand, reminding her that this scorched and freezing rice pudding had to be tasted without delay.

She queued a few more times as she followed Merlin Mwenda through Prague 4 and Prague 3. She liked the van's interpretation of vanilla ice cream, loved the avocado sorbet, was maybe too strung out to appreciate the pistachio option by the time she tasted it—and for the price of three more ice cream cones Hero learned that, according to Merlin Mwenda, the novella he'd written was an account of Casanova's humiliation on the night of *Don Giovanni*'s premiere in October 1787. The performance itself Casanova barely noticed; it was merely a pretext for the after-party. He'd come down from Northern Bohemia specially, blowing a month's castle librarian wages on a night's accommodation in a gigantic hotel suite well situated and furnished extravagantly enough to shock and excite the women he planned to carouse with until sunrise. The supreme seducer started out aiming for seven women, then five, then three. After a couple of hours he decided: all right, just one unforgettable nymph will suffice. Finally he was reduced to begging: "Five minutes, just give me five minutes of your time; don't you want to uncover the deepest secrets of desire?"

Prague's incurious womenfolk told Casanova to go to hell with all that, just as the operatic version of him had. Each of the pretty Praguers who condescended to let him have three minutes of conversation with them spoke only of the crush she now had on Mozart.

Casanova tried to make them see that he was the seed the opera had sprung from, but the pretty Praguers only shrugged.

You don't seem to understand who you're talking to . . . ladies, it's me! Giacomo Casanova, the great adventurer.

Good for you, sir, but all you've done is live a dissolute life . . . it's Mozart who's made music of it.

And as Casanova stumbled drunkenly home, he felt Prague's derision stalking him along the tapering alleyways and through the flinty picture frame that served as the gate between Old Town and

New. "I am Casanova! THE Casanova!" he cried aloud. No sooner had the final echo of his voice fallen from the arches than an androgynous figure festooned with tulle and paste diamonds (a true sophisticate knew the difference) leaped into Casanova's path, wove to the left, wove to the right, ran around him in a circle, then pulled the ribbon from his ponytail and ran off waving it like a flag. Dizzy and angry, he made a retaliatory grab for this person's tiara, but they were too fast for him. There was no mistaking the contempt with which Casanova, or perhaps the very factuality of him, was being opposed.

Merlin paused. "You know, I wrote the book a really long time ago, Hero. The memory of writing it is almost as distant as the memory of having two eyes. So I can only tell you what I think I was thinking while I was writing about Casanova slinking off back to Teplice with his tail between his legs, and maybe cheering up once he realized he could still score once he was out of Prague's reach. I think I wanted to say to anybody else who's here or has been here: Hey, you've noticed it too, right? That this city might not actually be a city, but . . . a dissociative state of some kind? A non-stop paternoster lift that's too fast for history to step into without severed ankles? Could this Prague be . . . a break? A snapping of the world's wire? Isn't this why any faction that has occupied this city has known deep down—must have known, unless they were complete idiots—that the more they seemed to get their way the less they were in actual control of anything at all around here? I just wanted to, you know, ask that and see if asking brought anything to mind for anybody else . . . and I can tell by the way you're looking at me that this is the first you've heard about *Paradoxical Undressing* being a Casanova story."

"Well, that and—actually I was thinking, Mr. Mwenda . . . it's not that I don't believe there were things you wanted to say . . ."

"But?"

"I thought—and sorry if this is a very pedestrian way to attribute motivation—I mean, it's my understanding that you wrote the book because somebody led you to believe your days were numbered if you didn't? Or was that part of the story's story?"

"No, that's as true as any of this is. Wendell's threats were the chronological beginning. I guess I dwell on the other beginnings more because it felt like they were thoughts that wanted to come to me. And they were OK with being written down. Like: *Sorry to hear you've been driven to this, mate, but here I am . . . chuck me in there if you want.*"

"Sorry . . . I just—did you say 'Wendell's threats'?"

"Did I?" Merlin looked past her, trying to remember. "I meant Hynek. Hynek's threats."

"All right. I'll just have to take your word for it, won't I? But there's something else I'd like to hear from you. What do you think happened when you finished writing your book?" Hero asked. "I mean, surely people have come to you saying things like *How come every time I look at this book it's become another book?!*"

Merlin had temporarily halted ice cream vending by then, and was parked right in the middle of a ring of tower blocks. People kept approaching to try to start a queue, but he shooed them away. He took a swig of beer and closed the eye that wasn't covered with an eye patch for a moment. "You first. What do you think happened, Hero?"

"Maybe you were so . . . open, or left the book so open that something entered it? Something like a genius locus that, instead of simply being, also wants to find out where it is—'where' in time and space, I mean—and that genius locus started looking for a person willing and able to tell them . . . ?"

Merlin smiled at her. "Oh, I'd love it if such mayhem could be brought about by the written word. Well, I'd love it but I'd also be shitting myself. Nah, my take is heaps more . . . what did you call your way of thinking? Pedestrian? Yeah, that."

Thunder had begun to sound while they were talking. The more they talked, the louder the thunder rumbled, until, feeling that the weather wasn't taking kindly to having its monologue interrupted, they both went quiet. Lightning appeared; this was no longer a monologue. Merlin continued: "Pick ten people, tell each of 'em the same thing—use exactly the same wording each time, then go back and ask of the ten what you told 'em. It's guaranteed you'll hear ten things you never fuckin' said. Hardly anybody talks about what it is they've actually heard or read; we only say what we were thinking about while someone was trying to talk to us. And when all's said and done, that's only natural, isn't it . . . and that's all that happened with *Paraxodical Undressing . . .*"

Hero could feel that she was being prevailed upon to change her mind. But for all that this place was every place that went through people's minds as they read about it, Hero still didn't want to stay. Her mind was always changing anyway; that was what minds did. And she refused to forfeit the possibility of being in places other than . . . these ones. There was nothing left for her to do aside from finish her ice cream and ask the author if he had a spare copy of *Paradoxical Undressing* lying around anywhere.

Merlin checked his watch. "Sure. I have a ton of copies at my place; wait a couple of hours and you can have as many as you like—take them all off my hands if you want."

There followed a glint of near-blinding coincidence; lightning bleached the sky and two keys landed on the concrete between them—along with a handful of coins. Chilled to the bone (just a couple of millimeters to the left or to the right and she or Merlin could have been hit), Hero peered up the ladder of blue squares that ran from the tower block's ground floor to its twentieth. Many, many floors above there was a hand, waving.

"That'll be Božena," Merlin said. "She loves a grapefruit and Campari sorbet of a Thursday afternoon, though she shouldn't touch it, really; I think the grapefruit interferes with her medication . . ."

He tied his apron on, prepared a sorbet cone, and handed it to Hero along with his customer's keys. He showed her which one was for the main door of the building: "And you can't use the second key all willy-nilly. You don't burst in on Božena, you knock first, and then you let yourself in when she says you can—"

Hero was halfway through her rebellion against these instructions—her hand was just returning the napkin-wrapped cone to Merlin, and he was saying, "Quickly now, or it'll melt long before the eighteenth floor"—when her name was shouted across the court-yard. Somehow holding on to the cone without crushing it, she looked over her shoulder and caught sight of Wendell Wechsler skipping her way, happily singing her name.

He was uniformed as a courier (so this was his other job), and he waved a stiff brown envelope that matched all the others she'd rejected.

"Oh no," she said, running for the door Merlin had pointed out to her. "Wendell, are you really . . . no, you can't be doing this to me!"

Safely enclosed in the tower's block vinyl beige interior, she took her time climbing the stairs, cupping her hands to contain the orange slush that wouldn't be undermining the efficacy of Božena's medicine today. Once she got up high enough, she'd look down and wait Wendell out. That rat, that Judas, that snake in the grass, taking on this delivery assignment after she'd told him that there was only one thing in the world she wouldn't read. He'd looked so pleased about it too.

She had two moments to breathe once she reached the top floor. Two moments before Wendell Wechsler stepped out of the lift with envelope outstretched. She read the sender's name: *Gaspar Azzouz*, just as she'd known it would be.

There was one more staircase, and Hero ran up it with dripping hands—it felt as if her hamstrings were liquefying too. The staircase led to a hatch in the roof—she went up through that, too, and so did Wendell. Out in the mist of black organza that now stood in for sunlight, he drove her to the gable's edge: "Take it—it's for you. This is for you. You're the only person in the world these words were written for. He's made it so simple, that man you made a story of. You don't have to respond in words—you can't write back, anyway, what can you say, he's already gone, right? He wrote his ending. All you have to do is read it. Don't you see what a chance this is? A chance to perfect something . . ."

Hero was listening—and disagreeing—but she was also looking down, and oh, the vertigo. These heights laid her low. They cut her legs out from under her, flipped her horizontal, and let the ground plummet toward her.

"Fuck off, Wendell," she shouted. "Get back. Please, please, I don't want to push you—" She would, though. She would push him. If she didn't, she would drop into the map that moved beneath them like multicolored sand.

Wendell pressed the letter into her chest with one hand and caught her arm with the other; she stayed upright.

He shouted something, but she saw him without hearing what he said. The thunder and the lightning were closer than he was. For a second—a second that seemed to skip forward and rewind at random—she was absolutely certain that they'd been struck. But Wendell lowered his knees onto the tiles, grappled his phone out of some pocket or other, and gestured to her to sign the screen with her finger. That wasn't something any living being would have the presence of mind to do after being struck by lightning, so they must have escaped for now.

And Hero gave up: she knelt down with him and signed, leaving orange globs all over the phone. The clouds burst and gave everything a good wash anyway. But there was more to a proper downpour than its cleansing qualities. Rainfall was night and it was day—that was the head-spinning factor . . . the inundation of radiance and gloom. A slippery thrum ran through her skin—not painless; the sutures above, beneath, and on Hero's jawline weren't liking this at all. This was a puffing, panting deluge; rain that pummeled her with indignant questions as it fell: *How could you, how could you, how dare you . . .*

Instead of answering, Hero took each slap without lowering her head.

Wendell was hopping around on one leg; his arms were raised, if he'd been wearing a crucifix, he'd probably have been kissing it—no footballer celebrating a hat trick could have shown more elation. He was drinking raindrops and laughing and weeping and holding his hand out to her; in a minute she'd go to him. If he hadn't slipped off the side of the roof by then.

First there was this letter to take care of. She slid it out of the envelope—a single sheet with nine or ten words on it, that was all—and she let the storm pull it from her open hand.

Blinking took longer with this much water trickling her eyelashes . . .

. . . by the time Hero Tojosoa blinked twice the last words were just another form in the glittering free-for-all.

June 1, 2021, to February 6, 2022
Prague, Czechia

Acknowledgments

Thank you, Vítězslav Nezval; thank you, Dr. Cieplak; thank you, Tracy Bohan; thank you, Petr Onufer; thank you, Jin Auh; thank you, Luděk Brož; thank you, Sarah McGrath; thank you, Alison Fairbrother; thank you, Delia Taylor; thank you, Jordaine Kehinde; and Louisa Joyner—thank you.